THE SHE

THE SHE

TERRY GRIMWOOD

NEWCON
PRESS

NewCon Press
England

First edition, published in the UK September 2023
by NewCon Press
41 Wheatsheaf Road, Alconbury Weston, Cambs, PE28 4LF, UK

NCP314 (hardback)
NCP315 (softback)

10 9 8 7 6 5 4 3 2 1

ISBN: 978-1-914953-63-7 (hardback)
978-1-914953-64-4 (softback)

Main cover image 'Killer' by 'Sam Williams
Cover design by Ian Whates
Editing and typesetting by Ian Whates

CONTENTS

THE SHE

Philippe was dead...

Breathing hard, crushed into the narrow alleyway between two fire-scarred houses only a few feet from my lover's corpse, I slotted a fresh magazine into my Sten sub-machine gun and wondered at what point I should bite the muzzle of the weapon and put an end to this.

Dead, he was dead...

No tears.

If I lived, there would be plenty of time for grief. Philippe and the rest of his cell were beyond help, their guts smeared across the alley wall beside me, their blood sprayed on my face and clothes.

A few members of the German patrol who had ambushed us had taken cover in the shell-blasted *boucherie* on the opposite side of the street. The rest of the bastards could be anywhere, moving in, wanting me alive, a plaything for the Gestapo.

I was supposed to be going home, meeting a Lysander in a meadow on the outskirts of this hamlet. But I had one last job to do on the way out, an extra, radioed in from England last night. Something of a mystery though. All any of us knew was that we were supposed to rendezvous with somebody in this ruin.

And now the only man I have ever loved was dead –

An object arced out of the *boucherie*'s broken window, tumbled end-over-end and landed on the road only a few feet from where I crouched.

Grenade.

Instinct shoved me onto my belly, arms crossed over my head.

The world disintegrated into an endless white roar.

*

God knows what got me back onto my feet. I wanted to lie quietly in the smoke and mud, with the wreckage of my lover. I wanted to rest...

But suddenly I was up and running into the swirling cloud and stink of the explosion. The lingering white roar of the detonation, my own blood-roar.

I ran towards the *boucherie*.

The Germans were suddenly in the street in front of me.

I felt the Sten hammer in my hands, but heard nothing. The Germans stood motionless, bemused, no doubt, that this crazed Englishwoman could have survived the explosion, then shocked and screaming. I saw them fall, bullet-ripped and bleeding.

Into the shop, scrambling over broken glass, splintered lathes and slabs of fallen plaster. Bullets whined and chomped at the already shattered fabric of the place. It was dark, treacherous with debris, choked with dust. I slipped onto one knee, twisted round and saw a figure crash into the doorway. I used up the Sten's last few rounds. Its brief chatter finally broke through the grenade-deafness.

Town square, broken fountain, a bicycle's twisted rusting corpse, burnt-out car: weeds, nettles, fallen masonry. The village had been devastated in a British rear-guard action on the road to Dunkirk and never rebuilt.

Drizzle washed the world into a grey blur. The air was sodden and cold. I saw a church and a different instinct drove me towards its black mouth.

Figures erupted from the ruins, fast, strong. Someone took me round the waist, my legs were pulled from under me.

When they removed the blindfold, I found that I was in some sort of attic. Dull, rain-greyed light forced its way in through a small window set into the sloped ceiling. It had little effect on the shadows gathered into every corner of the room.

A woman sat at a dusty table. She wore a Royal Navy duffel coat. Its raised hood hid her face.

"Sit." The woman's English was accented, possibly Russian.

I took the only other chair in the room then looked up and was startled to see that my two captors were also women; one young, tall, graceful and black, the other white, middle-aged, scarf worn as a turban. Both carried rifles.

Another order, and I was alone with Duffle Coat, who pushed back the hood to reveal a face that was shockingly, impossibly old.

"I'm sorry for your rough treatment," the woman said. "But caution has been my life." She pushed a wine bottle across the table. "For you as well I think."

I drank from the bottle. The wine was startlingly sweet. "My mother was French, married to an Englishman and living in London," I said. "So, perhaps you're right."

"The English don't like foreigners. You were bullied as a child, yes?"

"There were those who tried."

The old woman chuckled.

Voices snapped across the beat of rain, German.

The old woman must have noticed my concern. "They won't find us easily, and if they do, there are enough of us to hold them off for hours."

"Us?"

"The Order of Shadows and Whispers." Her voice held an undercurrent of self-mockery. "I am Sister Anna."

"Christine Brown." I answered. "The Order of Daring Deeds and Loud Bangs and…"

The grief hit me then, rising from somewhere deep; grief for Philippe, who had emerged from a darkness sodden with terrors even my brutal training couldn't assuage. I was in the middle of a big, open field in occupied France, fumbling with my parachute and silently pleading with the now distant Halifax bomber that had delivered me to come back and take me home. Philippe grabbed me and said, "Get a grip." I told him to get his filthy Frog hands off me so I could get on with sorting out this bloody parachute.

We both laughed and that was the last time I panicked.

And the first time I wanted a man simply because of who he was and not because convention decreed that a young woman was only complete on the arm of the first decent chap who offered to be her husband.

Get a grip…

"I have heard of you," Anna said. "The assassination of General Schumann."

Operation Jael, my reason for being in France, and named for the ancient Judge of Israel who seduced an enemy General into her tent then nailed his head to the ground while he slept.

"Yes, but how did you know —"

"The murder of such an important Nazi by a common Parisian prostitute does not go unnoticed. Only the woman who slit his throat and stole his wallet was neither Parisian nor prostitute, was she, Christine. Very audacious, and clever. Such a sordid death requires cover-up rather than reprisals."

Bed, floor, walls, my hands, my skin, all red-splashed, his body, twitching, white, pig-like, everything wet and stinking of raw meat and shit and piss…

I trembled at the memory, my gorge rising. I needed to change the subject.

"I didn't think a Bride of Christ like you would approve of that sort of operation."

"Who said I was a Bride of Christ?"

"So what sort of Order are you?" I asked.

"This Order is an ancient one. It has advised kings, emperors and even popes for centuries."

"Why so secret?"

Anna shook her head. "Christine, look at me, look at us. This is a world of men. When we do our work in secret we are tolerated, venerated even. Whenever we emerge into the light we are vilified, persecuted and burned as witches.

"In recent years, many of us who thought the time right to show our hand were named as anarchists and thrown in gaol.

"Some of us hide under Holy Orders, concealed in plain view by the very church that burned our ancestors but has always known our worth. Others work in the world but are protected under the church's wing. But there is a price for that protection. Have you heard of Lise Meitner, who helped discover the terrible energy that holds the universe together, or Nettie Stevens, who discovered that it was a man's seed that decided the sex of a child?"

"No, but…"

"Of course you haven't. They hide in the shadows of the men with whom they worked. There are so many like them who have been forced to keep their genius secret. That is the price. It has been that way from the very beginning. Why were you in this ruin, Christine?"

"I'm not going to tell you that —"

"Of course. I would have been disappointed in you if you did. But I know the answer already. You received new orders, your evacuation was delayed."

"So, you were the people I was supposed to rendezvous with. And that's why you knew so much about Operation Jael."

"The plan was for you to have met one of us, someone you would have assumed to be simply a member of the resistance. We did not anticipate having to rescue you from an ambush, but I am glad we have met." Anna smiled. "You have to take an important person with you."

"Who?" A downed pilot, another agent…

"Just a frightened male child who came to us for comfort and advice." Anna stood. "Christine, you are a Sister. You have been since you were born." She held out a package, wrapped in a dusty looking cloth. I took the bundle and found it to contain a notebook and a revolver.

"Look," I said. "I appreciate you wanting me to join your Order but I have no intention of locking myself away in a convent —"

"There is no need for you to lock yourself away. You have been doing our work all your life, ever since your first childish rebellion against the restrictions imposed on you as a girl. Read the notebook. It is transcribed from the most ancient of writings. Some of it from Dead Sea scrolls supposedly burned. It tells the story of our… how do you say, our founder."

"Sister Anna, I don't have time. I have a job to do here. And I have to get back to London. There's a plane —"

"We cannot complete the mission until nightfall," Anna said. "So, read."

She was right. And if this *was* a trap, then I was well and truly snared, not much I could do about it now. I opened the book. The pages were handwritten, neat and easily read.

In the beginning Is *made the world. It created light with a word and the heavens and the earth from nothing.* Is *made creatures that crawled and swam and flew. Then* Is *made man and woman, creating them both from the earth itself…*

…The She tore her way out of the translucent cocoon in which her seed had grown. Fluid spilled onto the lush riverbank vegetation as the sac bulged and ruptured. The She's back rose out of the amniotic mess. An arm flailed free. A hand opened and closed. Her head appeared, long hair smeared wetly against her scalp.

The She rolled clumsily into the grass and gasped unfamiliar, dry air. Then she curled back into a foetal ball and screamed. The screams quickly quietened to a melody of low moans and gasping sobs. Her distress wouldn't last. She had been created for this world, its sensory richness as vital to her survival as the air she breathed.

Quiet now, the She was on her hands and knees, face hidden by a tumble of hair. Her flesh was a cloud-map of shades and tones, a physical manifestation of her role as mother of an entire species. She was taller than her offspring would be and her womb, more spacious.

"You are the first woman." *Is* said

She knew that the slight-built, hairless figure who stood over her was her creator. She knew that it had no name she was allowed to utter. The creator existed, simply *is*.

"You will be called Lilith."

"Lilith, yes."

"You should bathe in the river" *Is* nodded towards the gently swirling waters. "Clean yourself before you meet your mate."

Lilith stared at the creature-being-He. This one's eyes were dark (ah, so this is dark) and shot through with filaments of blue.

Is, whom Lilith had followed to this place, turned and smiled.

"This is Adam, you are his helpmeet."

Lilith watched Adam and Adam watched her. Beautiful as he was, there was something dull in his stare. He made no sound.

Is looked from one to the other then said, "Everything in this Garden is yours. You can walk where you will and do what you will. Nothing will harm you." *Is* paused before continuing. "There is one angel you must never speak with. It will offer you the knowledge of good and evil. Ignore it or you will die. And death is a dark, cold nothing."

"How can it be nothing?" Lilith asked. "There must always be something."

"Death is nothing," *Is* said firmly. "I will explain it to Adam and then Adam will tell you in ways you can understand."

"Lilith." Adam's voice was low and gruff. He was pleasing to look at with his mottled skin and long mane of many colours. His face was squarer than Lilith's (she had seen her own reflected in the river) and roughened by thick, dark hair that grew about his chin. Lilith stared at the thing hanging limply between Adam's legs and felt a deep part of her body swell and grow moist. She breathed quickly, unable to find words even though she had many to say.

Adam stood directly in front of her. She wanted to hold him and for the man to hold her. She wanted other things that she couldn't understand. Adam stared at her but made no move. She took a step towards him and reached out and touched his face. He grunted softly and covered her hand with his. She took his face in both hands and drew him to her and pressed her lips on his. His breath was hot.

His arms encircled her and gently lowered her into the thick, soft grass where she cried out his name and received him.

Adam and Lilith wandered The Garden and all was colour and sound. The ground beneath their bare feet was soft with moss. The air was sweet with flower scent.

Everywhere there was life; from the buzz and scurry of tiny flying and creeping things to the crash and lumber of giant beasts with long, long necks and legs like the trunks of trees. There were animals that flew and creatures that crawled, slitherers and leapers, flutterers and soarers. Nothing harmed Adam and Lilith and, in turn,

The He and The She harmed no living thing. Time was the light of day and the star-dusted dark of night and its passing was of no consequence. Adam and Lilith slept when tired and ate fruit, leaf and root when hungry. They named each beast and plant they encountered.

Sometimes *Is* would come to them just as the light turned gold and the day faded. They had taken to resting in one particular clearing at night. It seemed right to them that there should be a place they always returned to. *Is* would enter in a breath of cool air and when it appeared, all the animals of the Garden would fall silent.

"Adam," *Is* said each time. "Walk with me."

"And me?" Lilith asked.

"No, just Adam."

This night Lilith asked a question just as *Is* and Adam set off for their walk.

"Why should we not speak to the angel?"

"Because I order it," *Is* said.

"But why?"

A moment's hesitation, then, "I will explain to Adam and then he can explain to you." *Is* became gentle. "You are Adam's helpmeet, you exist to serve him. You should not trouble yourself with these matters."

"What did *Is* tell you?" Lilith asked when Adam returned, deep in the night. She had tried to sleep but could not. This had never happened before. When she was tired she slept, but not tonight.

"It's too big."

"Too big?"

Adam sighed. "I cannot tell it to you."

"We were both made from the earth so why won't *Is* speak with me?"

"*Is* speaks to me," Adam replied.

Lilith had asked the question many times and always Adam gave her the same answer

The world was still peace and joy; it was warm and it was cool, there was scent and sound. In the morning the world was wet with dew, as were Adam and Lilith, but the sun soon dried them. They walked and saw and heard and they loved and wanted no one but each other.

But then, with the oncoming dark, *Is* came and took Adam from her once again. Lilith sat up and watched them walk away and fade into the shadow and moon-splash confusion of the garden. She lay down on the soft grass and tried to sleep, but she could not close her eyes. She rolled onto her back and stared up into the bright, sparkling night sky. Still her eyes would not close. So she got to her feet and set off into the dense forest in search of Adam and *Is*.

She tripped and stumbled, strained to hear their voices.

"Lilith."

She started and felt a pounding in her chest she normally only felt when Adam touched her. The voice was strange, not Adam and not *Is*. Stems and branches rustled and then a figure stepped from the patchwork of shadow and light.

"Don't be afraid?" It was a He.

"What is afraid?" Lilith asked.

The figure laughed softly. "You really don't know, do you."

"Are you the angel?" Lilith asked.

"Oh yes, but you can call me Lucifer."

"I am not to talk to you."

"Why?"

"Because I will die."

"And have you died?"

"No."

"So, you *can* speak with me."

He came closer, into a patch of moonlight and she saw how beautiful he was. Taller than *Is*, fair-haired, his eyes fire-bright. Like her, he was naked.

"I can teach you as *Is* teaches Adam."

Lilith struggled with Lucifer's words. He seemed wise. She felt the same power, the same ancient presence as she did when she was with *Is*.

"Yes," she said. "Teach me."

And later, after they had talked for many hours, hidden deep in the garden, Lucifer drew close and touched her. The gentlest touch she had ever known, and one that took the breath from her throat.

15

From then on, Lilith followed Adam and *Is* whenever they walked in the Garden. And each time she met with Lucifer.

Gunfire interrupted my concentration. The window shattered, fragments of glass waterfalled into the room. I dropped to the floor. As I clutched at the dusty, mouldering boards, I wondered how in the name of God this was going to end.

Silence fell. I struggled into a sitting position, coughing, frosted with dust. I tasted grit and spat it onto the floor.

"Are you all right?" I asked.

"Yes, yes," Anna sounded impatient with my concern. She waved me away when I tried to help her back to her feet. "Read on, please."

"We're not going to get out of here," I said.

"Don't underestimate us, Christine."

We stayed on the floor. It seemed safer down there. I retrieved the notebook. Nothing else I could do but read the thing. At least it was reasonably compelling.

"Lilith."

She awoke, almost uttered Lucifer's name, but found herself looking at *Is*. She sat up quickly, trying to cover herself with her arms. *Is* stood over her, fists clenched. Adam crouched nearby. He stared at her, face crumpled in confusion.

"Why have you disobeyed me?" *Is* sounded gentle, but there was something frightening beneath the softness of its voice. "Why did you speak with the angel?"

"I..." She could not find the words. Lucifer had told her so many things but it was as if they had been thrown to the top of a tall tree out of her reach. She trembled and understood that this was what Lucifer had called fear.

"At night," *Is* said quietly. "When I talk with Adam, you crawl out like a snake to meet with the usurper."

Lilith struggled to her feet. She had to stand, she would not crouch before *Is* any more. *Is* watched her, eyes burning.

"I am compassionate," *Is*'s voice had fallen to a whisper. "I can forgive, but you must never meet with that creature again. He is a monster, puffed-up, a traitor. He dared to challenge me. I forged him and his... his horde, and saw that they were good. And now I would vomit them out of my mouth." *Is* paused. Then, "Will you do as I ask Lilith?"

She closed her eyes and painted pictures in the red darkness. She saw herself huddled here, in the clearing, as Adam and *Is* walked away to talk. She saw Lucifer waiting. She saw herself alone, weeping, crying for his voice, his kindness and wisdom, and his touch.

"No." It was as if someone else had spoken the word.

Is threw back its head and roared and the sky was torn and darkness boiled through its wounds. The air raged and whirled and shrieked through the garden, shredding leaves and breaking bough and stem. Lilith was driven to the ground. She saw Adam, curled and shivering.

The sky flashed and spat and answered *Is* with loud crashes and rumbles that seemed to shake the earth itself.

"Go," *Is* howled. "Go from here!"

Lilith ran into the angry darkness. The air swirled and twisted about her and contorted the trees until they groaned. She fell, clambered back onto her feet then drove herself on. Something was coming, something terrible bearing down on her. She could hear its song in her head.

The garden ended.

Lilith stumbled to a halt. The whole world stopped here, as if it had been cut open and below, beating itself against the edge of the wounded earth far below was a river that was so huge she could not see the far side.

Then it came, plummeting from the broken sky, vast and shining, wings spread, and with a face so beautiful Lilith wept. It was bringing her death. She stood at the end of the world and watched as it became everything she could see, hear or feel.

In a blaze of light and roar of song, Lilith was torn from the earth and up into the cold, restless sky.

The world tumbled about her. The impossible river raged far beneath. It was some time before Lilith understood that she clung to the feathers of a huge flying beast and was sitting astride its back. The creature's neck was long, its beak lined with rows of long, sharp teeth. Its wings barely moved as they caught the currents of air that swept the creature higher then sent it into long, shallow dives towards the grey, restless water. Fierce as it seemed, the bird offered no threat. Lilith felt safe. The dizzy swoop and climb of the flight was exhilarating. She laughed.

The horizon thickened and became the far bank of the vast river. It was a dark garden where there were no trees, but huge mountains that spewed fire and smoke. Blazing orange water poured from their mouths, hot even from far above.

The mountains gave way to a bleak place, where the ground was damp and covered with clumps of trees and plants and where huge creatures walked. This wet, hot garden grew denser and denser until it lapped like a river at the base of a great rock.

On the summit of the hill were other rocks, these carved into shapes, some tall and graceful, others low and solid. In the centre was an immense tower, so high its top was lost in cloud. As they came closer Lilith saw figures climbing and ascending a great stairway that spiralled about its flanks, figures that looked like Adam and herself.

The bird landed amongst the dwelling places and crouched to allow Lilith to clamber from its back. She was dizzied by the noise, the smell of smoke, the dust, the voices, and the crowds of tall, beautiful people who had gathered around her. Confused, she turned back to bird. It was gone and in its place stood Lucifer. He smiled and offered her his hand.

Lucifer spoke to the others and they quietened. Lilith could not understand his words but when he had finished many of them dropped to their knees and lowered their faces to the hard, smooth ground. Lucifer took Lilith's hand and led the way into the nearest of the dwellings. Inside it was like a cave but clean and bright. There were places to lie and to sit and food that was already prepared.

"Eat, Lilith," he said. She did so. The food was better than anything she had tasted in the garden. He watched her for a while then spoke again. "We are the same, you and I."

"But you are a He —"

18

"True enough," Lucifer laughed. "What I mean is that we both questioned *Is*. We both sought to think and act as *we* saw good and have been cast out." He smiled. "I am an angel, second only to *Is* itself." He leaned forward, dropped his voice to a whisper. "I am building a tower that will reach to heaven."

"Heaven?"

"The garden where I was made, my rightful home." His smile faded. "Lilith, you are more beautiful than you could ever know. You will be my queen and the mother of an entire race. Your beauty and strength mingled with mine, your human seed with the seed of a god. We will people this world with titans."

Lilith stayed with Lucifer, and as he promised, she was soon with child.

I looked up from the notebook. I was still seated on the floor, thinking it wiser than raising my head above the table. Anna was a few feet away, slumped against the wall. From her rhythmic breathing, I deduced that she was asleep. The light had faded. It would be dark soon. I was suddenly swamped by my fear and, for a moment, wanted to give in, to make this go away.

Get a grip.

I breathed deep to steady my nerves and returned my attention to the story.

When many years had passed, there came a night when Lilith's dreams were torn by cacophony. She opened her eyes, lost in the brief hinterland between sleep and wakefulness. The sounds made no sense to her, until she heard the screams. She sat up, staring wildly about the familiar room. The white gossamer drapes drawn across the huge open window were ruffled by a cold breeze. The air was wrong, the smell, no longer fresh and sharp. It was tainted.

Smoke.

Lilith struggled to her feet, once more heavy with child (a daughter, always daughters) and crossed to the window.

The city burned.

And the tower, Lucifer's vast stairway to his home, was crumbling. Its gorgeous masonry boiled and melted. Above it, black,

black smoke painted a sky already darkened by monstrous clouds. Their bellies flickered with flame which licked at the tower and struck down at the city.

My children…

Lilith's cry was silent, trapped inside her by grief and fear. She could not understand what she saw. The city was burning and the city was filled with her children, and her children's children. And now they were dying.

She ran along the corridors, ignoring shouts of warning. She choked on smoke and dust. She reached the stairs and stumbled down. Others followed, calling her name, promising to get her to safety.

Then Lucifer was there, running towards her up the stairs.

"You should have waited," he said. His face, ageless and beautiful was wrought with grief. "I was coming…"

This time Lilith gave voice to her anguish. "My children."

"The city is lost. *Is* will not be defied." Lucifer grabbed her arms, held them tightly. "My people and your children are fleeing, they will be scattered across this world. We will build another city."

Lilith crumpled. She fell forward and was suddenly astride a great cat, black and sleek, which bounded gracefully down the steps and out into a world fogged with smoke, hot from flame and choked with dust and debris and the stench of the dead. Vast, red-glowing fragments of masonry, blown from the great tower arced through the sky to smash into once beautiful buildings. Each impact shook the earth and would have flung Lilith to the ground if it had not been for Lucifer's arm tight about her.

Then Lilith saw birds rise from the chaos, her children on their backs. The vast flock swirled into the shape of a vast black funnel then burst apart and disappeared into the boiling night-black cloud.

"Take me home," she whispered to Lucifer. "Take me back to the Garden."

"No Lilith –"

"Take me home."

Lilith knelt on the cliff edge. Stretched out before her the Garden was as lush and glorious as she remembered. Sweet scents drifted from its depths, birdsong punctuated the pulse of the waves and gentle rhythm of Lilith's weeping.

Behind her, the ocean beat at the foot of the rocky wall and, somewhere in the sky, Lucifer was swept across the clouds in search of his scattered peoples. He had held her, kissed her and wept his own tears, tears that burned and sang as they fell.

"Always," he whispered. "Only call my name and I will come to you."

Then he had turned, leapt skyward and was gone.

Lilith got to her feet, weary but knowing there was little time. *Is* would not tolerate her in the Garden.

The dense beauty of the place revived her, the coolness of the grass beneath her feet, the perfumes of flowers and music of bird and beast. She walked and came, at last, to the clearing.

Where a woman sat, alone.

Lilith took a step towards her. "I am Lilith."

The woman, childlike in her curiosity and lack of fear, said; "I am Eve."

I sensed that someone else had entered the attic room and closed the notebook. There was a familiar smoky scent. A cigar.

"Miss Brown?" The new voice was sonorous.

And shockingly familiar.

I closed the book, the act oddly furtive, and looked up, slowly, to face the newcomer who was on his hands and knees.

"I am impressed, young lady, that you were able to break through that ring of steel," Winston Churchill rumbled. "Perhaps I really will see England again."

I stared at him, bewildered, and shaken by his *humanness*; by the solid fact of his skin and clothes, of the sound of his breathing, and by the weariness etched deep into his face.

I took a last nerve-steadying swig of the miraculously unbroken wine bottle, which had been blasted onto the floor beside me by the German machine gun, then offered it to Churchill. He crawled awkwardly over to sit beside me, accepted the bottle and took a deep and enthusiastic draught. He then produced a half-smoked cigar and box of matches from his coat pocket and lit up. The smell was oddly reassuring.

"As much as I appreciate your faith in me, sir," I said. "I don't think we'll break through this time. The Jerries have this place surrounded."

"You will," Anna said, suddenly awake, if she hadn't been all along. "The Germans won't know which way to run."

On cue, another burst of gunfire. We would be lucky to survive the wait until full darkness, let alone make it out to that meadow and the rendezvous with our Lysander. I was bloody scared. The fear was familiar now, almost a friend.

"Why are you here, sir?" I asked. Stupid question, why on earth should he tell me? It was just that talking helped.

"I think the good Sister has told you already, Miss Brown," Churchill answered. "The burden of leadership is a heavy one. I am faced with a decision. Our new American allies demand Europe, my instinct shouts North Africa first and a thrust into Herr Hitler's soft white underbelly."

"But why here? Why these people?"

Churchill glanced at Anna, who nodded.

"This Order is an ancient one. It has advised world leaders for centuries. I have a war to shoulder. My ministers are frightened sheep. My allies shout and grow impatient. My sleep is sodden with nightmares. This is the only place left for me to turn. Not all great strategists are men, Miss Brown, though I suspect they are the only ones who will be remembered."

"And have you made your decision?"

Churchill nodded. "It will win me few friends."

One of the Sisters appeared in the doorway and spoke to Anna in a language I didn't recognise.

"It is time," Anna turned to me. "A little faith is needed. I will provide a diversion."

The building was a large house. The stairs ended in the dusty ruin of its entrance hall. Doors hung open, the ceiling was denuded, lathes exposed, bowed, splintered. The floor was awash with plaster. Shattered furniture littered the hallway. The front door had long been blasted from its hinges. Two Sisters crouched on either side of the gap. Both clutched rifles, Lee Enfields, British army issue by the look of them, left behind in 1940 or perhaps parachuted in as supplies to the resistance. One of the sisters was bleeding from a head wound. The blood cut a trial through the dust that caked her face.

I saw a third sister, sprawled on her back just outside the door.

We dropped to our haunches against the wall and away from the doorway.

"This diversion had better be good," I muttered to Anna. I knew I had no choice but to trust her.

Anna merely smiled. The smile swept away the ravages of age. "When I tell you to run, you must run," she said.

I glanced at the door and at the body. Bullets rattled against the side of the building.

"Insanity," Churchill growled. "We will not last one moment out there, and as for running..." He chuckled ruefully. He was suddenly frail, small, childlike even.

Abruptly Anna moved over him and took his face roughly in her hands. "Why did you come to me?" she demanded. "Why did you risk your life to step into enemy territory?"

The man nodded awkwardly, the way a schoolboy does when undergoing a reprimand. Then he seemed to gather himself. "I suppose I have been lucky until now. I survived the South African war, a motorcar accident and a threatened invasion. There seems no reason why I shouldn't survive this." He chuckled. "And if I don't, well, it will be a heroic end. Except no one would know, would they. It would have to be a heart attack, a stray German bomb, an assassin even. Never the truth, eh madam?"

"One day," Anna said.

He turned his attention to me. "Come along then, young lady. I'm in your hands."

I gritted my teeth, checked the revolver (fully loaded) and moved to the doorway, motioning Churchill to crouch behind me as I did so. He grunted with effort. He was right. His crouching and running days were long over. This was madness.

I stared out into the square, at the relentless streams of tracer arcing out of the gathering dark to slam against the walls. These were my last moments. A final breath, a movement and it would end. The vastness of it engulfed me. The notebook was tucked into my coat pocket, against my heart, but scant protection. Yet I knew it was important, oddly huge in the white-hot chaos of thought and feeling.

Let it be quick, for God's sake let it be quick –

"Now," Anna snapped.

I whispered his name as I plunged into the fire-torn dark.

Philippe…

I was outside, in the cold air, exposed, running and strangely free. This moment was dreamlike, bright with euphoria. I heard shouts, the clatter of small arms. I saw tracer reach towards me. I wondered, curiously, how painful the first bullet would be as it seared its way into my guts.

I heard Anna cry out. A name.

Then there was light.

An explosion, a flare…

Dazzling, shimmering. Light that turned the night brighter than day. Light filled with… figures, sweeping over us; figures, shapes, terrible, beautiful. There was a song, so heart-wrenching I wept.

As I grabbed Churchill's hand and dragged him into a shambolic run, I glanced back and was sure that I saw Anna in the arms of a man, a being, something indescribable.

Even more startling was Anna's face, altered, melted back into youth.

And astounding beauty.

Then the light became fire, and the song the screams of dying German soldiers. We ran on, through the burning ruins and out towards the field.

From somewhere distant came the drone of an aircraft.

"I am Eve," said the woman. "Helpmeet of Adam."

"No," Lilith said. "You are not."

Eve seemed confused, yet even in her confusion there was a spark, a light. "But..."

Lilith wandered to the edge of the clearing and found fruit, ripe and succulent. She picked two and offered one to Eve, who regarded it with suspicion. "Adam tells me what I must eat, and *Is* tells him."

"It is just a fruit, Eve. Look." Lilith bit into it and revelled in its sweetness.

Eve reached out tentatively and took the fruit for herself. She sat down and Lilith sat beside her. "You are a She. You are a soul, a life. You are wise and more powerful than you could ever know. The He is stronger of arm, so you will need to use another tool, another weapon; wisdom, Eve, the knowledge of good and evil will set you free. So listen to what I have learned..."

LAUREL

He had confessed. Walked right into the station and told the Desk Sergeant that he was responsible for all three Battersea Cannibal murders. It was the same every time. Nutcases queuing up to admit their guilt. Did these idiots have a death wish? Found guilty, the real murderer would hang.

Tired and irritable, Detective Chief Inspector Walters sat down at the interview room's battered old table. The confessor was a good-looking bugger, fair hair, tall. No trembling, no tics, no hint of madness. Needed a square meal, though, by the look of him.

The man had brought an odd smell with him.

Walters lit up then said, 'Talk.'

The man talked.

Oflag VIIIg Prisoner of War Camp, Germany, December 1944

Lieutenant David Robertson had only been here for five days when the news came. His home was Hut 33 which he shared with fifteen other Royal Marine Commandos. This place was luxury, compared with the succession of cramped cages and transit camps he'd experienced since his capture. There were even spare bunks.

But something was amiss. For a start, Oflag VIIIg was an officer camp, yet the commandos in Hut 33 were a mix of the commissioned and non-commissioned, which meant that they had been sorted and separated.

A bad sign.

Then there was the atmosphere.

Major Hunt, the hut's hatchet-faced senior officer, or Combine Leader in Prisoner of War parlance, had welcomed Robertson with a

27

handshake, but that was all. A wall of ice separated Robertson from the other men in the hut. He was puzzled by their hostility. There were good reasons to be wary, of course. It took a while to trust a newcomer, and who was to say that he wasn't a Jerry informer? There was also the fact that Hunt's group had been together for a long time. They had been caught at Dieppe over a year before Robertson turned up. So, he could understand that it made him a bit of an outsider. But he was still one of them, a Royal Marine Commando. Surely that should count for something.

On top of all that, there were frequent arguments and at least one fight every day, usually over something trivial. Even the light in here was grubby. And there was an odd smell and a taste in the dusty air. He couldn't put his finger on what it was exactly, but it wasn't pleasant.

So, day five, three days before Christmas. It was late afternoon. The light outside had faded and it was bloody cold. The stove in the centre of the hut was failing in its duty to heat the place (another thing Robertson noticed, no matter how much they stoked that thing, the air in here was always chilled and dank).

Robertson had been for a walk, wandering the slushy streets and side-alleys formed by the neat rows of the camp's wooden huts, then out towards the barbed-wire perimeter. Not too close. The guards in the brooding watchtowers were no doubt bored, cold, bad-tempered, and ready for some shooting practice. Robertson walked a lot. There wasn't much else to do. The camp did boast a theatre group, but he didn't see himself as an actor. Perhaps he should get involved with building sets or operating the lights. Anything to relieve the boredom.

He sat on his bunk, drank strong tea and pondered joining the hut's eternal card game. No one had invited him in, but he had cigarettes, the currency of the prisoner of war camp. Surely, that would grant him a space at the table.

The door opened. Silence fell instantly.

A guard entered, anonymous in his greatcoat. The German stamped the muddy snow from his boots and removed his helmet.

"I am Sergeant Richter," he said. His English was good. He was an older man, lined and tired-looking.

"Sergeant." The speaker was Major Hunt. "What can we do for you?"

"I have bad news." Richter glanced over his shoulder, a nervous gesture. "I should not be telling you this, but I think it fair that you know."

"Know what?" Hunt said.

"The Führer has issued an order –"

"Makes a change." This was Corporal Trent. Robertson didn't like Trent. He was a sarcastic bastard who showed little respect for rank, or for anyone or anything else, come to that.

"Corporal," Hunt snapped, but there was little bite in the warning. "Carry on, Sergeant."

"The Führer has ordered that all commandos caught behind our lines are to be shot."

"Hasn't your Führer heard of the Geneva Convention?" Hunt said coldly.

"I am sorry Major." Richter said. "The order was issued some time ago. There is a detachment of SS on its way here. They will transfer you to another camp after Christmas."

"I don't think we'll get as far as another camp, do you, Sergeant? I think we'll be lucky to get past those woods out there."

"Fucking bastards," someone snarled.

"I thought you should have time to write to your families and make peace with God." Richter shook his head. The gesture denoted both sorrow and bewilderment. "I fought your fathers and older brothers in France during the last war. *We* did not shoot prisoners." He drew himself together, saluted smartly then left.

Robertson glanced around the room. He found it hard to breathe. Yes, he'd faced death before. It was his duty, but there had always been a chance, a way out. Not this time. They would be slaughtered like animals in an abattoir.

"Listen to me," Hunt snapped. He had the floor, everyone's attention. "Laurel's our only hope."

"Laurel?" Robertson asked "Who's Laurel?"

Hunt looked as if he was about to answer when a big, surly sergeant named Kane interrupted him. "Wait a minute, sir. Do we trust him?"

29

"Of course you can trust me." Robertson was tired of this. "I'm a Royal Marine."

"Your concern's noted, Sergeant, but we don't have any choice." Hunt turned to address Robertson. "The camp had two tunnels; Laurel, ours, and Hardy, which was dug from the Village Hall."

The communal hut, used as the theatre.

"Hardy was the real tunnel, Laurel, the decoy, which means it was never intended to be finished. Ironically, the Goons discovered Hardy, but not Laurel. So, we have, what, four days, a week at most, to put our tunnel back into service. Can we do it, Trent?"

"It's probably caved-in," Trent said. "But like you said, sir, we don't have a choice."

"What about clothes, fake identity cards?" Robertson said.

"To hell with all that," Kane answered. "We have to get out of here."

"We head west," Hunt said. "Try to meet up with the Allies. We'll have to live off the land and stay out of sight. We can do that, can't we men?"

There was a ragged chorus of, "Yes sir!"

"We don't stand much of a chance," Kane said. "But I'd rather die on the run than be machine-gunned like a fucking sheep."

"And me," someone shouted.

"And me."

"And me," Robertson joined in. He meant it, but he was already in a cold sweat. The thought of facing premature burial in a second-rate tunnel had awakened a horror within him deeper than fear of any firing squad.

The last time he'd known that horror had been the hold of a trawler. It stank of rotten fish and the vomit, farts and fear of the other commandos in his company who were crammed down there with him. It was a place of utter darkness and confinement that had stopped his breath and crushed his heart. Now, as the loose boards in the corner of the hut were ripped up and the tunnel shaft revealed, Robertson felt the old terrors return…

That night had been moonless and warm. The dingy bucked and tumbled over the waves as it was rowed in towards the shore. There was a moment, a stomach wrenching, nauseating moment when he was convinced that he was going to be thrown out into the Channel, but then the craft settled and skidded out of the waves and onto the beach.

One glance back. The trawler was invisible now, blacked out and silent in the darkness, waiting to take them home when this was over.

Robertson was out, quickly and quietly. Bent double, he moved up the beach towards the low cliffs and the safety of the shadow they cast. Dangerous as this place was, it was a thousand times better than the trawler's hold. He could move. He could breathe.

For a moment, as he rushed up the sand towards the dark wall of the cliffs, he thought of the thousands of men who would be charging over beaches just like this one in only a few weeks' time. The landing zones were a little further south, but a beach was a beach and a machine gun a machine gun. They would probably hit the beach in daylight, or at dawn. They would be visible, vulnerable. Many would die.

Robertson shut the thought out and forced his attention back to the job in hand. They had a boffin with them, here to take samples of the sand. Sergeant Pullman and a handful of men would keep him safe. Robertson and his platoon would, meanwhile, scale the cliff and reconnoitre a German artillery emplacement situated a half-mile inland. They had two hours before the trawler turned for home.

Robertson reached the base of the cliffs and waited for the rest of his men to cross the beach.

"Ready, sir?" Corporal Wight said as he dropped to a crouch beside him.

"Get on with it, Corporal."

Wight and another man began their climb. The cliff was low, but it still seemed to take an interminable amount of time before Robertson heard Wight's low all-clear whistle. Robertson sent up the next two. He would ascend with the third pair.

A long moment then another whistle. Robertson took a deep breath, shifted his Thompson round onto his back then, accompanied by a marine named Kingston, set to work. Halfway up, he was beginning to think that they might get away with this and go home.

A flare exploded directly overhead and the world turned blood red.

Robertson crouched at the mouth of Laurel and watched Trent, naked but for his underpants, clamber, backwards, into the vertical shaft then drop, about seven feet to its floor. He was slight, wiry and hard-muscled. A perfect tunneller's build.

"Candle and trowel," Trent snapped.

Kane handed the items down to him and the darkness was pushed back far enough for Robertson to see the tunnel entrance. Trent pushed the candle inside, squirmed and contorted himself onto his belly then slithered out of sight.

"Your turn, sir," said Kane. He held Robertson's eye. There was a challenge in his stare.

Robertson took a deep breath, then forced himself to crawl backwards into the shaft and slide downwards. His bare chest and belly scraped painfully against the edges of the floorboards. He hung there for a moment then let himself drop.

"Here," Kane said and passed down an armful of pillow cases that were to act as soil sacks. Kane stripped off his tunic and shirt. He was going to enter the tunnel directly behind Robertson, blocking any chance of escape.

Robertson struggled onto his belly, as Trent had done, and slid into the tunnel.

Immediately there was horror.

Because the walls pressed in on his arms and the roof was only a few inches from the back of his head. The flickering glimmer of Trent's candle seemed a long way ahead. Robertson used it as a focus.

Think only of the candle, not the million tons of earth bearing down on your back. Watch the candle...

He felt the first of the wooden bunk slats that formed the sides and roof of a tunnel support. There were few such supports and dirt fell in a steady gritty rain as Robertson slithered on.

He could hear the scrape and shuffle of the trowel and there was Trent, silhouetted by the shifting light of the candle. Robertson waited. He tried to slow his breathing. Lying here, Trent's feet in his face, and surrounded by a mad dance of shadows was worse than crawling. Now he could think. Now he could ponder how low the roof was, how close the walls were.

Now he could hear the heartbeat.

He wasn't sure when he had become aware of it, but here, deep in the earth, his own shuffles and grunts of effort silenced, he could distinguish every beat. It was not his own. It was slower, deeper. It vibrated through the earth. It was close and vast. It was dirty and foul.

"Sir!"

Robertson started. It was Trent, who had rolled over and was waiting to pass the first of the soil-filled pillowcases back along the tunnel. Robertson worked himself over until he was supine. Dirt dribbled onto his face from the fragile earthen ceiling which was only a couple of feet above him. He tried to swallow, tried not to hear the heartbeat, tried not to see its owner clawing up through its bed of dirt to drag him down to Hell. He reached back over his head and accepted the pillowcase from Trent. He fumbled the bag, which was heavy and soft, over his face then down over his body so that Kane could take it from him. There were three pillow cases, all full. Trent was working at a prodigious rate. For all his faults, the man was tireless.

Voices now.

Take us home.

Robertson worked himself back onto his belly.

Take us home. Take us home, sir.

He clamped his hands over his ears and the heartbeat became vibration that hammered out its plea along Robertson's nerves. *Take us home. Take us –*

"Stop it! For Christ's sake shut up!"

"What's wrong, sir?" Kane sounded almost concerned.

"Nothing... Just a bit..."

"Gets like that down here. Hold on, sir, we'll be changing shifts in half an hour or so."

Robertson was pathetically grateful for Kane's reassurance. It was the first hint of friendliness he had received since coming to Hut 33.

It grew worse when he went to bed. Filthy and sweat-dank, Robertson slithered under the rough blanket and lay there, trying to shut out the voices and dampen his agitation. The work went on, he would be awake again and doing his share in three hours' time. The voices of the other prisoners were like grit against his skin. And all the time, underlying every other sound, were the whispers; soft but scraping over Robertson's skull.

Take us home, sir. Please take us home…

Flares. Light. Then the clatter of machine-gun fire. Kingston cried out then fell. More firing, from the beach, screams, shouts. Bullets cracked through the air. Robertson heard them thud into the cliff. Little explosions of sand stung his face. He clambered upwards, energised by panic. There was too much light.

A flash, loud bang. A grenade, below. More firing and screams. He glanced downwards and saw bodies, starkly outlined by the flares, sprawled on the beach. There were three more, back towards shoreline. The boffin and his soil samples were not going back to England.

The climb had no end. More bullets slashed by, but none hit him. A bloody miracle. He reached the top of the cliff, grabbed at the coarse grass that grew there and slithered up and over with the last of his strength. Every part of him shook. He couldn't think. There were Germans everywhere.

A searchlight. He saw a body. Corporal Wight. He saw the others who had preceded him up the cliff, on their bellies, firing back. Tracer arced out of, and into, the light. Robertson crawled into shadow. If he fired, the Germans would see him. He needed to keep still. There was nothing he could do for those men.

As if reading his thoughts and driven, it seemed, by the need for one last act of defiance, the three surviving commandos from Robertson's platoon scrambled to their feet and hurled themselves at the Germans concealed within the glare of the searchlight. They fired their Thompsons from the hip as they ran. The first of them was hit within seconds. Robertson saw the bullets explode bloodily out of his back. Face pressed against the ground, hands clawing at the grass, Robertson never saw the rest of it. He heard their screams though. He knew that he would always hear their screams.

He should fight. He had nowhere to go. He mustn't be caught. He'd spill everything once the Gestapo started on him. But he couldn't move. He couldn't throw himself into that moment of hell as the others had done. So he lay there until he heard a shout. "Surrender. You are alone. Surrender!"

The German's English was good. Robertson lifted his head cautiously and saw them approach through the glare of the searchlight. Still on his belly, he lifted his hands. A moment later a jackboot was driven into his side. As he rolled over to curl himself about the pain, a rifle butt crashed into his belly and he could no longer breathe.

Despite rough handling by his captors, there were no visits to Gestapo HQ for Robertson. Instead, there was the humiliation of failure, a handful of transit camps then Oflag VIIIg and Hut 33.

The work went on round the clock. The guards must have known. Roll calls that included dishevelled, tired and dirty commandos from Hut 33 should have made them suspicious. But they acted as if nothing was happening. Perhaps it was the Wehrmacht's alleged hatred of the SS that closed their eyes and stopped their ears, or the knowledge that the Allies were advancing eastwards and that defeat was inevitable. No one wanted to be pointed out as a cruel bastard when liberation, and rough justice, arrived at the Oflag gates.

Or perhaps they really didn't suspect. It was bloody cold, and dark most of the time. Who in their right mind would want to stroll around the camp looking for tunnels when they had a nice warm guardhouse to hide in?

Work, however, came to a sudden halt on Christmas Day.

Robertson was lookout that morning. He'd not been sent down the tunnel since the first digging session. There was plenty of other work and he'd done his share. He stood outside, freezing and miserable despite the voluminous greatcoat he'd borrowed from

Kane. He leaned against the hut door, smoked steadily and counted the seconds until he was to be relieved.

A group of figures emerged from the sleet.

Robertson rapped his knuckles against the door at his back. Three sharp knocks then three more. He heard a shout from inside and an eruption of noisy activity as the tunnel was evacuated and floorboards replaced.

Robertson felt his strength fail. Who the hell would brave this storm and make a beeline for Hut 33? The SS that was who. Christ, it was too late.

Then he heard laughter, a snatch of song, badly sung, and finally a loud and drunken, 'Happy Christmas.'

The visitors were from the neighbouring huts. They had a stock of homemade hooch and they wanted a party. The crowd shoved Robertson aside and burst into Hut 33 before anyone could stop them. Suddenly the hut was full of PoWs and Laurel was quickly forgotten.

Robertson saw resignation on Hunt's face. The day was lost.

The drink tasted foul, but after the first two cups the taste no longer mattered. There was a rule regarding prison camp hooch, or so Robertson had been told by his new friend Sergeant Kane: stop when you feel mellow, because the next cup will reduce you to a vomiting, shivering mess. Few men followed that advice and Robertson decided that he too needed the oblivion the hooch would provide. Anything to silence the voices. Anything to make him forget Laurel.

There was food; black bread, some meat and soup and a collection of small Red Cross Christmas puddings.

The party was raucous from the start. A few prisoners played musical instruments, also supplied by the Red Cross, leading to dancing; noisy and rough. The first fight was not long in coming, over some slight quickly forgotten in the drunken, messy brawl.

Robertson leaned against the wall and watched. The light outside had faded to dark. The room was hot and ill-lit. Dust, the by-product of tunnelling, was kicked up from the floor by the dancers. Mingled with cigarette smoke, it formed a pungent, yellow-brown fog that hung, curtain-like, over the proceedings.

There were other figures among the dancers.

Robertson shook his head in an effort to clear his vision. The figures were shadows that whirled and pirouetted madly in the spaces between the drunken revellers. And pulsing from the core of the raucous ugly music, came the heartbeat. Robertson could feel it as it thrummed through the floorboards under his feet to punch into his belly.

Panic-stricken, Robertson pushed himself off the wall and tried to locate the door. He couldn't see it. He was trapped in here. He had to get out.

Take us with you, sir.

No, he couldn't. Why didn't they understand?

Please.

The room spun and shuddered. The floor and ceiling twisted and distorted as if the whole world had become trapped in a fairground mirror.

Robertson groped his way along the walls, feeling for the door. He needed to get out. The walls were soft under his hands. Soil. The hut was made of soil. It was a grave, a tunnel. Worms oozed from the earth, fat and white, their heads human, their tiny mouths open as they pleaded with him to -

Take us home, sir. Please...

Shouts and crashes replaced the music as the party deteriorated into a riot.

The door.

He slammed it open and fell out into the freezing darkness, staggered a few yards then doubled up to vomit into the snow. A horde of bodies erupted out of the dark. Someone grabbed him, shoved him around and yelled at him in German.

"Was it you?" Hunt was furious.

He towered over Robertson, who had been forced to sit in a chair in the middle of the Hut. The others were gathered round. Violence emanated from them like a stink.

"What?" Robertson mumbled back at the Major. He was sick and cold and wanted to lie down and sleep.

"Did you call the guards? Being the good prisoner were you?"

"No. I was ill. I had to get out –"

"Fucking liar," Kane snarled. Robertson, flinched, sure that the man was about to punch him. No blow came, though Kane's fists were clenched. His nose ran. He shivered. All the men were red-faced with cold. The Germans had made the party-goers stand out in the cold for an hour. To 'sober up and calm down', according to the enraged Camp Commandant, who had sounded as drunk as the miscreants he was punishing.

"I stood out there with you."

"So what," Trent said. "The Jerries aren't about to wrap their rat in a blanket and make him a cup of cocoa now are they? Give the game away, that would."

"What the hell are you talking –?"

"You're a fucking informer," Trent snarled.

"I'm a Royal Marine. I'm one of you."

"Bloody prove it."

"All right," he answered and lurched to his feet. God, he was dizzy. He stumbled across the room, dropped to his knees and clawed up the floorboards. No one offered to help. The tunnel shaft was exposed. Robertson dropped into the darkness. "Give me a bloody candle."

"Get out of there," Hunt called down to him. "None of us are in a fit state to –"

"Give me a fucking candle. Sir."

A moment, then. "You, Trent, do as he says."

The trowel was already down there, as well as a bundle of pillow cases. Robertson struggled onto his hands and knees and set off into the tunnel.

He didn't need the candle. There was light down there already, a strange, golden light that seeped from the walls and ceiling.

He knew immediately that he was not alone. He could feel them slithering through the dirt, like fish swimming in an earthen sea. He heard their whispers and their pleas to be taken home. But, at the same time, he knew he was safe. The light down here, the light they gave him, was warm and comforting. It brought long-dead memories of the womb; the closeness of its walls, the beat of his mother's heart.

Once at the tunnel face, Robertson set to work and was strong and tireless.

Come on, sir, you can dig all the way to the end and we'll go home.

Yes, home. That was where he wanted to be, back in England. Soil fell and slid around him. He should bag it up, it was in the way.

The heartbeat, was stronger than ever, each pulse, a jolt of electricity to his muscles. He laughed, panting now. The air was thick and cloying, but that didn't matter, they would help, his men. They were here now, just behind the dirt wall to his left. Fighting to break through. Come on, chaps, we're almost there.

Impatiently, he scooped handfuls of soil into the first of the pillow cases. There was no time to waste clearing up. He had to dig. Dig, dig and fucking dig. Soil cleared, he resumed slicing at the tunnel face.

"Stop. You bloody fool. Stop!" Trent's voice was a distant thing. *Hurry, get us out. Go on, sir. We need to get home.*

So close. Robertson pressed his left palm against the wall. He felt movement.

"Corporal Wight, is that you?"

No, no don't touch us. Don't –

Something uncoiled and broke through.

"Corporal, thank God –"

A snake-like limb thrashed into the tunnel. It slid across his forehead, flesh-textured and cold. There was urgency in its writhing, panic almost, like the desperate thrashing of an earthworm exposed to the light.

Robertson howled and struggled, suddenly trapped in the tomb he was building. No room, couldn't get out. Couldn't bloody move -

The roof caved-in.

It was a horror beyond anything he had experienced before. It was a brutal, suffocating nightmare. He was alive and he wanted to be dead. He was sealed in.

He screamed into the blanket of soil. He screamed and begged to God for release. He tried to move. Christ, how he wanted to move. He wanted light, wanted to breathe. There was no air, only dirt that poured down his throat, gritty and foul.

He wanted it to end.

And somewhere, beside him, around him, was that creature he had touched. It had deceived him. His men were dead. Now that the thing's trickery was discovered it would come for him. He could feel it, clawing its way through the soil.

Then it had him, tentacles wrapped about his legs, dragging him into itself. He tried to scream but there was only earth and silence.

"Got him, the stupid bastard." The voice was full of anger, and familiar, Sergeant Kane. "Let's get him out of here."

After the beating they gave him, Robertson could do nothing but lie on the floor at their feet, filthy from the cave-in and bloodied by fists and boots.

"It'll take us fucking days to clear that lot!" Trent had screamed.

"Then get to bloody work," Hunt shouted at him. "The SS will be here any time now and then none of it will matter. Sharp, Cooper, barricade the door. If they do come, it'll give us a little time. You men, yes, you three, smash the chairs and bunks and make some clubs. We're going down fighting." He was breathing hard. His eyes were wild. "And you two, drag this bastard onto his bunk, then get on watch. And if he tries to get up, give him another pasting. Understood?"

"Yes sir."

The two men assigned to the task were not gentle.

"The rest of you, digging and dumping soil. At the fucking double. Come on!"

No effort was made to hide the tunnel soil. It was piled up anywhere there was space. Robertson lay on his side and watched as the men worked. There was madness here. Robertson could feel it emanate from the filthy, sweat-slicked figures labouring in the dim light of the afternoon and then bathed by the unwholesome illumination of Hut 33's diseased electric lamps.

He wanted to warn them about the monster in the tunnel, but he could barely speak. Ribs had been broken, his jaw was swollen and his mouth still muddy with dirt.

At some point, deep in that endless, pain-sodden night, Hunt came over to crouch down beside him.

40

"We should tie you to this bunk and leave you to the SS," Hunt growled. "But you actually helped us." He shook his head, as if bemused. "Once we cleared that fall-in, we found that you'd dug a hell of a lot further than one man should have been able to. So, I'm going to let you follow us out once I make sure all mine are safe. And once beyond the wire, you're alone. I don't want you anywhere near my men. Understood?"

Robertson managed a stiff nod.

Then the hut door burst open.

Everyone froze as the intruder stumbled in, accompanied by a swirl of snow. He closed the door then took off his helmet. Sergeant Richter. Apparently the two lookouts hadn't seen him coming. Asleep at their posts, perhaps.

Richter stood, grim-faced, and surveyed the heaps of soil, the hole the floor and the gangs of filthy, sweat-soaked men.

"They are here," he said. "The SS are at the gates."

"God help us," Hunt growled.

"My men are trying to delay them by checking their papers and being obstructive, but they will not be able to hold them back for long. Major Hunt, please get your men out of this camp."

"I'm trying," Hunt said. "Lads," he ordered, without taking his eyes off Richter, "Tell Trent to break through. Now."

"There will be no alarm or search parties until long after dawn," Richter said. "There will be confusion and diversions. Hopefully, none of us will be shot for incompetence. Good luck, Major."

"Thank you, Sergeant. I wish I could repay you for this."

Richter shrugged and smiled. Robertson didn't like that smile.

Hunt was the last to climb into the tunnel. The hut was suddenly empty.

"And you, Lieutenant Robertson? Are you staying or going home?"

Robertson struggled into a sitting position then got to his feet. He almost fell back onto the bunk as faintness greyed the room. Blood sang through his head and he fought a wave of nausea. How the hell was he going to crawl through that tunnel? And once out, he would not be able to run. He was doomed, but he would die a free man.

41

He shuffled towards the tunnel entrance, then stopped and looked back at Richter.

...or are you going home?

Home.

And he knew.

"The SS are not here, are they? They're not coming."

"No, they're not. The order was given, but there was an oversight in the paperwork. Hunt's men were forgotten." Richter smiled again. "You're very perceptive, Lieutenant Robertson."

"Was there ever a Sergeant Richter?"

"Yes. He died on the Somme in October 1916, defending his trench from yet another fruitless British attack."

"You wanted Laurel opened again, is that it?"

"I was disappointed when it was abandoned. I am very ancient and very lonely." Richter drew a pack of cigarettes from his greatcoat pocket. "I want to see the world again. I want to taste it. And to do so, I need a friend. You're my friend, Lieutenant."

"Who are you?"

Richter shrugged, then placed a cigarette between his lips and lit up. "You cannot imprison me with a name." He exhaled and faded, somehow, as if part of him had melded with the smoke. "Now, you should go. The guards won't treat you well if they find you here alone. An example will be made to discourage others." Then he was shadow, a stain on the already infected light of the hut.

Robertson crawled back into the hell that was Laurel. Everything hurt. Each movement. The pain overwhelmed the terror of the crushing smallness of the tunnel.

Sir take us home.

No.

Sir, please. We'll give you light.

No.

There was nothing but darkness. It choked him. It ground into his eyes. It crawled over him and whispered and pleaded and begged. Those men who died while he survived. He heard the creak of the earth above his head. He heard the shuffle of the men further in as they awaited their turn at freedom.

The monstrous thing was back. He felt its vibrations through the rough floor. He heard its voice. He heard his men begging him to take them home.

I can't.

You can. You must.

No.

You don't understand, sir. You must gather us to yourself.

He saw light, far ahead, a dim shaft that pierced the black of the tunnel. The lighter darkness of the night outside. Trent had broken through.

"Off you go, Trent." That was Hunt, passing on the message from the rear of the queue. "Make for the woods and wait there."

Robertson hung back. They didn't want him near. He closed his eyes and tried to shut out the voices and the beat of the tunnel's rotten heart. Silence. Waiting. Then.

The brief rattle of a machine gun, short and sharp. A distant cry. Then an eruption of shouting, screaming and panic, and Hunt's desperate yell of "Back!"

Then the world was shattered into a million, bloody, white-hot shards.

Grenade. Christ Almighty. The Jerries were tossing grenades into the tunnel. Robertson coughed on the billowing fog of smoke and dirt. He pushed his face hard into the soil of the tunnel floor. A moment later the world bucked and shuddered once more; a second grenade. This time the roar of the blast ripped away his hearing and replaced it with a ringing sound so loud it hurt more than his bruises and fractures.

Help me. Please. Help me. He prayed into the dirt. He clawed at the floor and begged for salvation.

When he opened his eyes, he saw the bullets from a Schmeisser cut and slice their way through the surging, screaming tangle of wounded and dead escapers trapped in the tunnel. Some brave soul must have crawled, head-first into Laurel's exit to finish the job. It went on and on. And then it stopped. Everything stopped.

Take us home, sir. Take us home.

"Yes," he said. "Anything. I'll take you. I'll take you home."

He didn't feel the arms of the thing as it surged out of its earthen home to embrace him and fill him. He remembered it, though, in his nightmares.

Battersea Police, Station February 1949

"By the time I came round, it was quiet." The confessor slumped in his chair, exhausted and pale. "Another deceit. The SS *had* arrived and what better way for them to cover-up their dirty work than burying their victims in a tunnel. It's why the guards pretended not to know. They let us dig our own grave. Meanwhile, that monster, Richter, or whatever it is, seized its opportunity. Luckily, the death squad didn't seal Laurel straight away so I was able to crawl over what was left of the others and get out. I was the creature's host. Hunt and the rest were its food. It was hungry again by the time I made it home, so I fed it. Three times. And now I've had enough. I want it gone.'

Walters stubbed out his cigarette and immediately drew another from his pack. He had a confession. He had fingerprints and witnesses. If they all married up it was case-closed and a celebratory pint in the Hammer and Nails.

He breathed in a lung-full of tobacco smoke, hoping it would smother the smell of freshly dug earth that hung about the room. Yes, a beer and some noise. Anything to shut out the whispering.

STUKA JUICE

1938... Tonight it started. You could feel it. Something that burned through the music like electricity. All your doubts about the bargain were gone now. The moment you closed the deal and the amulet was pressed into your palm by that black blues singer, Johnson, that was his name, you had felt it coming, like a storm building. The singer was drunk, making all kinds of wild claims. No harm in trying, though, even if you believed it to be the ramblings of a whisky-sodden fool, but you and your band were going nowhere, so what was there to lose? You gave him the bottle of Bushmills you had bought him and held out your hand, and at that moment, in that grimy back alley, in that hot and humid little Southern town, you heard it: the music, and you felt strong and knew what you had to do. Johnson had said he was giving it away because he was scared. There was, he said, a price; your soul, to be checked-in before your time was due. Well, to hell with your soul, because tonight the music was alive and hot and the world was going to be yours.

1: GOD

It was when the old man looked up, and Dietrich saw the fury and the fire in his eyes, that he recognised him and understood that he was in the presence of his god. The realisation sent him to his feet with such violence he knocked his chair backwards to the floor.

"Heil Hitler!" Dietrich snapped, arm extended.

"Sit," said the Führer. "Major, please, sit."

Dietrich did as he was told, after first retrieving the overturned chair, an action that made him feel clumsy and foolish.

"Thank you Mein Führer," he mumbled. *Mumbled!* He was a major in the Wehrmacht.

He had fought for the Fatherland since the invasion of Poland. He was a leader of men, had survived the apocalypse in Stalingrad, and now, suddenly, a mere table-width away from the deity he had worshipped for almost his entire life, he was as tongue-tied as a love-sick boy.

And what was that god but a sick, tremulous old man? Dietrich could hear the Führer's every breath, see every line etched into his face.

But he could still feel his power.

A table-width. That was all.

The Führer leaned forwards. "You are a hero, Major Dietrich," he said. "An Iron Cross, yes?"

"At Kursk, Mein Führer."

In Hell, Mein Führer, a hell of flame and smoke and shattered flesh, of endless slaughter and ignominious, bloody defeat.

The Führer closed the distance between them further still, his eyes bore into Dietrich, and it was if the walls of the Bunker were drawn in around him, transformed into a halo of concrete and shadow. "I was betrayed," the Führer growled. "Generals they called themselves. Hah! Cowards, incompetents, all of them. They would not listen to me. *Me*, their Führer! And when I am betrayed, my soldiers are betrayed. Is that not so, Major?"

"I do my duty Mein Führer." A careful answer.

"I know." His hand came to rest on Dietrich' arm. *His* hand, the Führer's hand. Dietrich could feel the man trembling. "How are the defences?"

"Strong Mein Führer. The men are in good spirits."

The *old* men and young boys assigned to Dietrich on the eastern borders of Berlin *were* in good spirits. Afraid, but confident that they would hold the city against Stalin's peasant hordes. Dietrich had been relieved to be called away, here, to the Bunker. He had not relished being present at the swift destruction of his rag-tag command.

"Good. Good," the Führer said, and smiled for the first time since Dietrich had been in his presence. "Now, Major, you have a special duty to perform for the Fatherland."

Dietrich felt his strength drain away. He was exhausted, sick of war. He longed for the Americans and the British to break through and put an end to this nightmare. Treacherous thoughts, he knew, but he had seen what the Russians did to the conquered. And Germany *was* conquered. Only a fool would think otherwise.

"There is an artefact, lost, now found," the Führer said. "You must fetch it."

"An artefact?"

"To be returned to its owner, who has promised his help, has promised victory."

"Forgive me, but I don't understand, Mein Führer," Dietrich said carefully.

"This war, this total war, is only the surface of an even greater struggle. Forces you can never imagine, wrestling for supremacy, armies that could crush an entire world if unleashed. And they will be, when we return this lost possession to its rightful owner." The old man's grip tightened. "I have seen this... this being, and I have seen his armies. The only advisers I can trust, they have shown me."

The rumours were true then; a cabal of charlatans who called themselves wizards or some such, whispering magical nonsense into the Führer's ear.

"Your name will go down in history, Major, as the saviour of the Thousand Year Reich."

The Russians on the outskirts of Berlin, cities pounded to rubble day and night by Allied bombers, and he, Major Paul Dietrich, a soldier of immeasurable experience, survivor of an entire war, was to be sent on a fool's errand to fulfil the fantasies of his broken, deluded leader. He should refuse, he should drag this idiot out into the rubble and show him the Truth –

"I will do my best, Mein Führer."

"I know you will, Major, because you are a true German."

The Führer smiled and spoke with such fatherly warmth that Dietrich's anger instantly dissolved and he almost wept with love and gratitude.

2: STUKA JUICE

There was darkness, made worse by the stunted beam of his waterproof torch, darkness that pressed into his eyes. Darkness that had debilitating, bone-crushing *weight*.

There was also cold, absolute, blood-freezing cold.

And there was loneliness, down here under these millions of tons of water. A loneliness so intense, he found himself believing that he was not alone at all.

She's here...

Stirling brought himself up short. This was the bloody English Channel, not the Pacific or the Atlantic. It was a ditch, a few miles of cold grey water.

Besides, Christine was up there, waiting for him on the *Fox* with the rest of the boat's crew. And he certainly wasn't adrift. Connected to his heavy, brass diving helmet and waving gracefully in the icy currents far above him were the pipes through which he breathed and had his being.

So, Stirling my boy, you have nothing to be afraid of. You've spent most of the war underwater; folded in half for hours-on-end in sweaty, stinking mini-subs, sneaking round the barnacle-encrusted keels of enemy shipping with Buster Crabbe, crawling out of the waves to recce the Normandy beaches on the eve of D-Day. Took it all in your stride, didn't you. So don't go getting the frighteners now, not when the bloody show is almost over.

He trudged on, Frankenstein boots sinking into the soft, sandy seabed. The cold seeped through the heavy canvas suit and into his flesh. Into his nerves, his thoughts, his soul.

Traitor... she knows... did you really think she wouldn't find out? Do you think she's going to forgive you? Unfaithful, murderous bastard... All she has to do is snip that pipe... cut the cord...

It's the Stuka Juice. It's not the truth. Stirling repeated it over and over, made it his prayer. Breathe enough of it and it sent you mad. They warned him when he volunteered for this. Hold your nerve, they said. Keep your thinking straight, laddy.

But you did betray her, Christine, your wife... while she was in France, playing the hero... Do you know what the Gestapo would have done to her if they'd caught her? You can guess, can't you? You can see it, here in the dark... Weren't thinking about that though, were you, laddy? You'd found yourself a bitch in heat and you were sniffing at her like a mad dog...

Sixty metres. Bloody deep, and he needed to go a lot deeper. So breathe it in, breathe in the old Stuka Juice, that magic mix of helium and oxygen. It was the only way to survive at this depth. They *had* to get it right. Before the Yanks did, before the Germans. So he had to stay down here until the test was over. He had to drop into this icy black hell over and over again until they got the mixture right and the monsters stayed under the bed.

Who is the monster, laddy? She knows what you did that night... she's going to leave you down here, alone, with the...

He could feel them now, moving towards him. Slithering through the thick, thick water. Hungry. Whispering. He jabbed the weak torch light about him, punching its beam into the darkness, seeing them flit aside, hiding.

She's bloody angry... and she has a knife, laddy... She will do it... you'll breathe in and there'll be nothing but cold water... and the dark and the loneliness and them...

There! And there. Circling him, human faces, featureless black eyes, rotten white skin. And she was going to leave him here. The slut was going to abandon him to those things.

But why shouldn't she?

Get me out of here! He yanked at the lifeline.

To hell with you, Christine screamed back. You can rot down there forever you bastard...

"Get me out of here, please, please..."

3: CHRISTINE AND HELEN

He lay on the deck, stripped of the cumbersome suit and helmet, wrapped in a blanket and shivering. Faces looked down at him. Then Christine came into focus.

"To hell with you," she whispered. "Next time I'll leave you to rot down there forever you bastard."

"No." He felt like crying, like a baby. "Please, Christine, don't do that."

"Do what, my darling? What's wrong?" She looked at the others. "This is the worst he's been. How many more times does he have to do this?"

"We have our orders, ma'am –"

"But look what it's doing to him."

"Sir, are you all right?" Harper now, the *Fox's* skipper. Big man, beard, gruff.

"Yes, yes, it's wearing off." Stirling struggled to sit up. Christine crouched beside him, hand on his shoulder. "Bit of a bad show, that one," he said to her. "Seeing things, hearing voices."

"Do you think you'll be able to go down again tomorrow?" This was Walpole. The boffin. In charge of mixing the Stuka Juice, trying to get it right. He was skinny, pale and out of place on the *Fox,* which was a fishing boat, a rough-and-ready vessel at the best of times. The crew were no fishermen, though. Royal Navy, in mufti, half a dozen of them, hand-picked for the job.

Stirling felt Christine's hand tighten on his shoulder, but he still said "Yes, of course I will."

"Why?" She wasn't angry exactly, but the question was like a whiplash. Stirling had known it was coming.

"You know why," he answered. "You of all people."

They were below decks, in the cramped space laughingly called their cabin.

"Yes, me of all people. But you can stop this, at any time. What I did, what you did back then, neither of us had a choice."

"You volunteered."

"I was asked. Do you seriously think I could have said no?"

"I can't say no to this Christine."

"You can and you must. The war's almost over, you could be tucked up safe behind a desk. You've done your bit, Jim. You've done everything that was asked of you."

Christine sat on the bunk, a slight, dark-haired woman. She looked deceptively delicate, fragile, the effect heightened by the heavy Navy-issue pullover she wore. She was the only person Stirling was afraid of, and the only person he trusted with his heart.

Christine's mother was French, her father English. She had spent her childhood in Brittany until the early death of her mother drove father and daughter home to London. When war broke out, Christine joined the Royal Navy as a WREN. It didn't take long for the SOE to find her. A year later, Christine was parachuted into a night-dark French meadow. She came back, whole and hearty, or so it seemed. When she slept, though, the memories clawed their way to the surface and into her dreams. Her midnight cries still woke Stirling and he would hold her tight until the terrors went away.

She agreed to go again.

Somewhere between those two operations, she met Lieutenant-Commander James Stirling. They had married quickly and quietly. If you wanted something in these times, you had to take it. There would probably never be a second chance.

"I'm sorry," Christine said. "A tiff is the last thing we need right now. It's just that… I'm afraid of losing you. I always have been. Even when I was in France, with other… things to think about."

"It's all right," Stirling said and pulled her to himself. "Look, the whole thing really is a piece of cake. It's like going to see one of those ridiculous Bela Lugosi films, only it seems as if it's real. But if you keep telling yourself that it's all nonsense, well, you can get through it."

"I'm hardly in a position to interfere, am I?" Christine said. "I shouldn't even be here."

She was along as an 'Observer', strings pulled, favours called in.

"Darling, one more try and then no more, I promise," Stirling said.

He flopped onto the bunk behind her. She turned and stroked his hair.

"I love you," she whispered.

"And I love you."

He always had, from the moment he saw her.

So how could he have been in love with Helen Howard as well?

He had been at a US Eighth Air Force base in East Anglia that day, invited in to lecture aircrew on survival after ditching in the sea. The Bomb Group had completed their first one hundred missions the day before and, to celebrate, the Glenn Miller band were booked for that evening.

You wanna come, Lootenant? Sure it's okay. Don't need no tickets for this one. Hey, you'll feel right at home. We invited a bunch of local girls, all in the interest of co-operation with our British allies, you understand.

Helen was a 'local girl'. She was pretty, knowing, fun. No harm in a dance. God, Christine was probably holed up with some charmer from the French Resistance at that very moment. So it was only fair.

Wasn't it?

The music was loud and exciting. They danced, drank too much, and danced again. They both missed their respective lovers. They were both lonely.

It was wartime.

Stirling woke, suddenly, confused. There was shouting, thuds, footsteps, then the bark of weapons.

"What is it, Jim? What's happening?" Christine mumbled

There was a rattle of automatic fire. A shriek of pain. More gunfire.

"Schmeisser," she whispered. "Bloody Jerries…"

Stirling rolled off the bed, thankful they had fallen asleep fully clothed. He scrambled for his kit bag and the revolver he kept hidden there. Christine was up as well, now crouched at the foot of the cabin's short ladder, unarmed. Stirling moved across to join her. Still a little befuddled by sleep, he climbed the ladder to the door itself.

"Ready?" he said. Christine nodded, directly behind him.

He opened the door, carefully. The night dark was a confusion of movement, torn open by the jagged flicker of muzzle flashes. Stirling saw another vessel drawn up alongside; fishing boat, like the *Fox*. Then he saw a body, another, a third, sprawled on the *Fox's* small deck.

A figure rushed out of the dark, sub-machine gun in hand. Stirling fired. The figure grunted and fell backwards. Before he could stop her, Christine scrambled past Stirling, to crouch by the body, scrabbling for the weapon.

She was suddenly bathed in white. Searchlight, on the other boat.

Stirling saw her freeze, saw three men move in, weapons aimed at her head. Two he didn't recognise, the other was Walpole.

"Throw down your weapon, Stirling," the taller of the two strangers said. His English was only slightly accented. "I won't hesitate to shoot her."

4: SOLDIERS

Sometime later, in the small hours, two members of the German boarding party hauled Stirling up from below decks. His arms and legs ached from being trussed-up with his wife in their cabin. Christine was still down there.

Stirling was shoved into the tiny chartroom behind the wheelhouse. The boarding party's commander was seated at the table. Stirling was forced down onto a chair opposite. The men were dismissed.

The officer was thin, almost gaunt, his dark hair streaked with premature grey. Like his men, the German was out of uniform, dressed as a merchant seaman. He regarded Stirling with deep-set, blue-grey eyes.

"You dive at first light," the German said.

"Where are the crew?"

"They were enemy soldiers and we are at war."

"You haven't answered my question."

"They were given as decent a sea burial as is possible out here." *Dumped over the side then.* "We are not barbarians."

"That's a matter of opinion."

The German sighed, then repeated "Lieutenant Stirling, you dive at first light."

"No I don't."

"You must. Otherwise… Well, your wife is on board. Need I say more?" Matter-of-fact, no sadistic pleasure, just weariness at the prospect.

Stirling sighed. He had known there would be a threat to Christine and that, in the end, he would have to do something like this. Why else would the German boarding party have kept him alive if not to go down into the water for them?

Into the cold dark. Christ, down there, breathing that bloody nightmare juice. He couldn't...

"Look, what do you really need me for?" he said. "The new gas mixture is on the boat for the taking. The boffin, Walpole, he's yours anyway. All you've got to do is haul the tanks aboard your ship and it's done. Bit of bad news, though, the stuff doesn't work."

"I know nothing about the gas mixture. That is Walpole's responsibility."

"Bloody traitor."

"Is he? He is being true to his beliefs. After all, he did march with Oswald Mosely."

"He'll hang when this is over."

The German shrugged. "None of my concern. Or yours. You simply have to dive and retrieve an artefact." The German lit a cigarette. "From the wreck of an aircraft, to be precise."

"Secret weapon is it?" Stirling sighed. "I need a smoke."

The German held out the pack.

"Can't you untie Christine? There's nowhere for either of us to run." Stirling's wrists and ankles still ached from returning circulation. He noticed that his skin was bruised and rope burned.

"She stays where she is." The German regarded him for a moment. "Why bring your wife out here? The war isn't over. The sea is still a dangerous place."

Stirling didn't answer, but drew deeply on his cigarette and concentrated on working out how he could get them out of this fix. So far there were no ideas forthcoming.

"The wreck should be directly below us," the German said. "It is a small aircraft, a Curtis Norseman, which crashed last December on its way to France. There was a passenger, an American bandleader named Glenn Miller, you have heard of him?"

Glenn Miller? Glenn Bloody Miller?

Heard of him? Was this some sort of divine joke, God paying him out for what he did that night?

Like a dog sniffing at a bitch on heat.

But that wasn't the worst of it, was it...

"I thought no one knew what happened to his plane."

The German ignored the comment. "Miller came by the artefact, many years ago. He was struggling, going nowhere as they say. He met someone and struck a bargain. His soul in exchange for fame and fortune. The bargain was sealed with an object. An amulet. That is what you must retrieve for us."

Stirling took another deep drag. He stared at the German. "You don't really believe that rot, surely."

"What you or I believe is not important." The German looked directly at him and Stirling saw the depth of his weariness and realised that it must mirror his own. "I promise that both of you will be released if you bring the artefact back from the wreck."

"Why should I believe you?"

"You have my word, soldier to soldier."

"I assumed you would like tea. You're British, the British like tea." Dietrich offered the mug. Christine turned her head away.

"Untie me and I'll drink it."

"I'm sorry, I cannot. Not until your husband has completed his task."

Christine sighed and strained forward to sip at the drink. She was lying on her side on the bunk, hands behind and bound, in turn, to her ankles, legs bent double. "My last meal?" she said.

Yes, it is. You were a spy, and, as such, condemned to death. The Führer's orders.

"Not if your husband is successful."

She spat out a cynical laugh, which was surprisingly painful to him. Why should he care about the opinion of an enemy?

Because there had been another woman, just like this one. You shot her in the back of the head as she knelt by the grave she and her fellow partisans had been forced to dig. You pulled the Luger's trigger and the bullet smashed a hole in the back of her skull and tore open her face. She was still alive and screaming when she pitched forward into the trench.

He was feeling pity, for *partisans?*

Then there were the villages selected for reprisal. The men and boys shot out of hand. The women thrown to your men as a reward for their dogged heroism. Mothers, sisters, wives, daughters, screaming as their houses burned and their humanity was ripped away —

Dietrich stood, abruptly. He was breathing hard, drenched in sweat.

"I give you my word," he growled. "As a soldier."

5: THE DARK

Stirling slammed boots-first into the sea and the old panic tore at him like a thousand knives. The water closed over his helmet and there was grey, bubble-fogged gloom.

Then came the cold.

It seeped through the thick canvas suit to wrap itself about his flesh and mine its way down into his bones. He gasped for breath, afraid, panicked, fought to claw back up towards the surface. But he was falling into the dark.

He could not stop falling –

He flicked on the torch and its beam sliced into the murk. He aimed it downwards and it was worse. Nothing for an eternity, until at last he glimpsed a dim-lit circle of seabed.

He landed, softly but firmly, his boots kicking up an explosion of silt that billowed through the torch beam and surrounded him like gritty fog. He panted for breath and was already fighting the urge to remove his helmet.

Stirling relaxed a little, tasted rubber-tainted Stuka Juice. He was alive. He could breathe.

Because the enemy *were keeping him alive, the bloody Germans, cranking the pump and squirting gas into his lungs.*

Which way to walk?

The ocean bed was a vast, empty wilderness. The chances of finding the wreck were remote. He would walk in a leftward spiral, slowly working outwards. Carefully, because disorientation came quickly down here. But he had to try –

Christine, dirty, bruised, clutching her sten-gun, face white.

Down here, pounding through the water, closer, closer.

He twisted round, the movement slow and cumbersome.

And there was empty blackness.

But she is down here, laddy, plenty of places to hide out there in the dark...

Who was down here? He struggled to remember, thought made difficult by the music racketing through his skull. Bloody Glenn Miller. It was giving him a headache. He grabbed at his helmet.

No… Stop you bloody fool… STOP!

He let go. The darkness swirled in. He calmed. Lifted the torch and resumed his walk.

He could still hear Glenn and the boys. *Chattanooga Choo-Choo.*

Distant, close, waxing and waning. They'd danced to that, hadn't they, Stirling and Helen, the dog and the bitch-on-heat. They'd danced, then rutted and suddenly Stirling was plunged into a desperate, breathless affair. Ravaged by guilt, consumed by his need to be with this woman until he wanted it to stop. He told her, in a cheap hotel in Brighton as the grey sea raged outside and cold November rain pounded the window.

She shouted and swore and tried to scratch his face. Then she cried and pleaded, went down on her knees. He turned away and walked out. A week later she was dead; wrists hacked open with a bread knife, the bed in her cottage, the one on which they had made love for the first time, sodden red with her blood.

There was light, wavering in the swirl of dark water. Light, where light shouldn't be. And the music, rolling through Stirling's head, big band, dance music yet hard to name, dissonant, discordant.

None of it was real. It was the Stuka Juice, it-was-not-real –

Stirling resumed his trudge, heading now towards the uncertain, shifting glow. He sensed, *felt*, others walk beside him. Yet when he looked round, there was only darkness. They were there all right, moving in closer with every step.

Who are they, laddy? What are they? Is she *among them? The* other *woman? Is she, eyes a-bulge, wrists all torn and bloody?*

Shapes began to form in the gloom. Christ, shapes, figures, people. Moving in time to the beat of the music. No longer dissolved by the stunted reach of the torch beam, yet at the same time insubstantial.

Faces erupted out of the black, excited, laughing, shouting, men and women. They rushed at him, then shattered into tornadoes of spiralling bubbles.

Turn back.

Now.

Tug the life-line. Get out of here, scram and scarper. Save your sanity, laddy.

He stumbled on, making for the dancers, starting as more of them ran by, shrinking from their terrible faces. But it was the only way to keep Christine alive. So he trudged through the madness, until he saw what was in the light.

Dietrich paced, smoked, then went to the rail and looked out at the cloud-heavy morning sky. A few feet from where he stood, Walpole oversaw the men who operated the pump, their exertions keeping Stirling alive via the pipes trailed over the boat's side and into the choppy, foam-flecked water.

A black, rotten dread sat in Dietrich's belly. Was this moment of insanity really the salvation of the Thousand Year Reich? He barely believed that Stirling would even find the wreck down there, let alone locate the amulet in the dark and mud. Dietrich knew little about Glenn Miller, had been aware of his music – condemned as degenerate by the Party – remembered something about the man's disappearance, but had cared little, if at all.

His briefing had been detailed, much of it given by one of those charlatans he had come to despise once he discovered that they were real. The man had worn the uniform of the SS, though Dietrich doubted he had ever held a rifle, let alone seen action. He was intense, fervent, and Dietrich had wanted to break his nose. "The amulet was stolen centuries ago," the man declared. "Bought and sold by the unscrupulous, its energies abused for personal gain. But now it is within reach and can be brought home to its rightful owner. The rewards for the Fatherland will be uncountable."

The man opened a map on the table, general co-ordinates, taken from the report given by the fighter pilot who claimed to have downed Miller's aircraft. And, more precisely, from the magician's own 'inner searching and questioning'. His long finger stabbed down onto the chart. "Here," he said. "This is where you will find it."

Dietrich threw the last of his cigarette outwards over the water. It trailed a brief stream of red sparks then vanished. Like us, Dietrich mused. Like all my old comrades. So few of them left now.

Stirling and his wife would join them soon, a bullet in each of their skulls. The thought of it sickened him; odd, since he had killed so many over the last five years. Why trouble his conscience over two more?

Dietrich pushed himself back from the rail and lit another cigarette.

It had to be done.

Duty, he told himself. And expedience.

And the saving of his own neck.

6: IN THE MOOD

It was an aircraft, silhouetted against the glare. Whole and undamaged by the look of it, sitting on the sea bed as if brought in for a perfect landing.

The music was loud here because of the band arranged around the aircraft. The musicians could be glimpsed between the dancers. All were indistinct in the wild mix of ocean dark and blazing light, but Stirling could see that the men were in US Air Force uniform, and the women in dresses that swirled in the water as they moved and settled slowly when they were still. The dancers' polished boots and high heels billowed the silt around their legs and then upwards to hang over the scene like the fug of cigarette smoke.

Stirling came to a halt at the edge of the dance floor. He had to get out of here. He should turn round and walk away. This was dangerous. This was so bloody bad. He fought for breath. He lifted his hand to wipe the sweat from his forehead but met brass and glass instead. The sweat trickled and itched. If he could just get this bloody helmet off –

Then a woman emerged from the dancers and stood about six feet from where Stirling waited. She smiled.

Helen. He had known she would be here –

No, not her. She was dead. He knew she was dead because…

Because you killed her, laddy. Remember that, do you? Remember her face as you swung round and walked out of that hotel room? You knew what she was going to do. In your heart, you knew, and you still walked away.

I couldn't betray Christine any longer, don't you understand? I couldn't do that to her.

Of course you couldn't. You did what was best.

Helen's eyes were bright, lips red and slightly parted in that way that had driven him mad. Her skirt, and her hair, unpinned and loose, undulated in the water. She held out her delicate, white-gloved hand.

But it's all right. Dance with me.

Stirling's breath caught and he realised that he was crying. "I'm sorry... I didn't mean... I couldn't stop myself..."

Dance with me, Jim, hold me close.

He reached out and felt her hand in his and followed her into the whirl of dancers. The music filled his head. He pulled Helen to him and felt her close, despite the heavy suit, despite the helmet. They were together, crushed together. He saw the band now, their leader conducting with one hand, trombone at the ready in the other. Light glinted from his glasses. Glenn Miller of course. Who else could it have been? The band roared on behind him. Stirling couldn't see their faces. He didn't want to, because there was something wrong with them, something too shadowed.

Then there was nothing but the music and the swirling crowds and Helen and they were dancing, dizzy, buffeted by other couples. Stirling could smell cigarettes, beer, perfume and sweat. The music roared and filled everything; *In The Mood.* Helen clung to him, hot and soft and sweet-scented.

The bandmaster's conducting grew wilder with each beat, until he resembled a jerking, frantic puppet. He turned to the audience.

Dead. His face was dead, eyes wide, mouth an open black hole.

Stirling saw the band then, human, yet not human, bestial, red-eyed, perversions torn from mediaeval images of Hell.

"Kiss me." Stirling felt Helen's breath on his face, inside the helmet, a butterfly wing dancing on his flesh. "Kiss me, please, kiss me..."

Despite his terror of the monstrous band, of the shadowed darkness hiding the dancers' faces, Stirling wanted her. He grabbed at the helmet clasps.

"I'm doing it now," Dietrich said.

"Sir?" Sergeant Baeker looked up from the pump.

"I'm dealing with the woman now."

And I don't have to explain myself to you, Sergeant.

"With respect, sir, the Britisher won't co-operate if she's dead."

There was a look in Baeker's eye; he saw it in all of them. He'd known the handful of infantrymen he'd picked for this mission a long time. They were his men, yes, but they were also his friends. The three sailors who had been assigned to him were strangers but also war-hardened and reliable. A fine team.

But now he heard their muttering, their whispers. He saw their unease.

Something has happened down there, something has been disturbed —

Nonsense. He was a soldier, not some superstitious old peasant woman.

— which means that he's found it. Which means we can go back to Berlin and fight for what is left of the Reich. And if the Führer's magicians are right...

"Your respect is noted, Sergeant. Your job is to keep the bastard alive, do you understand me?"

"Yes sir."

Dietrich crossed the deck. He paused outside the door to the tiny cabin where Christine was being held. He swallowed dryly and pulled the Luger from its holster under his coat. He had to do this now, before his nerve failed and it was too late. It would be simple, quick, painless.

A bullet punched into the back of her skull, her face ripped open by its exit. Still alive and screaming as they pitched her into the sea...

He opened the door.

7: 44-70285

No...

Stirling pushed himself back. Helen stumbled, her hair and dress billowed. Her face twisted into shock, then hurt. She threw herself at him but Stirling shoved her aside and drove into the dancers.

Jim, don't. Listen to me, please listen, you mustn't...

The dancers crowded in, spinning impossibly fast, bodies pressed together. Stirling battered his way through, each blow, each punch delivered with dreamlike slowness. He glimpsed their hell-horrible faces, felt teeth and claws tear at his suit and beat at his helmet.

Then he was through, hauling himself along the fuselage of the aircraft, until he found the door. He leaned in and saw what looked like a pile of sticks. Bones, picked clean. A pair of glasses. And there, a chain, a pendant, caked with silt.

Jim, please. Helen, her arms about him, cheek against his back. *Don't –*

His hand closed around the pendant. The music stopped, the light went out and he was alone. But that didn't matter, because he was filled with a joy so intense it ripped a howl of ecstasy from his throat. He saw a glorious, vast, unstoppable army, and glowing, golden hosts singing songs that pierced deep into his soul. He felt strength flow into him, the strength and the will to fulfil any desire, to bring any dream to fruition, and understood what it had given to Miller and a thousand others before him.

He reached up and grabbed the lifeline. One tug and his feet would lift from the seabed and he would be on his slow journey back to the surface, out of the dark and the cold.

Dietrich stepped into the cabin. Christine had turned herself over so that she had her back to him. He saw her cramped, bent-double legs, her hands, purple from loss of circulation, and grazed from what looked like determined efforts to free herself.

"Do I get a last cigarette?" she said.

Dietrich couldn't find an answer.

"At least let me stand up and face you. I don't want to die like this."

"It makes no difference," Dietrich said and moved to the bed.

She grunted, and twisted over onto her back. "Yes it does. It makes a great deal of difference."

Dietrich brought the weapon up. Christine watched him, unflinching, even when he placed the muzzle against her temple. Her eyes never left his. Dietrich wetted his cracked, dry lips. He blinked away a trickle of sweat from his eyes.

"Do it," Christine whispered through gritted teeth. "For God's sake get it over with."

His finger tightened, he felt the trigger give under the pressure –

The amulet pulsed in Stirling's hand. He could feel its energies, its power. He could feel what it might do.

And that couldn't be.

Even for Christine's life – which was lost anyway. He had never believed the German's promises.

Christ, Christine...

"I'm sorry my darling," he wept. "I'm so sorry, for all of it..."

Stirling turned away from the scattered, rotten remains of the aircraft and opened his fist to let the amulet drop slowly into the darkness. The band immediately struck up and all was light and music once more. Stirling let the dancers whirl around and imprison him. He waited for Helen to step out of their ranks; hair and dress a-swirl in the currents, arms out, red, red lips apart, awaiting his kiss.

The moment she did so, Stirling began to unclasp the big brass helmet.

Can you hear them? Women thrown to your men as a reward for their dogged heroism. Screaming as their houses burn and their humanity is ripped away –

Now. He must do it now. He could hear Christine's laboured breath, hissing through her clenched teeth, could feel her shaking, waiting for that final, explosive fragment of pain.

Can you hear them? Can you? All of them? Men, women, children, soldiers and civilians, clawing their way into your soul, daubing it with the blood you shed from them. Can you hear their rage –

Dietrich relaxed his grip on the Luger's trigger and slumped back to kneel on the wooden floor. He heard Christine's gasp of shock; half sob, half laughter.

A moment later, someone pummelled at the door, shouting. "Sir! Sir! The Britisher has gone. We have lost him!"

"Why didn't you shoot me?" Christine asked him. She and Dietrich were in the wheel house, watching as the last of the German's party boarded their own boat. She hadn't cried. Dietrich could see her grief clearly, but knew she wouldn't weep for her husband until long after they had gone and she was steering the *Fox* back towards England.

"A change of orders from Berlin," Dietrich said.

A doomed city. There would be no demonic armies to save them now, only exhausted soldiers, their ranks swelled with young boys and old men.

And nothing to save you when the Führer hears of your failure.

"You're lying," she said.

Dietrich shrugged and made to go.

"Major."

He stopped, halfway down the steps to the deck.

"Yes?"

"You do know that if it had been you lying there, I would have pulled the trigger."

He looked back up at her. "I would have expected no less."

THE MAN WHO WASN'T DEAD

1: Cops

The oldest of the three detectives in that stinking little interview room leaned towards me and said, "So, you were in the army." His name was Lieutenant Morrison and he had a wrinkled kind of face. He was all smiles, like your favourite uncle, but I could tell that he was as mean as a polecat. "D-Day. Omaha Beach. That makes you a hero."

"Yeah, I was a hero."

"Master Sergeant Tom Hanson."

"First prize in the lottery. Look, what do want, you're using up a lot of my valuable time."

"Busy eh?"

"Yeah, busy."

The smile turned sarcastic. "So when *was* your last case, Tom Hanson, Private Eye?"

"Thanks for the coffee." I stood and grabbed my coat from the back of the chair. "Now, if I'm not under arrest, I'll be moving along."

"Private First Class Bannerman, remember him?" the big one, Sergeant White, asked. He was jowly and heavy, equipped with the kind of flab that hides a lot of muscle.

I sat down. "Just quit the games and tell me what you want."

"What happened to Bannerman?" White again.

"Killed, like a lot of guys on that damned beach."

"So *you* say."

"Yeah, so *I* say."

"What happened to his body?"

"How the hell do I know what happened to his... It was four years ago, I don't remember much about it." *Liar.* I remembered everything. Every second of that day was branded, red hot, into my brain. "Come on, what is this, some kind of joke?"

"He was found halfway up the beach, one Kraut slug in his gut, three others through his chest," White said. "He was tagged, ready to be buried, and that's the last anyone saw of him."

I was angry now. "That beach was a mess, it was chaos."

"Maybe he never died." Morrison said.

"I saw him go down. He was dead before he hit the ground."

Morrison and White exchanged looks. The third cop moved in. He was a short guy, dark hair, neat, a cigarette clamped between his teeth. Smoke stung my eyes. This one was Desoto. He dropped a report in front of me. There was a photo, and that was what I saw first.

No doubt about it. The face staring up at me was Rick Bannerman. There was a woman beside him, in a bridal veil. Rick wore a suit, sported a buttonhole. The document was a missing person report.

"The lady, his wife, Angie, reported him missing five days ago." Desoto shook his head. "Doesn't make sense, seeing as you saw him die on June 6th 1944."

"This is some kind of mistake —"

Morrison sat down opposite. Desoto moved away. Morrison offered me a cigarette. "It's not a mistake," he said.

"You telling me he came back from the dead?" I tried to be sceptical, but I was unnerved.

"Looks that way, don't it."

I sucked in smoke, closed my eyes then asked, "What do you want from me Morrison?"

"I want you to find your old war buddy."

"Why me? You're the cops." I took a deep drag on the cigarette and noted that my hand was shaking.

"We're too noisy. He'll hear us coming." Morrison leaned back. "Besides, you were his buddy, you know him. He'll talk to you."

I shook my head. "Find another sucker —"

"Interesting choice of clients you've had lately, Tom."

"You bastard. My clients are my business."

"Not when their activities are police business, which makes your business..." Morrison leaned forward and fixed me with a hard stare. "Our business."

He was right. Times were hard. I'd stopped being fussy about the jobs I took on. I'd stopped asking for references, and started making no-questions-asked deliveries and drop offs in out-of –the-way places, picking up tight-lipped, scary-looking guys with bulges under their jackets from airports and railway stations, and ferrying cheap women to expensive addresses. Anything to make enough dough to pay my rent, alimony and bartender.

"And when I find him?" I said.

"Get him to tell you what the hell is going on."

"Going on? You think this is some commie plot to raise the dead?"

Morrison smiled the way an alligator smiles at mealtime. "Maybe, or maybe its monsters from outer space. You going to do this or not?"

"Do I have a choice?" I asked.

2: Cellar

The cops gave me an address and that afternoon I drove there.

Rick's bungalow was on the side of town that even looked nice in the rain. There was no car and no sign of life. You could tell, even before you rang the doorbell. A deserted house looks... dead somehow. I rang the bell anyway. Nothing.

So there I was, already calling it Rick Bannerman's bungalow. Like I believed in all this hogwash.

I went round the back, where there was a lawn and a patio. A peek through the doors revealed a kitchen and dining room, all space and clean lines.

"Hello?" It was an elderly but sprightly-looking woman, standing on the other side of the fence that bordered the yard.

"I'm looking for Richard Bannerman," I said. "I'm an army buddy of his."

Always goes down well, army buddy, as if anyone who put on a uniform during the war was a hero.

"Oh, is that so? Well, I was beginning to think Richard and Angela didn't have any friends," she answered.

"Rick was always a bit of loner," I lied.

"Yes, I suppose he is, but very friendly and polite, a nice man."

She was right there. Rick had always been a nice man, the kind who'd give you his last dime for a bus ride then walk home himself.

"What's your name?" the lady asked. "So I can tell him you called next time I see him."

"Tom," My real name. Easier than lying, and she would never find out who I really was. "Tom Hanson." I gave her my best all-American smile and held out my hand, and that seemed enough to dispel any suspicion she might have had.

"He'll be glad to know you called."

"Yeah?"

"Well, things have gone a bit... His wife walked out on him a couple of weeks ago and he hasn't been home for days."

"I'm sorry to hear that. Nice girl, Angela," I ventured.

"Yes, yes she is."

"Do you think he went off to find her?" I asked.

"I doubt it, it was a terrible argument. He hit her. I saw it. I nearly called the police."

Nearly?

"But you don't interfere in that kind of thing."

I made a show of leaving, waited in the car until it was dark then hugged shadows all the way to the back of the house. I had a set of keys that could get me into most places. I should have handed them back when I left the police department before I signed up for Uncle Sam in '42, but it slipped my mind. I've been meaning to return them ever since.

Inside. Flashlight on. The kitchen and dining room were impeccable, all gleaming white and chrome. The sink, however, was full of dirty dishes, at odds with the feel of the place. Hallway; a potted plant by the front door, coats neat on their hooks. Lounge;

neat as well, except for the mug on one of the tables, full of congealed coffee and accompanied by a mouldy sandwich.

I shivered, and not from being cold. I shivered because I had begun to feel that I was not alone in here.

Scared? Just like that morning on that beach? You were a real hero that day weren't you...

Out in the hallway again I froze, glanced round. Was sure... *there*, picked out by the flashlight, movement, a flicker. Gone, nothing.

Swallowing dryly and telling myself that there really was no one but me in this house, I forced myself into the larger of its two bedrooms. The bed was unmade. There were men's clothes, discarded, on the counterpane and on the floor. It didn't look like the work of an untidy mind to me, or a burglary. It looked like someone in a hurry.

The place screamed *Marie Celeste*, abandoned in moments, food served but left uneaten, coffee made, but undrunk.

A sound, a *feeling*.

I wasn't armed. I never carried a gun, not any more.

On my feet now, back against the wall, behind the door. I waited. And waited. No one came. No more sounds, no more *feelings*.

Sweating now, shaking badly, I went back out into the hall. Nothing to help, no clues. Most of the mail I'd found lying around was for Mr R Bannerman, Mrs A Bannerman and Miss A Willcott; I guess that was Angie's maiden name.

An idea, a long shot, but sometimes long shots come up with the goods.

I found the basement door in the kitchen. It led to the stairway into hell; dark and steep. But I had to go down. I shone the flashlight into the thick, solid back. It pushed the darkness away a little, turned up spider webs and dust. I set off. My mouth was dry and I was scared. Yeah, I've known that before. That was bullets. That was real. This was my imagination. There was nothing here but dust and trash no one wanted, but couldn't throw away.

I made it down the steps and all the way to the bottom, I had to fight the urge to turn round and look behind me. Instead, I concentrated on the filing cabinets, and on the boxes of documents heaped up on an old table that had been stashed down here because, I guess, no one could bring themselves to throw it all away.

Something had followed me down here...

Something had *not* followed me down here.

So why could I feel it, close and cold?

I started pawing through the paperwork; bills and invoices, catalogues, letters.

And school reports for Angie Willcot, a little yellowed with age.

I poked the flashlight around me; things moved in the dark. Shadows, that was all. There was nothing else that could move round here. I started leafing through the reports and found what I was looking for; the School Kid Angie Willcot's address. Her parents would be middle aged now, maybe a little older, so they'd be settled and not keen to move. The address was local, a few blocks away.

When you run away, where do you go? To Mom and Pop, if they're still alive.

It was a long shot, but it was something.

I wasn't going to find Rick easily, so the next best thing was his wife.

I tore out the page I needed, folded it and put it in my coat pocket. Then turned to go. Somehow, I had to get back to the steps. So, what was the problem? Why was my heart hammering? Why could I hear the rattle of those godamned kraut machine guns and the screams of the wounded? Why could I hear the waves lapping on the beach?

Figures, in the torch light.

Ghosts.

Shadow men wearing helmets, battledress, holding rifles.

Christ... Them.

Them.

The temperature dropped even further. I shrank back against the table, whimpering like a dog.

Panic twisted me around to reach for the dank, crumbling basement wall, to slither past, crushed against the brickwork, willing them not to touch me; because if they did, I would break down and hammer my forehead against the filthy floor of the basement until my skull cracked. If anyone found me down here, they would take me back to the same crazy house they sent me to when they scooped me off Omaha Beach, babbling and ranting and pissing my pants.

The shadow men, Morrow, Peabody, Jason, Hogan, they were closing in. I couldn't breathe, I wanted to bury myself, in the dirt, to claw my way into the concrete.

I'm sorry... I'm sorry...

I saw the steps, ran for them, and scrambled upwards on all fours. They were coming after me, weapons at the ready.

Wait for us, Sarge, why're you so scared? Do you really want to live forever?

Back in the kitchen, in the hallway, bumping off the walls, tripping and scrabbling at the front door, handle, the Yale lock. Behind me, God they were behind me. Cold, close – The door gave and I half fell out into the sharp, cold night. I scrambled away from the bungalow, clawing my way through the dark towards my car.

3: Ashes

Angie's parents' address was a non-descript apartment block in a non-descript street. Non-descript, that is, until I saw it. The place was a burned-out hulk, squeezed between two others that looked to be occupied, even though their facades were scorched from the smoke and heat of their neighbour's demise.

One thing wrong though, one thing that stopped me turning tail and giving up on this lead. There was a light in one of the windows, up on the third floor, flickering, weak and yellow. Angie's mom and pop's address was on the third floor. For some reason I was sure that the light came from what was once their apartment.

I decided to finish my cigarette before I got out of the car. It was my third since leaving Rick's bungalow. It was going to take more than a lung full of smoke to stop me shaking tonight.

It was them. Those ghosts, my platoon, my guys, my brothers in arms...

I didn't need to ring the bell this time. What was left of the front door was open. The black hell that had once been the foyer stank of ashes and rain. I cast the flashlight about and saw blistered woodwork, and charred lathes through gaping wounds in the scorched plaster. Debris crunched under my feet as I picked my way to the stairs. The light caught the cage of the lift, giving me a glimpse of twisted steel and dark emptiness. The lift itself had never made it down to the first floor.

The staircase was an iron spiral, scorched and, like the foyer, strewn with debris. I corkscrewed upwards towards the third floor. There were too many shadows here, too much fire-scented darkness. Shapes and imaginary horrors skipped through the beam of the flashlight. It was damned cold, my teeth clattered, my arms and legs were stiff. If I needed to run, I wasn't going to get very far before the bogey men caught me.

Out of breath and shivering like a scared puppy, I made it to the landing. There was a short passageway. The smell of burning was strong here.

The flickering yellow light spilled weakly from the apartment I wanted. The bubbled, charred cadaver of the door hung open. As I stepped inside, I heard someone breathing, hard and fast.

A bad sound, but human, mortal.

She was in the smaller of the two bedrooms. I caught a glimpse of her, huddled against the wall, candle flickering on the floor beside her. Then the dark was ripped apart by a yellow-white flash, which was followed by a sharp, deafening detonation. I threw myself to the floor and felt the bullet's shockwave, as it hurtled overhead to thud into the wall behind me. I rolled, gathered myself into a crouch and threw myself at the woman.

Angie Bannerman held the gun in two hands, shaking and screaming. I grabbed her arm and swung the weapon away to her right. The gun clattered heavily to the floor. I held her until she went limp in my arms. When I let go she drew herself even more tightly into a shivering ball in the corner of the cremated room.

I crouched down. "Are you okay Angie?" I said as gently as I could.

"Who are you?" she whispered. There was little warmth in her voice.

"Someone who's on your side." Was I? No way to tell as yet, but it felt like the right thing to say. "Tom Hanson, I'm a Private

Detective and I'm trying to find Richard Bannerman." No use beating around the bush.

"It wasn't him," she said, urgent now, gripping my arm this time. "He was never cruel to me, not like that."

"What did he do? Did he slap you around Angie?"

She nodded. I saw her bite her lip. She became earnest. "He didn't want to. I could see it in his eyes. He didn't want to hit me. He had to make me go away somehow. I see that now."

"Is that why you left him, because he was cruel?"

She nodded. "He was scared. People were watching us."

It was getting too cold to speak. I was shaking and thinking things I shouldn't and I needed a drink. But I pressed on. "Who was watching you?"

She didn't answer. She had gone rigid, I became aware she was looking over my shoulder. The look in her eye, the fear in the shadow ravaged lines of her face made my skin crawl. She gasped a single word.

"Mom…"

I spun round and there they were.

A man and a woman, featureless, made out of shadows. Both of them were whispering. I couldn't make out any words and realised quickly that the voices were in my head, scratching around and not meant for me, meant for Angie. The smoke smell grew stronger, made it hard to breathe.

"Go away," Angie whispered. "Please go away, leave me alone."

I scrambled for Angie's gun then up onto my feet. "You heard her," I said. "Get lost, scram." I raised the weapon.

More of them boiled into the room, through the dead mouth that was once the doorway. I knew these ones, Christ, I knew these ones well. Now I could hear their whispers, their babbled accusations, their rage. They moved closer, spreading out to surround me, to press in with their cold, dead-hate.

Angie surged to her feet, the candle in her hand, and thrust it towards the ghosts. They swirled back on themselves, like blown smoke, then reformed and rushed at her. She cried out, more in grief than fear and held the candle the way a vampire fighter in a movie, holds a crucifix towards Dracula. For a moment we were engulfed,

73

and autumn night turned to June daylight and the air was filled with the hot tearing of machine-gun bullets and the whine of mortar shells, then the darkness was blasted outwards, over me, through me, cold, cold darkness, that sliced me open like a stiletto, and was gone.

"Mommy… Daddy," Angie sobbed. "I'm sorry…"

I grabbed her and hurled us towards the door. I felt the remnants of the things as we brushed by them. Tiny electric shocks that stabbed into my flesh. Angie gasped in pain but we were through, out onto the landing and heading downstairs where there were more, ghosts. I forced myself through them, each touch, a memory, a darkness revealed.

City-night was a friend, cold as it was, and wild with shadow from the wind-blown, leafless trees in the orange street-light. For the second time that night I shut myself in my car and whimpered out my terrors. Only this time, I wasn't alone.

"Let me out!" She was suddenly frantic, slamming at the door as I drove.

"Angie," I yelled. "For Chrissakes."

I drove fast, headed downtown towards light and people where ghosts couldn't go (could they?). But even here, as we raced past brightly-lit bars and allnight stores and diners, there were still plenty of shadows, plenty of gaps and dark spaces from which they could slide.

"Are you one of them?" She was screaming at me. I smelled the booze then, mixed with cigarettes and stale perfume.

"I don't know what you're talking about –"

"Let me go, please, oh Jesus, please let me go."

She collapsed into helpless, exhausted sobbing.

"Who do you think I am, Angie? Tell me."

"One of the watchers, the followers."

"The shadow people?"

"No, not them. We were being watched. I was so scared. We were being watched and Ricky was going mad and then he started an argument, over nothing, shouting and throwing things around. Then he hit me…" The sobbing took over and she finally collapsed.

That's when I slowed the car and steered in close to the sidewalk. Hookers, pimps and punters swirled around us in the gaudy neon pandemonium. Not a good place to stop, but now I had a gun.

"Had he hit you before?" I was gentle again, Hanson the Patient Guy.

She shook her head. "Of course not. He loved me."

"Who were these watchers?"

"I don't know, how should I know?"

I lit up.

"Can I have a cigarette?"

She took one from the pack. I held my lighter to its tip, the brief flare illuminated her face and showed me desolation.

"He was scared when they started following us around, parking outside the house," she was quiet now. "He changed."

"What about the ghosts? Were they part of it?"

"No, not then." She shuddered, sighed. "Not until I tried to find him. When I called… I heard whispering on the phone. Then they came. I ran away, home, I don't know why. I didn't know where else to go, I was too mixed up – hey, I don't trust you, let me out of this car, or I'll scream the place down."

I reached inside my jacket pocket and drew out the gun. Angie gasped, scrabbled for the door handle, until she saw I was holding it out to her, grip first. The thing was ugly and vile to the touch, like a steel rat. Angie stared at it.

"It's still loaded," I said. "You can have it back."

Finally, after an eternity, she reached across and took it from me.

I said; "You say you called someone. Who was it? Rick?"

"I thought I knew where he had gone, but when I tried to drive there the shadow people were in the car, Mommy, Daddy, only it isn't them, it can't be."

"Why not?" I knew it was cruel question, but I needed to ask.

"Are you really trying to help me?"

"I have a client who wants me to find Rick."

"A client?"

"The cops. They think he's in danger. They know about the watchers. They think they're agents, Soviets." Mostly a lie, but the situation was delicate. I needed her on my side.

75

"Why would the Soviets want to hurt Rick?"

"I don't know. He was war hero. I knew him back then, we were in the same outfit." I was his sergeant and I let him down and got the guy killed. "Look, you don't have to help me, you can open that door and get out of this car any time you like. I'll even take you to a hotel somewhere."

A pause. A moment. Then,"My parents died in that fire. Five years ago, before I met Rick. I was a bitch, a hellcat. We had a fight, I made my mom cry, my pop… He was a good man, I broke his heart. I stormed out, slammed the door. When I headed home, it was late. I was drunk, hanging myself round the neck of some no-good son-of-a-bitch, just to make a point… I saw the fire from two blocks away. I knew, I just knew…"

I waited a decent time, before taking a step back and asking; "You said you called Rick, so you must know where he might be."

"No. No, I don't trust you." Angie grabbed at the door handle.

"Go ahead." I shrugged. "You're not my prisoner."

I heard the door click, but she didn't move.

4: North

There was a bungalow, a few miles upstate, on a deserted beach where Rick and Angie stayed when they wanted to get away from the city. It belonged to a friend. They could use it whenever they wanted to. Angie never met the friend but Rick had a key. It seemed a good place to start.

So we headed north, and we were followed. By the cops, the watchers, the ghosts, hell if I knew. They seemed one amorphous, dark mass of harm, boiling into the darkness in our wake, spreading and reaching towards us. We could both feel them. Some sense, some tautening of our nerves, some icy dance on our skin. Neither of us said anything, but I knew she could feel it just the way I could. The engine droned loudly and the wipers fought their losing battle against the relentless rain. Occasionally another light would burst out of the dark, drench us in white then fade away. I was getting too tired to drive. I wanted to stop, get some sleep.

"How much further?" I asked, more to wake myself up with the sound of my own voice than because I really wanted to know.

"Couple of hours," Angie said. "We have to stop. I'm hungry, and I need the bathroom."

Stop? We couldn't stop, they would catch us...

But the idea of company, hot food and coffee was a good one. And rest, Christ, I needed a rest, my eyes were burning.

We found a diner. Not much of a place, lonely, not quite deserted. The warmth and comfort was almost too much to bear when I walked in. I wanted to stay here forever. We sat by the window. I faced the door. We ordered coffee and two steak sandwiches with fries. Angie disappeared into the restroom.

A car pulled up outside, a blaze of light distorted by the rain. I peered out but it was too dark for detail. The lights stayed on and the car didn't move. I watched. Why didn't they go, or come inside? Why the hell were they just sitting out there?

Waiting.

For us.

But who really meant us harm? The cops were the *watchers*, I was sure of that. And they needed us to lead them to Rick. The ghosts? They didn't drive cars. Did they?

The lights went out. A moment later a couple entered the diner. The man made a big deal out of shaking the rain from his umbrella. The pair of them were laughing, like kids. They were good-looking but middle-aged, which should have rung alarm bells. None of the middle-aged couples I'd ever known laughed together like that.

They sat at the counter, ordered coffee.

The sandwich arrived. I ate it like a starving man.

Angie was back. She picked at her food.

"Aren't you hungry?" I said. "You need to get your strength up."

"You sound like my pop." She smiled, for the first time since I had met her. It was also the first time I'd seen her properly. So far it had been candlelight and dark cars. She was tall and slender, with long black hair that was escaping from its prison of pins and perm. What make-up she might have been wearing when all this started for her, was gone and she obviously had no replacement. It didn't matter, black hair and fierce dark eyes were always good for me. She wore a coat that was a little dusty and scuffed, but looked expensive.

She gave up on the sandwich and curled both hands round her coffee cup.

Rain pattered at the window. The middle-aged couple laughed.

"Rick... What kind of a guy was he?"

"You said you knew him."

"Yeah, but that was in the army, the war. That kind of life leaves a mark on you."

"He never talked about it. He was kind, quiet, romantic. I felt protected when I was with him. Is that the guy you remember?"

"Pretty much, except for the romantic part." And it was. Solid, calm, even on that beach, even when his sergeant was belly-down in the sand, blubbering like a baby and the US army was being cut to ribbons before it could get more than a few yards from the tide line. He was the kind who just got on with his duty, and died for it.

Only he didn't.

"He was a good guy," I said.

"Was?"

"Is." Too late for corrections.

"You think... You think he's dead?"

"No, he's hiding from the watchers. I don't think they've found him."

"How do you know?"

"Hunch."

"Were you a cop? Before you became a shamus?"

"Before the war. Couldn't do it no more once I came home from Europe." The department doesn't employ anyone who's spent time in the crazy house.

She appeared to store this away for future consideration. "We should go."

The couple were making me antsy. They had brought something in here with them, something I couldn't put my finger on but it was cold and it was wrong.

A second car pulled up outside. The place sure was busy for the time of night, and the locality. I tore at the last of the sandwich.

The car outside still had its lights on. There was more of it out there, that dark ice.

"Yeah, one thing to do first." I headed for the restroom. I didn't like leaving Angie out there like that but I needed to do this, for more reasons than the obvious one.

I entered the restroom. A moment later the guy from the middle-age couple appeared and a gust of freezing air came in with him. He looked at me as we stood there.

"You okay?" he said.

I nodded, non-committal.

"We got your back buddy."

"Is that so?"

He smiled and nodded. He was a good-looking, square-jawed type. "Yep."

I buttoned my fly and swung round to face him. "Well, get *off* my back. I don't need you or your buddies. Got that?"

"Hey, friend, orders –"

"Disobey them."

"What are you talking about –?" His guileless protest didn't convince me. Wide-eyed, he might be, but something behind the mask of All-American duty-doer was laughing at me.

"Listen, you're about as discreet as a pack of wild dogs. Bannerman's wife is getting jumpy, I'm jumpy, and from what I understand, Rick Bannerman will be off like a rabbit if he gets the slightest hint that you're on your way. I can handle it, okay?"

"But –"

"Talk to Morrison, tell him what I said. Got that? Trust me or the deal's off."

The further we drove, the worse it got.

I checked the mirror. The action became a tic. No sign of headlamps, just the endless dark, strung out behind us. The radio whispered big band music, Angie went to sleep, her head on my shoulder. I reached out and put my arm about her. She was a client, she was a witness, I don't really know what the hell she was, but she wasn't mine. So what I was doing was bad, but at that moment, alone-but-not-alone in the rain-filled dark, driving towards God knew what, I was glad of the warmth of her.

The road behind stayed dark. The road ahead, the unseen that pressed in against the disc of light from the car's lamps, whispered and shifted and filled with ghosts. They were growing so strong, I began to cry.

Sometime, in the dark hours before dawn, I glimpsed the ocean. It glowed a little, no moon, cloud-hidden sky, but between the trees, those little sightings, I could see it, I could smell it.

Angie must have sensed it as well because she stirred, burrowed herself a little deeper into my shoulder then started awake. She slithered away from me as if I was a snake. She didn't say anything though. Just yawned and asked where we were.

"I was hoping you could tell me," I said.

"Stop the car. I need some air."

I did as I was told. We were on a cliff road. She got out and I followed. We stood by the railing, looking over the dark mass of the Atlantic. It was damned cold. I took off my coat and put it around Angie. She glanced at me and I think that was a thanks.

"I recognise this," she said. "Not much further."

I kept glancing back up the road. No sign of any cars. The All American agent was following orders, mine.

Christ, I needed a drink.

There was something good though, out here, between us. A bond, only a few hours old, yet it felt deep. We were silent as we stood there. Smoking, staring out at the sea but aware of each other. When I said we should get back into the car she looked at me for longer than was decent.

About fifteen minutes later she told me to stop again.

The dawn was turgid grey. The rain was back.

Down to our right, down on the beach, there was a bungalow.

5: Ghosts

Sand, soft under my feet. Hard to run on sand, hard to fight, but when you fall you can claw at it and burrow and hide...

The light strengthened steadily as we walked down the wooden steps onto the beach then headed towards the bungalow. The building was lonely, desolate somehow. There was no sign of life.

Then it no longer mattered, because the darkness that filled me was worse than any night could ever be.

They came out of the shadow of the leeward side of the bungalow. The ghosts. They came in droves. I saw Angie's parents again, I saw my buddies. I saw them half-crouched, clutching their rifles to themselves. I felt them rushing towards me then over and around and inside me.

I struggled on because you keep going, you get off your belly and run up that beach.

I burst out of the landing craft and run and the others are behind me because they trust me; Morrow, Peabody, Jason, Hogan... I run and scream and the world is ripped to shreds around me and flesh is torn and burned and men fall. I see severed limbs and guts and blood. They are all falling, all of them, falling, falling... My legs give way, my strength fails. Down, I have to get down. I have to get out of this, I claw and scrabble and swallow sand and sob like a child.

And now they were inside me and they were so damned cold and I was on my knees again and I wanted to lie down and feel the sand and bury myself like a worm, bury myself real deep, and keep going and going.

Angie was ahead of me, running and calling out to her mom and pop and reaching for them, trying to pull them to herself but she couldn't, because there was nothing there, except the ghosts.

The wall of shadow, of ice and pain and voices and the feel of those good, good guys was almost too dense to get through. But I had to keep going. Angie had the love of the man in that bungalow to keep her on her feet. Me. I had nothing but memories and the bottle and failure. So I had to keep going because this was the only way through.

Ahead, the sea pounded at the beach and threw up spray and blood and tipped corpse after bullet-torn corpse onto the sand.

I saw her hand. Angie's hand. I grabbed at it and held it tight and let her haul me on. I sobbed and muttered and shouted and my legs were so weak I could barely stand.

Morrow, Peabody, Jason and Hogan, they were all there, with me, pushing at me raging at me and screaming at me that I killed them all.

Yes, I yelled back at them. *My father was a hero, but I couldn't be the man he was. I couldn't do what he did...*

Then I slammed into the rough wall of the bungalow and they were gone. I pressed my head against the wood, heedless of the cold.

I was exhausted, as if I'd run a marathon. Angie leaned against the sun-bleached timbers beside me. No heat this morning, just the grey clouds and a savage wind blowing off the land towards the boiling, angry waves.

"You okay?" Angie said, so softly I wanted to take her in my arms and crush her till her bones snapped. I wanted to kiss her deep, so deep I lost myself forever.

"Yeah," I croaked at her instead. "How about you?"

She nodded. "We got through, didn't we, Tom? We made it through our ghosts?"

Now we had to go in. Face the guy. Find out at the hell was going on.

"Stay behind me," I ordered.

Angie nodded. I didn't trust her compliance though. Because she was a few feet from her heart's desire and coiled-up like a tightly wound watch.

I moved around the side of the bungalow. The wall was by my left shoulder, the beach stretched away to my right. Up ahead, the wind whipped a fog of spray from the wave crests.

I reached the steps. Then, before I could make my move, Angie shoved past me and ran up to the front door. She pushed at it, and to her obvious surprise, it opened. I followed as fast as I could.

He was sitting in a rocking chair, at the far end of a small room cluttered with ocean-related tchotchkes; ships in bottles, shells, and nets strung across the ceiling. It was him okay; Private First Class Rick Bannerman. A big, tall man with hair that probably started to thin the moment he took his first shave. He wore a suit that looked as if it had seen some hard labour, shirt open at the throat, feet bare.

Angie had stumbled to a halt halfway across the room. She uttered his name. Rick didn't reply. I stared at him, unable to make sense of the sight of him, sitting there, living and breathing, the man I had seen torn open by machine gun rounds.

"Rick?" I said unnecessarily. Just had to be said I guess.

He spoke at last "Sergeant Hanson. I wish I could say I'm pleased to see you".

"I wish I could say that too, but that isn't going to happen, is it." I sighed, suddenly weary. "I'm sorry. I… I let you down."

"No," he answered. "You didn't let *me* down. You let Private Bannerman down. He's dead. Too late to be sorry about that."

"Dead can mean a lot of things," I said, suddenly waxing philosophical. "Dead to friendship, dead to an old life, or just dead."

"This kind of dead," Rick said and unbuttoned his shirt. The bullet scars were livid, four of them, forming a rough diagonal across his upper chest, above his right collar bone, his right lung and his heart. The last one had probably gone into his stomach. No one could have walked away from that, yet here he was hale, though not so hearty.

Angie must have seen those scars many times before. I guess they didn't mean much to her. A lot of men had come home with the marks of war tattooed on their bodies. And on their minds.

"Why are you talking about being dead?" Angie said. "I don't understand."

Rick finally offered her his hand and she went to him. It took a few seconds for him to respond. When he did, he held her tight. When she finally drew back he said, "You have to go, get out of here as fast as you can."

"I'm not leaving you, Rick."

He sighed, infinitely weary. "I knew you'd say that, hon, and I knew you'd try to find me and I knew the ghosts wouldn't stop you, no matter how bad they got."

So, *he* had sent them to keep us away. But how? What the hell *was* he?

"I guess Angie hired you to find me," he said.

"No. The cops hired me. They want to know how you can be lying dead on a battlefield then appear, married and on a missing persons list four years later."

"What the hell are you talking about?" Angie had rounded on me, her face twisted in fury. "You're crazy, I knew I shouldn't have trusted you. Jesus, Rick, I'm so sorry..."

"It's not your fault." Rick stood up and took a step towards me. "You were a coward back then and now you're a dumbass. They weren't cops."

"I met them in the precinct house. They looked and smelled like cops to me, and I should know."

"Of course they did, just like I look and smell like Rick Bannerman." He made an odd movement and suddenly he was clawing at the flesh of his chest. I thought he was ill, having a heart attack, a stroke, Christ knows. Angie cried out and grabbed at his arm but he shrugged her off. The skin came away, like a torn shirt. Underneath were...

Underneath were fibres, tendrils that waved like plants in the sea, that groped at the air, black, hair-like, thousands of them. As I watched, they grew longer, as if exploring the new world they had been released into.

"I'm dying, that's why I'm here. These things are eating me from the inside. No, it's okay, it was meant to be like that. If we don't open the gate in time we destroy ourselves, it's called getting rid of the evidence. Time is running low."

"*Our*selves?"

"I'm not the only one Tom, didn't the cops tell you? The *dead* cops. I suggest you go to a library and look them up once you get Angie out of here; heart attacks, cancer, shoot-outs, all the usual ways cops die. We use the dead as vehicles. We set up home in your brain and nerves and muscles. We use you like shells, like godamned hermit crabs. We're the vanguard, the guys in the Trojan Horse. We're here to open the gate so the real visitors can come through to rape your world."

"You bastard," I said. "You defiled his body..."

"I'm not a bastard. I'm a virus, I don't have feelings." Rick's shoulders slumped and he shook his head. "Except I do."

"What did you mean, when you said that you came here to die?" Angie voice was so quiet I could barely hear her.

"Exactly what I said," Rick answered. "Maybe Bannerman was still alive when I infected him. You humans are damned hard to kill. Maybe a little part of him is still in here. Loving you Angie was only meant to be camouflage; Rick, the regular guy with the pretty All-American wife, but it wasn't like that. You... You've..." He straightened. "I don't want this world, *your* world Angie, laid waste the way the others have been. There needs to be all six of us together to open the gate. So I ran away, playing for time. But you, Hanson, you've brought the others here. You've slaughtered your own world."

There was nothing I could say.

"Just let me die." Rick sat down again.

"No," Angie knelt beside him and grabbed his hand. She held it against her face and wept softly. "You can't die. You can't!"

Rick stroked her hair. "I has to be, hon. Can't you see? There's no pain. It's okay."

Moments later the window behind me exploded inwards and all became shattered glass and whirling white fire.

6: Six

I was down, groping for Angie. The fire boiled above me, stinging me with a scourge of electric shocks. I trembled and twitched as each one stabbed into me, taking away control of my muscles, burning my skin and jangling my brain. I pissed myself, couldn't help it, and couldn't stop it. Pissed my pants the way I'd pissed my pants as I lay on Omaha Beach and my platoon were slaughtered around me.

A hand clasped mine and suddenly I was hauling Angie to her feet and we were scrambling for the door. It was only as we tumbled out onto the sand that I realised she was struggling and pummelling me with her fist and yelling that Rick was still inside.

I tried to drag her away. Tried to make her see that we had to get out of there, and that Rick wanted to die. That he *had* to die.

The car was where we had left it, across the beach, up on the cliff road. But there were two other cars now, a Ford Tudor and a Chevvy Fleetmaster, unmarked, but cop cars, no doubt about it. I twisted round to scan the beach, and saw them, spread out, walking through the morning murk towards the bungalow. I recognised the three 'cops', plus two others, the middle-aged couple we'd seen in the diner.

"Keep out of this, Hanson!" Morrison shouted. "Your job's done, get the woman out of here."

Angie resumed her struggles. She slapped at my face, clawed and thrashed and swore and called out to Rick. I clung on, trying to drag her away. I was scared, of these people who were not people. Suddenly they were monsters, too crushingly powerful and *other* for me to face down. I wanted to get away from them, to be gone, to warn the authorities, to call out the army.

They were moving closer, dark figures under the restless grey sky. Now they seemed larger than they should be, taller, their angles and structures all wrong.

In that moment, Angie wrenched herself free of me and darted back towards the bungalow. I froze, again, froze and felt my strength fade.

Another fireball arced towards us. It slammed into the sand and blew us off our feet. I heard Angie's cry of shock, then my body convulsed and shuddered as it was battered by the fireball's electric storm. A steam locomotive thundered through my head. I writhed in the sand, ending up face down, trying to bury myself, digging and digging and sobbing out my terror as the world was ripped apart around me.

Then Angie's screaming began again. The sound drove into my madness and I pushed myself up onto my hands and knees to see her in the arms of Desoto. No, not arms they looked like tentacles, gleaming, slippery and tight about her waist and neck. The 'cop's' suit was in tatters, too small now to contain what was inside. Angie stood motionless. I saw her face, and even from this distance I could see her raw terror.

"We will hurt her, Bannerman," Morrison called out. "We'll hurt her a great deal and for a long time, if you don't come and join us. What's it to be? Bannerman? Can you hear me?"

The locomotive was still rattling around in my skull, making it hard for me to remember why I was here. My attention switched to the guy I'd spoken to in the diner. He was carrying something that looked like a poker that had been dragged out of a fireplace. The end glowed red. A weapon, the fireball launcher maybe.

"Bannerman!"

"Let her go, I'm here." A figure appeared in the shattered doorway of the bungalow, naked, bleeding tendrils of that fibrous stuff from wounds all over his body.

"No, Rick!" Angie shouted back. "Ri—"

A hand, a pad of glistening membrane, muffled her shouts.

Rick shuffled forward, the diner woman and Sergeant White went to help him. The other three formed themselves into a rough, broken circle. The poker guy had his back to me. So why was that important? I wanted that damned train to stop so I could think.

Stand up, that was the first part; up onto my feet.

Rick stumbled to a halt, completing the ring. White and the woman stood on either side of him. Angie was still Desoto's prisoner. Morrison nodded to him and Desoto flung her aside as if she were a discarded soda bottle. Angie crashed heavily into the sand, and didn't move.

The dull, early morning light grew strange. I looked up.

There was a rent in the sky.

Cloud swirled and boiled at its edges. Blood-coloured light seemed to bleed into the grey, then spill onto the beach as tiny fireballs. They pattered into the sand like –

Bullets.

I flinched and cowered, but I had to do something. This time I couldn't hide.

The poker. It was the poker. *The godamned poker...*

I ran.

More red light, bars of it, connecting Morrison and Rick and the rest of them. They let out a cry and each one was wrenched backwards, their bodies arched at an impossible angle.

I ran.

The red light blasted upwards and tore open the whirlpool of cloud. Something unfurled itself from the hole in the sky. Something titanic, city-sized and many-limbed. More of them could be glimpsed behind it.

I ran.

The sky rumbled and roared, the world tilted under my feet.

I ran –

– and slammed into the poker guy and we tumbled violently onto the sand. The weapon flew from his hand. Tentacles lashed at me as I drove my fist at his face, again and again, feeling skin tear and bone crack.

There were shouts, shrieks and porcine squeals. More tentacles wrapped themselves about my arms and legs, something tightened about my neck. The light was back, hot on my face, the colour of blood. The circle had repaired itself, the gate was opening again. It was all fading away, I could no longer breathe. No use... No damn use. I'd slaughtered the world -

A single detonation broke through the haze.

Rick falling, his head, a bloody ruin.

Me, free and crawling across the sand away from my attackers.

Angie, on her feet, ashen-faced but determined, pistol in both hands.

Then there were five, not enough. A sound like the booming of a giant bell thundered through the air. I looked up, vast tentacles slithered back, the clouds rushed to cover the wound in the sky. Red faded to grey.

I crossed the beach to Angie. She slumped into my arms. The 'cops' made no move to stop us. As we turned to go back to the car, Morrison dropped to his knees, flesh splitting, fibrous tendrils breaking free. Desoto was next, then poker guy. We left them there, the rising tide would clear away the mess.

Rain fell.

7: Miracle

It don't happen the way it does in movies or books or fairy tales. I got Angie back to my apartment and she stayed there for a couple of days. It took almost that long for her to be able to speak again. It was good having her around, someone there when I woke up in the morning and someone there when I went to sleep again at night. She took the bed, I slept on the couch. I got principles, not many, but enough.

When she did speak, we were sitting in the lounge sharing a bottle of Italian red and listening to that Frank Sinatra guy crooning on the radio. He had a good voice I guess, but he was a flash in the pan.

"I killed him," she said. "I killed Rick."

So did I Angie, long before you did.

"It was for the best," I answered.

"Yes, I guess it was, because I loved him."

"You saved the world," I said. It sounded like a joke, and it had to, the truth was too big to handle.

She sat on the couch, I was on the floor, leaning back, careful not to touch her legs. I wanted to, but like I said, I got principles. Suddenly she reached down and stroked my face. "Thank you," she said. Then kissed me, gently but frankly.

In the morning she was gone.

My head told my heart that it would have all been too troubled, overshadowed by nightmares. All my heart could do was remind me of that kiss.

I managed to carry on, even picked up some honest employment. An errant husband to tail here, a stolen antique to track down there.

Then, one bright August morning over breakfast, the world changed. It was a report in the *Post*, read while I sipped coffee and ate toast. There had been a plane crash out in the boondocks. A Cessna, all in pieces, spread across a cornfield. Five passengers and the pilot had climbed aboard at the local airstrip.

There was no sign of them at the crash site.

No sign of them anywhere.

By all accounts, no one should have walked away from that wreck. But you know, said the farmer who owned the field and was first to arrive at the scene, miracles happen, praise the Lord.

So now I'm looking for Angie. I need her at my back before I go hunting those passengers. She's the only one who understands what's going on. I don't know where she went. But I'll find her. Like the farmer said, miracles happen, praise the Lord.

THE DARK ABOVE THE FAIR

Even in the heyday of the British seaside, this particular travelling fair had already gone to seed; its paint peeled, its scenic railway a rattling deathtrap, its ghost train a clunky monstrosity about as frightening as *Watch with Mother*. It should have curled up and died decades ago, but, dead or not, it's here today. And I know why. Nothing to do with its rickety, rolling schedule, nothing to do with coincidence.

The fair is here for me.

It's set up on The Common, as it was fifty years ago. Every year it was the same, a three-week stopover, which encompassed the height of Westerton-on-Sea's holiday season. The season included August Bank Holiday and, like those of old, this one is overcast and wet.

Another surprise is that The Common is still The Common. In my day, Westerton's residents generally avoided the place. It was scabby and scruffy, and speckled with litter from the out-of-towners' cars that congregated here for picnics and other less salubrious pastimes. I'm amazed that a property developer hasn't made a golf-course deal with someone on the council and turned it into a set of exclusive, seaside apartments.

But they haven't.

And here I am.

There are few other punters in sight, just the rattling near-empty scenic railway and the peeling yellow and orange roundabouts and dodgems. There's music. The Kinks' *See My Friend* – a song I remember from that day.

And beneath it all, beneath the rattle, rumble, siren-wail, and air-rifle clang, I can hear the fair's rotten heart, its beat, synchronised exactly to mine.

*

It didn't only happen in Brighton and Margate and exotic places like that, it happened in Westerton-on-Sea as well, in 1965, the year after the biggest and most notorious Mods and Rockers scrap of all. Yes, it happened here, in what was once a fishing town and, at the time of the battle, a high class seaside resort (that's what it called itself anyway). When Westerton looked in the mirror it saw Hove, or Frinton.

Westerton was not *common*, like Great Yarmouth or Blackpool.

Westerton was *genteel*.

Except for the travelling fairground, of course; that wasn't genteel. It was tolerated, because it brought in money, even if that money came from the sticky, grubby hands of the sort of people Westerton did not normally welcome. It was only for three-weeks, after all.

Westerton had another thorn in its side. Us. Its youth. Youth that, in the opinion of its residents, would have benefitted from a spell in the army. Youth who spent too much money on clothes and those wretched scooters they charged around on all day, when they weren't lounging around in the Sea Vista Café, playing dreadful music on its jukebox.

We all came from loving families who made sure we had a decent upbringing and a good education, the sort of upbringing and education that had already landed many of us well-paid jobs. A fat wage packet and a train line straight into London meant that me and my friends were always at the forefront, the trend-setters, the Kings and Queens of Westerton Youth.

We were Mods, Lambretta owners to a man (girls rode pillion in those days), our rides replete with mirrors, badges and gleaming chrome.

Oh, and my name's Michael. Back then, my dad owned Westerton's only plumbing company.

August Bank Holiday Monday, 1965, the year it was moved from the first to the last weekend of the month. There was a westerly breeze, so it wasn't hot, even when the sun peeked from behind the clouds.

Where were we? Lounging around in the Sea Vista Café, the Animals on the juke box. It was the usual gang, including Tony Harper, the local bank manager's son, slight, quick and neat, and gorgeous Sheila Weir, who was the property of the Lord of the Westerton Mods, Bobby Chambers. Good looking fella, Bobby, all blond hair, blue eyes and square jaw. Likeable, though, as long as you didn't take the piss. There were others, of course, laughing, joking around and annoying the more sedate clientele, who never stayed long. Karen Whitley was there as well. She wanted to be my girlfriend. She was pretty and kind-hearted, but she could never be my Great Love. I knew it even then.

It was sometime after three in the afternoon.

There was a sound, a deep rumble that became a jagged roar. It rose in volume until it drowned out our voices, then Eric Burden's, and rattled the café's big plate glass window.

Motorbikes, a dozen of them, black and chrome and ugly and, yeah, I'll admit it, terrifying.

Astride the bikes: Rockers.

They slowed and swarmed on the street outside the café, then shuffled their machines in to park. They surrounded our Lambrettas like Apaches around a wagon train.

Don't get these fellas mixed up in your head with Hells Angels. They didn't have long hair and big beards and they didn't wear German helmets or decorate their leathers with Iron Crosses. In 1965, Motorhead wasn't even a twinkle in Lemmy's eye and heavy metal could only be found in a steelworks. This gang was clean-shaven, their hair Brylcreamed to within an inch of its life. They wore leathers based on US Air Force flight jackets, and were laden with scores of motorcycle badges.

There were girls with them too.

Half a dozen, all wearing the same leathers and jeans as their fellas.

The Enemy.

They milled around outside for a bit. Then came in.

The place didn't erupt into a fight. There was no sudden silence like in a western when the stranger enters the saloon. Cups chinked as normal, the espresso machine hissed. But the atmosphere did tighten. The other customers were suddenly in a hurry to finish their sausages and chips. Behind the counter, Charlie, the owner, frowned and puffed himself up to his full, inconsiderable height.

And us Kings and Queens of Westerton? We stayed put, and were suddenly very quiet. We had never been challenged before and, apart from the odd little scrap and some pushing and shoving, we had never had to fight. It was easy to be tough when there was no opposition, but suddenly we were faced with a herd of characters who looked very battle-hardened indeed.

They ignored us at first and crowded around a couple of vacant tables near the window.

Maisie, the waitress, went over to them and took their order. Her voice was small and she looked scared. The gang told her what they wanted; not polite, but giving no reason to be challenged or thrown out. We huddled into ourselves and tried to carry on, but bravado was in short supply.

There was no music at this point. One of us needed to go to the juke box. I was single, no official girlfriend to weep over my grave, so I squared my shoulders, stood and reached into my pocket for some coins.

At the same time, one of the bikers got up, chair scraping noisily back. He didn't even look at me, but strode across to the machine before I could get anywhere near it.

The Last Time by The Rolling Stones.

I hated, and still hate, The Rolling Stones.

He looked at me and smiled. He had a missing front tooth. He raised his eyebrows, a small gesture, but a challenge. *What are you going to do about it?*

Humiliated, I went back to my mates.

"Next time, get up there a bit quicker," Tony snapped at me.

"*You* do it next time," I said to him.

"Yeah, I fucking will," he growled.

"Hey," Charlie snapped from behind the counter. "That's enough of that language Tony."

Tony coloured up. The Rockers sniggered.

I wanted to get out of there. So did the others.

The Last Time faded away. Another silence.

Tony wouldn't look at me. I got up. So did one of the Rockers. A different one this time; slight-built, fair hair. We made it to the juke box at the same moment.

Tolstoy wrote about chance and whim. There's a lot of it in *War and Peace*. Yeah, I've read it. Years after that Bank Holiday, though. I didn't time my rush to the juke box to coincide with the Rocker's attempt. It just happened. Just the way Leo said it could.

He held back. I swear to you. He held back for a fragment of a second so that I could get there first. Money in, no hesitation on my behalf, and The Animals were back. I looked at the Rocker. He looked at me. The stare was intense, and it went on too long. Then I went back to our table. There was a deal of back-slapping, and triumphant stares over towards the window.

The Rockers shook their heads and laughed some more, not caring about our victory. They mocked their representative a little and I saw him go red, but that was it.

Stalemate.

They were by the exit. Our scooters were hemmed in by their motorcycles. We needed to get out.

Bobby's girl, Shelia, was the one who said it. "We'll just have to get up and walk past them. They're not going to start any trouble in here." Weren't they? I admired her confidence, or was it naïvety?

We all took deep breaths, got to our feet and made for the door. The Rockers watched us coming. Except for the fair-haired one. He kept his eyes on the plate of sausage and chips in front of him.

Close. I could smell leather, I could smell cigarette smoke and I could smell grease and oil and sweat and the strong, cheap perfume of the girls.

Then we were out into the pale sunshine and huddled together on the prom. I sighed out my relief. Until I noticed Tony's expression. I turned to see the Rockers emerge from the café. They set off across the road. Straight towards us.

"We'd better run," Tony said.

"Fuck that," Bobby said. I could see that he was scared but trying to be tough. Not just a pretty face was Bobby. He glanced at his girlfriend. "You'd better get out of it, Sheel."

She stepped up to him and took his arm. Brave girl, braver than me because all I wanted to do was get as far away from that place as I could. But it was too late. The gang were almost on us. And I would never have deserted my mates.

"What do you want?" Bobby said. He stepped away from Sheila and stood in front of us.

"Nuffink," said the gap-toothed character who had beaten me to the juke box. "Just some of that sea air."

He smirked.

"There's plenty of seafront," Bobby said.

"Yeah, well, we like this bit."

"You can't have it." I said, wanting it over with and wondering how much it was going to hurt.

"Fuck," Tony hissed.

The gap tooth raised his eyebrows, then grinned and glanced at the others who had formed an arc about him. He nodded, and in they came.

It wasn't so bad, not at first. I suppose my own blood was up. Adrenaline, anger, fear, I don't know, but I went straight for the leader and grabbed at him. I remember the feel of leather in my hands and how cold it was, I remember the violence of the collision between us and how we were rammed close to each other and he was suddenly simply a human being and not frightening at all. I remember that he stank of sweat and cigarettes and his breath was foul. Then we were forced apart. I slipped and his boot flicked towards me and there was pain, a lot of it. It exploded outwards from my right side and I went down onto the pavement, which seemed to slam into me like a dirty, grey train. Another impact and suddenly I couldn't breathe. There was no air, only a horrible, agonised blank where there should have been taste and oxygen. Another kick. This one dulled, not the same shocking explosion as the first one. I curled up as feet shuffled around me and people shouted and swore.

Someone else went down onto their hands and knees. It was the fair-headed boy. He looked at me, and I saw blood dripping from his lip. I sucked in a breath. It hurt. Everything hurt. I struggled to my feet. Aware that at any moment someone could pile in and beat the shit out of me, but the battle had become a rout and I glimpsed Rockers running in pursuit of my mates, as they disappeared down the beach.

I stood. The Rocker looked up at me. He shook his head and said; "This is so fucking daft." He extended his hand towards me and without thinking, another of old Leo's moments, I took it and helped him to his feet.

"Thanks," he said.

I shrugged.

I saw the Rocker girls still standing across the road, smoking and watching. The boy rubbed his lips with his sleeve then reached into his pocket and offered me a cigarette. I took one.

"Ta," I said. "Michael."

He nodded. "Simon."

"Don't get mixed up in this," he said as he took the first drag. His accent was different to the others. He sounded... educated, I suppose that's what you'd call it. "I don't know why I am. Motorbikes. They're my bloody downfall. I started going to the Ace Café, in London, you know, where all the Rockers go, and somehow I got drawn in. It was Nick, he's a powerful bugger, you know, persuasive..."

I assumed that Nick was the one who had kicked me.

"It's because he thinks I'm posh," Simon said. He seemed in no hurry to leave and, to be honest, I wasn't in a hurry to go stumbling off down the beach to find the others either.

"What do you mean?" I asked. The cigarette was comforting, but it hurt my chest and burned my throat, and my ribs were on fire. I wanted to sit down, but suspected that that would make the pain even worse.

"My dad' he's a doctor. I suppose that sounds posh to people like Nick."

"He still let you join his gang," I said.

Simon chuckled, an old sound, as if he had suddenly aged by twenty years. "I'm a sort of prize. I make his gang different from the others. He's always boasting about Lord Bloody Simon. That's what he calls me."

"Why... Why don't you just leave the gang?"

He stared at me, hard. That stare, it made me uncomfortable, but I held it because there was nothing in the world I wanted more at that moment than to hold that stare. It drew me in, made me... Christ knows what it made me feel. I remember it, though. Every second of it. His eyes were blue and for those hours, days, seconds, the whole world was blue, and dark at the edges, like burning paper.

"I don't want to," he said at last and broke the moment. Then I swear I heard him say. "At least, I *didn't* want to." Perhaps he didn't say that at all. In my memory he did, and still does.

"I'd better find my mates," I said. My voice sounded dry and so bloody ordinary.

"Yeah. Look, lie low until we're gone. We'll be around until tonight. Okay? Nick and the others are looking for a fight. There's some nasty bastards among them. Don't try to, you know, get your own back or anything. Nick's... Well, he's a nutcase."

We'd have called him a psycho these days.

"Fucking sent him down," Tony said. "One fucking punch." He held up his fist. The knuckles were grazed. There was even a blood stain. "Split his lip. Blood everywhere." He sounded out of breath. They all did, my mates and our girls. I found them by the pier, bruised, grazed and huddled about one of its huge freshly-painted iron legs. There were no amusement arcades on our pier. There was a concert hall and, would you believe, an art gallery.

So, Tony was the one who had hit Simon. I was oddly angry about this, even though he was one of the enemy.

There was a lot of talk when I first arrived. Slaps on the back for me, and loud bravado, which quickly ran out. Karen shuffled over to me and tucked herself under my arm. The action annoyed me further, although I tried not to let it show. I wanted her to leave me alone. The sea raged and hissed over the shingles, waves bounced against the sea-buried legs of the pier. The light dimmed to grey as the sun disappeared behind yet another cloud. The scant warmth was sucked from the air.

I noticed straight away that Bobby didn't join in the war stories. He sat, arm about Sheila, brooding, his face like thunder,.

"Where shall we go?" someone asked, more to break the atmosphere than because they wanted a plan.

"The fairground," Bobby answered.

"No," I said. I didn't often argue with Bobby, none of us did, but Simon's warning was still fresh in my mind. "*They'll* be there."

"Scared?" Tony said. *He* was, despite his bravado. He wasn't the only one.

"That's why we should go," Bobby said. "No one comes here and thinks they can do what they fucking like." I'd never seen him like this. He ground out the words. He was breathing hard. He wanted blood.

"You weren't the one who got a kicking." I grunted in pain, and not just for effect. "And Nick –"

"Who the hell's Nick?" Bobby said.

"Their leader. He's bloody dangerous. I was the one who took him on remember?"

"Yeah," Tony said. "I saw that, before I punched –"

"How do you know his name?"

I should have told them, but I couldn't. "I heard someone shout to him."

I didn't like Bobby's stare. I didn't like the suspicion it contained. We were lifelong friends. We were supposed to trust each other.

"I'm going to the fairground," Bobby said. "Even if I have to go alone."

"I'll come with you." Sheila gripped his arm, scared, but determined.

"Me too," Tony said. The rest all chimed in bravely.

"Of course I'm coming," I said.

We started to get up, not easy for me, because the pain was getting worse.

"Not yet," Bobby said. It was almost funny, everyone frozen, halfway to their feet, as if we were playing Simon Says…

The world, blue, burning at the edges…

"Let's get our scooters. Then we'll meet back here at about seven. Right?"

Right, Bobby.

"Bring whatever you can get your hands on. Know what I mean?"

We knew. And now we were scared.

As I said. My dad was a plumber, so there was plenty of metal pipe stacked up in our back yard...

None of us spoke as we parked our Lambrettas and walked into the fairground. Anyone looking at us must have wondered what was wrong, because it's hard to act naturally when you have a length of pipe stuffed down your trousers or a knife hidden in the inside pocket of your jacket.

We strolled with studied nonchalance past the shooting gallery, the dodgems and the waltzer. Music blared from the speakers; The Yardbirds, The Beatles, The Kinks' *See My Friend*.

Bobby led us deeper into the fair and we all followed. We glanced left, right, looking for the enemy.

My own fear was complicated and deep. My own fear was tangled up with the pain in my side and the weight of the metal pipe tucked against my right leg, and the dread of the coming fight. And Simon. I had to find him, and warn him. I don't know when I had decided that. He was going to get hurt. We had knives and clubs and Bobby was after blood and we would do what he said because we didn't know how not to and we were together and none of us wanted to be left behind.

There was no sense to my need to protect Simon. I didn't know him. I had swapped a few awkward sentences with him. We had smoked together.

He had stared at me and I at him.

And the world had turned blue and burned.

"This is a bloody useless," Bobby growled. That's how I remember it, a growl, heard by all of us, even though we were being pounded by noise; music, the dodgem siren, the drone of the generators. "We should split up, come back in twenty minutes and meet here, by the dodgems, yeah?"

Yeah.

I was off, quickly before anyone else could volunteer to come with me. Karen, especially. She would have given her eye teeth to be alone with me.

My side hurt so badly it made me dizzy. The lights stung my eyes, there were people blocking my way, bumping into me, swirling around me.

Then a shout. Louder than the rest of the noise.

I saw them; a clutch of leather jackets by the shooting gallery, cigarettes hung precariously from their lips, sneers firmly in place. They were moving, towards me. Five of them, all coming for me. Five sets of fists and boots. One of them broke into a run. He carried a bike chain. Christ, they were armed as well.

It was impossible, too many people, too much pain. I could barely breathe. My side...

I fumbled for the pipe, tried to force my hand into my trousers. The waist band was too tight. I hopped and blundered through the crowd and almost fell. Then a hand grabbed my arm and propelled me forward.

We barged and battered our way towards a gap between stalls. The gap was dark and narrow. I knew, without looking, that the hand belonged to Simon.

We stumbled to a halt on the edge of its temporary car park. Behind us, light and noise. Ahead, the gathering dark, the shadowed huddle of cars. A few people made their way to and from their vehicles.

Simon still held my arm, and still clutched a chain in his other hand.

We were both panting, breathless. The pain in my side was intensified by every gasp for air.

"I... I thought... I thought you were going to wrap that round my head," I said.

I heard his laugh. "I don't know how to... I've never hit anyone..." His laugh became a cough. He released my arm so he could double-up and recover.

"You have to get out of here," I said, my breath steadier now. "Bobby... My lot, we're armed..." I wrestled the pipe from my trousers.

"Bloody hell, Michael —"

There were shouts, movement, dark shapes that tumbled from the side entrance through which we had just escaped. They stood for a moment, looking round. Simon grabbed my arm again. We stumbled between the cars, slipped and scrabbled over the scrubby, stony ground and on towards the woods that bordered The Common.

Then I heard motorbikes, a brutal, animal roar that turned my soul to ice. I glanced back to see their headlights sweep over the car park as they weaved towards us.

We plunged into the trees. I gripped Simon's hand and felt the tightness of his about mine. We careered through the undergrowth. The darkness grew more complete. We ran blind, tripped and careered over fallen trunks, bracken whipped at our legs and grasped at our ankles.

The night was sliced open. It became a tangle of light-blackened claws, a jagged web of white and dark. The motorbikes roared behind us, one of them in the woods. Nick, it had to be Nick, the mad one. Driven by whatever mindless need for revenge, violence or destruction that pumped the blood through his veins. He was close. I could smell the bike's exhaust. I could smell petrol fumes. I could smell Nick's hate.

We crashed out of the dark, suddenly back in the fairground, next to the generator lorries. We ran again. The crowds were thinner here, but quickly dense, until we were once again in an obstacle race. At least I couldn't hear the motorbikes any more.

The dodgems, we had to get to the dodgems, where we would find my friends and allies. I wasn't thinking.

I led the way now. I hauled Simon behind me, my hand tight about his. Unheeding. Too frightened and desperate to understand.

"Mike! Over here!"

I saw them; Bobby, Tony, all of them, looking hunted and frustrated. I lurched into the light. Tony grinned and took a step towards me, Karen beside him. Bobby made to speak, to ask where I had been? Had I found...

"He's all right," I said, meaning Simon. "He's not like —"

I wrenched my hand free. I sensed Simon take a step back.

"Fucking traitor," Bobby spat at me. "Fucking..."

He had no words. None of them had any words for what they had seen. Nor did I. All I saw on their faces was hatred and disgust. My lifelong friends. We were children running and laughing in the playground, we were the Kings and Queens of our town. Me, and these people whom I loved.

And who's love I needed more than anything.

I swung round. I had the iron pipe in my right hand. I can't remember all of it, only the first moments, the anger and the need and the way Simon staggered back but didn't go down straight away. I remember his face. The blood. His wide, bewildered eyes. Blue they were.

...and the world burned at the edges.

Right here. That's where it happened. By the dodgems.

I got away with it. There was confusion. It was dark.

You can bury the truth only for so long; weeks, months, decades. You can bury it but it will slowly claw its way back the surface.

Like a splinter.

The others managed to drag me off and we slipped away.

Our gang didn't survive long after that night. They all kept the secret though. I respect them for that. Me, I joined up, ten years in the army. Quickest way out. Some nasty moments in Belfast, but a decent life all-in-all. Eventually, I found love, and we set up home a long way from Westerton-on-Sea. We were happy. Seven months ago Tom noticed blood in his urine. Happiness never lasts forever.

A good life then, but formed about the tumour in my soul, layers of lies and guilt that could never stop its slow, relentless spread.

I didn't cry at Tom's funeral. I'm crying now. I have a mobile phone. Bloody thing, too awkward for my clumsy fingers. Only one number needed though, the same one, pressed three times.

Police.

I killed someone.

THE THIRD MAN ON THE MOON

For Allen and Sarah

You really think that a few weeks of NASA's home-made claustrophobia training, a little meditation and good old American willpower could ever be enough to prepare anyone for what I had to go through? Think again, bubba. They tried, of course. They buried me alive in a coffin, under six feet of dirt (I lasted about two hours before I was screaming into the mike for them to dig me up). They put me in a body bag, strapped a parachute onto it and then threw me out of a B52. They floated me in a sensory deprivation tank, they glued my eyelids shut, they turned off the lights, they folded me up and crammed me into every little box they could find, but none of it could compare with being squeezed into a tube which barely gave me enough room to blink, let alone breathe, fed through pipes jammed into every opening in my body, and then bolted onto the nose of a Saturn V.

When the Saturn sparked up, I was thrown into the sky with a roar that made my ears bleed. The ascent piled on so many gees I hallucinated that I was back in that coffin and that the lid broke and a million tons of dirt had been dumped onto my face and chest.

There were three others atop the Saturn that day, you've probably heard of them, Armstrong, Aldrin and Collins. It was okay for them, they had the luxury seats in the capsule. I was the legal stowaway, the secret cargo, stashed in a wardrobe at the back the Command Module.

I never volunteered. Problem was, I was a hero already. A Purple Heart won in America's dirty little jungle war. I'm Major Jack Kavanagh of the US Navy Air Force, a soldier from a soldiering family, so where else would I have been in 1969 but in Nam? My brother was out there too. I flew F4s off a carrier, he flew Bell Hueys out of some muddy, snake-infested clearing in the jungle. One day he didn't come back. Just disappeared with the rest of his crew and the handful of wounded grunts he was bringing back to base. When they ordered me home, I didn't want to go. I felt as if I was leaving him behind. But it was an order. And I'm a soljer.

I ended up in a place called Langley. I was taken to a meeting room and offered coffee. There was only one guy in there. He wore an expensive-looking suit and had steel grey hair and steel grey eyes.

Over coffee, he told me a story.

The Soviets had landed an unmanned probe called Luna 9 on the Moon three years before. The story goes that it sat there, took some snapshots then died. Well, there was more than a camera in Luna 9's belly. There was a little dog-sized rover which trundled over the moon's surface taking more photos and picking up bits of rock. Hell of an achievement, even if the samples would never make it back to Earth. The Soviets just wanted to know that it could be done. The rover made it to Mare Crisium and when it got there, it found something.

They didn't illuminate us on what. It was just *something*.

And it was dangerous.

It *is* dangerous, because it's still there.

"The Soviets have been trying to get back up there to take another look, maybe even bring a piece of it down to Earth. Our intelligence suggests that they're going to make an attempt at the same time as we land men on the moon's surface. Perfect timing, because the world will be looking the other way. We can't allow that, Major."

"No sir," I replied because I was a soljer and soljer's agree with their superiors, even those who wear expensive suits and manicured their fingernails.

"We have to put it out of reach"

If we can't have it, neither can you, nah nah nah.

I didn't say that, but I was surprised at how bitter I felt all of a sudden. Did that come from dropping napalm on villages full of women and kids and then losing my brother while he was trying to get wounded men to safety? Who knows. What I actually said was "Yes sir."

Space flight is silent. Oh, there was sound, the thrumming and hissing that was the Module's heart, nerves and lungs. But behind it there was a silence so deep and so visceral, it was as if some gigantic sea creature had its tentacles wrapped around the craft's hull and was crushing it like a rotten fruit. It was a black oil that seeped inside to contaminate my brain like bad acid. I drifted. One minute I was in the tube, its curved surface only a few inches from my face, the next, I was back in Nam where death-rotten voices called out to me from the wet shadows between the trees. They stank and had substance, bloody and viscous, which forced itself into my ears and eyes and poured down my throat when I opened my mouth to scream. I woke, choking and gasping, to an even greater hell. Then the silence was no longer monstrous, but there was my brother, tapping on the module's hull; please, Jack, let me in because it's cold out here, so fucking cold and lonely -

It'll end. It will end. I chanted it over and over again. It'll end, it'll end, *it'll fucking end...*

I blew a fever, I shivered and sweated and saw spiders and snakes and other things, shadow things that flitted around in the corner of my eye. I heard voices that shouted from a distance and that whispered to me. Things that were not my brother scratched and banged on the outside of the module.

Outside, where it was cold and airless and there was nothing.

And then, one day, the hatch behind my head swung open and I was ejected into the Command Module like a squalling new-born.

The Eagle had already landed and Mike Collins was tumbling and grinning like the cat in that fairy tale. Me, I floated around the cabin of the Command Module in a foetal curl, shaking, weeping and unable to comprehend all the bro-ha-ha.

"You okay?" Mike asked me. He was a nice guy. Shame he wouldn't get to set foot down there. At least his name would be known. Not like mine. Nobody would ever know my name.

"Sure," I lied. I'd stopped crying at last, but I was still shaky and needed to pull myself together. "They safe?"

Mike nodded. "It was close. They were running out of moon."

"And the Soviets?"

"They landed their craft a few minutes ago. Official story is that it crashed."

"On target?"

"Pretty close."

"It's my turn now; third man on the moon."

"Yep." Was that a hint of envy? Only a hint though. Mike was a professional. "You sure you're okay? You don't look too good."

I shrugged. Not easy in zero-gee because it sent me roofwards like a fish.

"We'll hit the darkside again in twenty minutes. You'd better get suited-up."

There were two lunar modules. One of them now sat in the Sea of Tranquillity and that was the one the world was looking at. The other hung in a geostationary orbit above the dark side of the moon, hidden from Earth. It had been assembled during the Apollo 8 and 10 missions. Risky business, EVA, working in pitch darkness, a quarter of a million miles from home. But they did it and now that second lander was out there, waiting for its pilot; Major Jack Kavanagh, US Navy Air Force.

There was to be no docking this time. I pulled my helmet over my head and secured it. The suit, even in weightlessness, was ungainly and awkward, but it was to be my universe for the next few hours. I gave Mike the thumbs-up, struggled into the airlock then stepped outside.

The first thing I was aware of was that there was nothing underneath me. I mean, nothing, forever. No distant canyon floor to fall into like Wile E Coyote. No faraway street alive with ant-like traffic. Nothing. No*thing*. I launched myself towards the lander, now lit up by a searchlight affixed to the Command Module's nose cone. The consummate pilot, Mike had decelerated the module to match the lander's orbital speed. He would need to accelerate soon, before his craft's own orbit began to decay. A hawser unfolded behind me, my umbilical, literally my *life*-line. But for that, I would keep moving at the same speed and in the same direction for eternity, or until the universe came to an end. The thought was a scream, from deep down in the raging moil of my subconscious.

I became aware of the moon.

The moon is smaller than the Earth, but here, now, it was infinite and so utterly, unforgivingly heavy and vast. It was a huge black slab of solidity. It loomed over me, shadowed and formless. Its sheer presence made me want to return to my foetal curl and hide.

Closer now. This lunar module looked thrown-together, no finesse, no style. Just the things needed for it to work, all bolted into place. I fell into the gap between two if its three sprawled legs and grabbed at one of them. There were no sharp corners. A split glove would mean a quick but horrible death. Worse still, it would be the biggest secret in the world. My body would float out here forever. No one would grieve for me. I had no family I cared to talk to since I lost my brother, and no wife since Laura decided that enough was enough and walked out. I'm no angel. I'm no All-American saint.

I hauled myself up to the lander's airlock and yanked at the lever. The hatch opened, I swam inside and unclipped the hawser. Hatch closed. Inside. Lights on. There was a seat, from an F4, so I'd feel right at home. The controls were basic, enough to get me down onto the surface and back up again. No radio. No temptation to call anyone and get the signal picked up and the secret uncovered.

Okay. Time to go. I had a Soviet moon rover to catch. No time for pre-flights. There was only one chance here. I reached for the ignition switch.

The engine exploded into life. The craft shook so badly I was sure the thing would just rip itself apart. I ignited the steering rockets and set my course for Mare Crisium. The thing bucked and shuddered so much I could barely see a damned thing. Sunrise limned the darkened curve of the moon's horizon and then there was light. I didn't see much of the moon itself, though. The moon was a blurred, jiggling image glimpsed through the tiny port holes. I held on, forced myself to stay calm and think. Like I said, I flew F4s and an F4 was a big box of iron and rivets with two Saturn fives strapped to its ass. It was a jet-powered cheetah on the straight and level, but a lumber truck when you tried to turn it. If I could put one of those down on a carrier deck, which looked as big as a thumbprint when you finally located it, I could drop this thing onto the moon, which was, well, big, and hard to miss.

I killed the main engine. The shaking stopped. The lander dropped into a decaying orbit.

Then I saw it.

Jesus, I saw the moon's surface. It was grey, no, brown, ash-coloured, hell, I don't know. I saw mountains, craters, a lot of flat nothingness. I saw the moon. Can you believe that? I saw the fucking moon.

Then there was dust. I brought the craft to a stop and dropped her down. Hard. As I said, there was no time for finesse. I cut the engine and the silence was like a physical thing that made me never want to hear silence again. It was total. It was thick as maple syrup. It was empty and it was cold. It made me hear my own body: my breath, my heart beat and the blood ringing through my skull.

I guess that Neil and Buzz had finished hopping around their little lunar backyard, a performance purely for the cameras. I had to trek, I had to walk. I was scared. I picked up the metal case I'd been given, then re-fitted my helmet and once more squeezed into the air lock. There would be no messages from the President for me, no games of golf in one-sixth gee, not even a Stars and Stripes to plant. I had to get out there and I had to walk.

Each cumbersome, bouncing lunar step was worth three or four Earth ones. But despite that, it didn't take long for me to sweat and feel tired. I tried to slow my breathing. I tried to look around and enjoy the view. I was on the moon for Christ's sake. I was the third human to ever set foot on this place. Hard to take in. Hard to comprehend.

It was a strange and beautiful place, no doubt about that. To my right, a lunar sea stretched away to the distant, oddly curved horizon. It was bright with sunlight. It was flat, but rose here and there to form crater rims. The ground was dusty. Dust that had stayed in place, undisturbed for thousands, maybe even millions of years. Now I was mussing it up with my big boots, kicking it into explosive puffs that descended back to the ground with disorientating slowness. Ahead, a clutch of jagged-looking mountains rose from the plain. Their flanks smooth, their low summits looked like broken teeth. They cast a long shadow.

That was where the Soviet probe had landed.

It was lonely out here. I kept looking round, awkward in the suit because you had to turn your whole body and the first time I did it I overbalanced and fell over. My suit was tough, more expensive and with a lot more oxygen capacity in its tanks than Neil's and Buzz's. It was why they only made one of them.

I walked.

The mountains were not much higher than a hundred feet. There was a crack in their flanks, which formed a passage. It was dark, but there was nothing that would hurt me. There were no aliens, no monsters. Only the silent, silent cold. I hesitated, looked back up at the blue beauty of Earth, maybe for one last time. Then went in.

I switched on the chest flashlight that was part of the suit and found myself in a ravine, Sheer walls of brown-grey stone reared over me on either side. The sky was a strip of indigo a hundred feet above my head. There were a lot of boulders and rocky debris on the ground. I tread as carefully as I could. I reached out to steady myself against the walls and touched the stuff of the moon with my gloved hand.

The ravine opened out into an arena-like space.

And there it was.

Luna 19.

It looked like a spider with a broken leg. It hadn't so much crashed as made a bad landing. It was bigger than I had imagined it would be. The thing was lit up, which meant that not everything was busted. What I needed to know was if it had discharged its rover. I checked the dust for tracks and saw none. I guess that meant that nothing much had happened since its moonfall. That made the job easier. I opened the case and pulled out the first of the two magnetic mines it contained.

Time to do my duty like the patriotic soldier I was. I set off towards the craft. The ground here was treacherous, debris, rocks –

Something moved.

I froze.

A metal ring that suddenly looked a lot like a hatch wheel made a handful of laboured rotations. Then a section of hull swung open. What now? A weapon? A robot arm? No, it was a hand. Then an arm, yeah, which, despite the white thickness of spacesuit sleeving, looked human.

Luna 19 was manned.

Christ, it was a lunar module and there was at least one human being inside it. A human being I had been close to blowing to little pieces.

Not that it would have been the first.

The arm was followed by a body that slid out and onto the surface with that odd mixture of grace and clumsiness that accompanied movement out here. Dust was kicked up around its boots. It wavered for a moment, then straightened. I didn't think it had seen me yet.

The figure's suit was similar to mine, apart from the letters CCCP printed across the top of the helmet. If I was the third human on the moon, I'd just met the fourth.

I suppose it would have looked funny to anyone watching: two space-suited figures frozen, identical but for the national emblems that decorated their helmets. We must have resembled a couple of toddlers who'd blundered into each other in the park and didn't know what to make of one another, or what to do.

Me, I felt guilty, caught red-handed, a magnetic mine in my left glove, obvious to anyone what it was and what I intended to do with it. CCCP also carried a case. I guessed that, like mine, his (or her) burden could inflict a lot of damage on both of us.

Not knowing what else to do, I raised my right hand as slowly and carefully as I could. CCCP mirrored the gesture. The world was filled with the sound of my own breathing and it reminded me that if I wanted to go on breathing, I needed to make a move. My air supply was finite. But what the hell was I supposed to do? Barge past my counterpart, say excuse me and slap a pack of explosives against the hull of his (or her) spaceship? Not that his (or her) spaceship was anything but a broke-down tomb to die in, anyway. Perhaps it would be a kindness.

One of us had to do something. We couldn't just stand there all day.

CCCP made the first move.

He (or she) bounced into sudden motion and blundered across the gap between us and almost careered into me. He (or she) managed to grind to a halt in a slow motion spray of moon dust only a couple of feet away from me. I tensed, waiting for a blow. CCCP steadied his (or her) self, placed the brief case on the ground then reached out carefully to lay a hand on my left shoulder. A moment, then the hand was removed and used for a come-with-me gesture as the cosmonaut set off towards the mouth of a cave, drilled into the rockface over to my right. Now that was dedication to duty. I would have admired it once. Not any more. Dedication to duty got my brother killed in a dirty little war that should never have been started.

This guy, or gal, was stuck out here a quarter million miles from Earth, with their only way home broken across a saddle of lunar rock. Why the hell didn't they just curl up and cry until the air ran out and the dark came in. But then, the cosmonaut was a commie. Commies were crafty, and they were cowards; brainwashed into doing as they were told. Or so I'd been taught. This fella, or lady, didn't seem brainwashed, crafty or cowardly to me.

That's why I followed him (or her).

I stumbled, windmilled, fell into the dust and wallowed helplessly like an upturned beetle. The sound of my laboured breath deafened me. I forced myself to lie still and stared up into the sun-drenched blackness above me. That blackness went on and on and asked me who the fuck we thought we were to decide who should live and who should die?

Jesus, three days in a coffin had really done some damage to my soldier-brain. I let my breathing slow and forced myself to stay where I was, against every damn instinct in my mind and body. Once my respiration was back to normal, I slowly rolled over then struggled up onto my hands and knees. By the time I was back on my feet, CCCP had disappeared inside the cave. I set off in pursuit. I wasn't sure what I was going to do when I caught up with the guy (or gal), all I knew was that I had to catch up. I broke into the nearest thing to a run you can do on the moon. A little warning bleep sounded. My air supply was near the point of no return.

Now I was scared as well as confused. I began to feel the first stirrings of panic over my air situation. CCCP had gone into the cave and I was not supposed to go any further than the entrance to that black, empty mouth. If the thing that the Soviets' rover had found was in there, then I was supposed to blast it shut. My orders were to 'put it out of reach'.

Too bad.

I threw myself into the dark.

My yellow-white flashlight beam cut into the blackness and showed me CCCP, who had waited for me. We stirred up a lot of dust as we trudged deeper into the cave. It hung like gritty fog and danced a slow waltz in the light. The walls were odd, ribbed, like the inside of the whale in Disney's Pinocchio movie. The roof was so high I couldn't see it. I was scared, my heart thudding and my mouth dry.

I almost blundered into CCCP's back.

"Holy cow!" I said.

There it was. The Forbidden, the thing I wasn't supposed to see. The thing that had stopped CCCP in his (or her) tracks.

I don't know if it was alive. I don't know if it was a machine. I don't know if it was something God put there or whether it was the work of Satan. It was beautiful and horrible and perfect. It was like a huge starfish, some ten feet across, its arms splayed over the rock of the cave wall. Its flesh was translucent and through it, I could see tubes or veins along which fluid was pumped as if driven by a slow heartbeat. The thing was lit from inside by an unsteady pale white light. The rock beneath its arms had been changed, unless moon rock really was soft and flesh-like and webbed with fine things that could have been fibrous roots.

CCCP hesitated a moment, then took a step forward, arm extended, hand open, as if to touch the damned thing. I threw myself at the cosmonaut, but the move was clumsy and slammed us both against the fleshy flank of the creature. Which gave and thrummed then reformed itself around us. I was trapped again, coffined again. Screaming as my mind crumbled.

I tried to push myself back but suddenly I was too weak then confused then filled with thoughts.

His thoughts, those that belonged to the guy in the CCCP suit; Anton, that was his name. Anton Avarin. It was an explosion in my head. I smelled perfume, felt the softness of pale, flawless skin and whispered a name; Darya. Then I marched, boots crunching along with a thousand others through Red Square on May Day and I looked up and there, on the balcony were the cold, brutal old men who would never relinquish power until they died and who I despised from the bottom of my heart. I flew, in a MiG. I laughed and was drunk and then Darya was in my arms and I kissed her and then I tasted her heat and her softness and I ran and walked and marched and laughed and cried and raged.

I was afraid.

I was guilty.

I was disobeying orders.

I was not going to destroy the creature. I was going to take something back. I would be arrested, shot... but it might work because those who would hurt me, the heartless and the cruel, would feel what I feel and I would feel what they feel and they would understand and throw away their rifles...

I cried. I was not going to make it back. I was never going to see Darya again, or my daughters, or my friends or my world...

And Anton cried because I/he would never see my brother again and because I/he had murdered and burned and fought for something I/he didn't understand.

I stumbled back, free of the creature, contact broken.

Panic stricken. I looked round for Anton. He was sitting on the floor, like a broken doll, a confusion of shadow and suit, his landscapes carved into pieces by the combined beams of our flashlights. I stood over him and offered him a helping hand. He reached towards me but as I opened my glove to clasp his, he dropped something into my palm. I looked down and saw an object that resembled a large jewel, like an overlarge diamond in some movie or cartoon. It glinted rather than sparkled and I understood that it was a fragment of the creature's flesh. He closed his hand about mine, the object crushed between our palms.

Anton was going to die here, in this cave, close to the creature, but I had to go back, I had to take the fragment to Earth. It would change everything. It would tear down walls and barbed wire. That's why the Power didn't want it brought home.

I nodded, the gesture, no doubt lost in the confines of my helmet. Anton knew, though. He was me and I him. I turned and headed towards the cave mouth.

Once outside, I looked up at the blue wonder that was Earth and began to retrace my everlasting footsteps towards the lander. It was long walk. The air supply warning bleeped constantly now.

I would try. I am trying. Maybe, just maybe I'll make it back.

Just maybe…

WHEN THEY UNMASKED

We will always remember where we were when they unmasked.

Nathan and I were changing the tyres on a white Range Rover. I gave a running commentary as we worked. Nathan was *Fast*Wheels' mint-fresh apprentice. Seventeen years old he was, intimidated by the noise, activity and struggling to separate his arse from his elbow. His overlarge, crisp red company overalls made him look like a kid trying to be grown-up.

Suddenly he frowned, took a step back and looked up at the dirty girders and corrugated metal roof beyond. I released the trigger of the compressed-air wheel-wrench and snapped at him to pay attention.

He ignored me and, before I could bollock him back into line, reached up to grab a handful of his scalp. His hair was Grade One short, no flowing locks to grip, only that tight, no-give skin that covers the top of our skulls. I thought he was having an epileptic fit, although he wasn't convulsing and was still on his feet. He just stood there, a serious expression on his face, and pulled his own flesh. He had a handful of it. You can't do that. I've tried it since. You can't grab a handful of your scalp the way you can grab a handful of your belly.

He pulled.

And drew his face upwards so that the corners of his eyes were impossibly slanted, his mouth distorted into a nightmare clown grin and his nose yanked into a grotesque impression of a pig's snout.

I knew I should act. We had all passed our First Aid refresher about a month before, but they hadn't told us anything about self-flaying.

The skin slid up over his face. *Slid*, a word that doesn't begin to describe what I saw.

117

There was no blood. No tearing or crackling of ripped flesh. Up it went, smooth as you like. What remained was no Nathan-shaped skull. No steaming red muscle. No bulging eyeballs and grinning teeth. This wasn't Nathan.

This wasn't human.

His new face, his under-face, was smooth and oddly innocent-looking. Its skin was white and veined in blue like marble. His eyes were small, blank and black, set on the surface rather than sunk into sockets. He had no nose or ears. His mouth was a hole that opened like a wound.

I couldn't move or even shout or swear. The wrench was in my hand and would have made a good weapon, but I simply could not grasp what had happened.

I noticed that Nathan (what else could I call this thing?) still held the skin of his head in his right hand. It was a floppy, rubbery membrane, complete with a sad, hole-eyed face and ears and a crop of bristly hair. It was, at that moment, more horrible than anything.

Then someone did shout. It was Unit, the exhaust specialist. He shouted a rude word, which was followed by the clang of a dropped tool. The noise broke my paralysis and I spun round to see Unit backing away. He repeated his expletive with each reverse step. Unit was a rough, tough, built-like-a-brick-shithouse, ex-submariner. I had never seen him scared before. He had scrambled from under the ramp on which perched the Ford Ka he had been working on. Another figure emerged from its shadows. It should have been Stu. The figure wore red overalls and was as tall and lean as Stu. It even walked like Stu. But he didn't have Stu's head. He had a new head and it was identical to Nathan's.

There was more swearing, more dropped tools and shouting.

Livvy appeared from the far side of a battered old Micra (rear nearside puncture), repeating the word, "No," over and over again. Each *no* was louder than the one before. It took a few moments for me to locate the source of her shock. Then I saw that someone in a suit had entered the workshop. The suit looked expensive, dark blue, open-necked white shirt. Cufflinks visible. His head...

There was a sudden flight of red overalls, scrambling through the oily obstacle course of equipment and into the reception area, where the thing that used to be Kahn was at his laptop, staring at the screen with his two, dead, black eyes. He looked up as we blundered in.

"Oooo," he said.

The sound echoed from the workshop. It was a sad, song-like noise, not at all threatening, but strange enough to drive us out into the cool March sunshine, where the first thing I saw was a woman pushing a baby tripper. She wore an expensive-looking parka with a luxuriously fur-edged hood. I recognised the coat and tripper as belonging to the owner the Range Rover. She had been an attractive brunette when she entered the reception. But not any more. Neither was her baby the cute, gurgling little beauty it had been when I first saw it.

The *Oooo* sound was coming from all over the industrial estate now. From the electrical retailer across the road, from the door specialists beside us, from the woman climbing out of the delivery van parked in front of Auto-Parts.

We, that is Unit, Livvy and me, stood in a frightened huddle in the parking area that fronted *Fast*Wheels and looked wildly around at the things who had been people until a few minutes ago. The aliens who had been our workmates, customers and neighbours.

We were outnumbered. We could see, and hear, more marble-heads (the name just slipped into my brain) than normal human beings.

"Bastards," Unit growled. He held a large spanner in his oil-grimed, bear-paw fist.

I was suddenly conscious that I had no weapon. Neither did Livvy.

We waited.

The woman in the parka continued to push her pram. The delivery driver went around to the back of her van and reappeared a moment later with several packages. Behind us, Kahn continued to enter data onto his computer. Tools and machines whirred and clattered from the adjacent squat and ugly industrial units. And from our own. Tyres were being changed and exhaust systems replaced.

It was as if the marble-heads were unaware of what had happened.

A car raced past, gears grinding and I glimpsed its human driver and saw his fear. A couple of people hurried by, a woman in a blouse and skirt, a man in dark blue overalls. They held on to each other and glanced nervously about themselves as they walked. Normal people. People with faces. Frightened and trying not to run. They weren't alone. Humans poured from various industrial and commercial units all around us now. More and more cars had started up and were trying to leave, jamming up the exits in their panic. Horns blared, windows were rolled down and the shouting and arguing began. I heard screams. I heard yells and cries of fear.

"Fuck this, I'm going home," Unit said and was making for his car before any of us could reply.

He was right. We had to get out of here. Home. That was the place to be. The marble-heads might be peaceable now, but their time was coming. Their moment.

The trouble was, I used the bus for work. Would they still run during an apocalypse? Only one way to find out. I set off for the entrance to the industrial estate. Yes, I left Livvy behind, but there seemed to be no imminent threat. She owned a car and neither she nor Unit had offered me a lift. Twenty-minutes into the End of the World and it was already every man and woman for themselves.

Groups of humans were gathered together on both sides of the scruffy street that fronted the industrial estate. The English need for personal space appeared to have been overridden by pack instinct. They were arguing, staring, and sometimes shouting at any marble-heads who passed by on foot, on bicycles, or in cars and vans.

I hurried towards the bus stop.

There was an outbreak of pushing and shoving ahead of me. A figure stumbled onto the road and fell heavily. He was a man in a leather jacket and tee-shirt, human but for his blank, vein-marbled head. He lay in an ungainly heap, struggling to get up. As I slid through the mob, a big, shaven-headed human broke free and kicked him in the ribs. The marble-head curled about his hurt. There were cheers that sounded like the baying of animals.

Cars swept past, many driven erratically by terrified-looking humans. I heard a crash, a thud, the tinkling of broken glass, the never-ending dirge of a jammed horn.

I walked on. Head down, unwilling to catch anyone's eye, whether normal iris-and-pupil or black button.

As I took my place in the dirty glass shelter, I felt suddenly foolish. The world was ending and here I was waiting for a number seven bus.

I watched the chaos from my flimsy sanctuary. The street was already snarled with traffic, people ran in all directions. I glimpsed scuffles; human-on-human, and human-on- marble-head. Outside a mini-mart, which broke the uniform line of terrace houses opposite to where I stood, a middle-aged woman in a black business suit threw a punch at a male marble-head as he tried to walk past her. He too wore a suit and carried a briefcase. He ducked and danced to one side. The punch missed and he hurried by. Unbalanced by her wild southpaw, the woman fell against the shop's plate glass window. It held. Thank God.

The jammed horn blared on.

There was no fire yet, no looting, just confusion, fear and bewilderment, but I sensed that it was only a matter of time before things escalated to the next level.

Another car crash, directly in front of me. Head-on this time, in that familiar, startling detonation of shattered glass and bruised metal that made me flinch back. A large man with a shock of curly hair oozed out of the bigger of the two cars, a slight-built female marble-head climbed from the other. Curly's red-faced anger dissolved into abject fear. He spun about and fled as fast as his bulk would allow. The marble-head simply stood and watched him go.

Another marble-head appeared, draped in an expensive looking brown coat. She walked steadily, brief case in hand. Another followed close behind, a burly male in a bright orange high-viz, a tool case in his left fist. They both paused by the female driver. I heard their *Oooo* speech. The driver responded and they went their separate ways.

I saw it then. In that encounter.

The truth.

The marble-heads were carrying on with whatever business they had been engaged in at the instant of their change. I bet the compressed air tools at *Fast*Wheels still clattered and chattered. I bet delivery vans were still arriving at Auto-Parts and circular saws continued to whine at Finch Bespoke Doors and Windows (est 1949). All the aggression, so far, all the panic and damage, was down to us normal-heads.

A police car raced by, lights on, siren blaring. Another jump-scare. Then as if to balance things, I saw a police officer striding down the other side of the street, minus his helmet, head featureless, white and marbled. His chest-holstered radio squawked and crackled. I wondered if his control realised that he wasn't human any more.

Any *more*?

Was this a change or an unveiling?

To my amazement, a bus appeared and I did the only thing I knew to do and stepped out from the shelter, hand extended.

The bus glided to a halt. The doors hissed open. I stepped inside. The driver looked at me with featureless, black-pebble eyes and froze me in place. I glanced at the other passengers on the bus. Most of them were marble-heads, although there were a handful of humans, huddled near the back. They held onto one another or gripped the rails of the seats in front with white-knuckled desperation.

"Robin Street?" I said.

The driver nodded. He opened his circular lips and uttered a soft "Oooo".

Hand trembling, I passed him a five-pound note. I had nothing smaller. I didn't expect change, but the driver handed it to me as if nothing was wrong at all. The ticket chattered out of the machine. I tore it off and headed into the bus. I heard the doors close. I was entering the realm of the enemy. I was surrendering myself to their will. I sat, halfway down on the left. Away from any marble-head passengers and separate from the other humans. I trusted neither. I just wanted to get home.

The bus rattled, the engine revved and away we went.

The marble-head passengers were silent. Some looked my way but there was no threat, just fleeting interest. The tension was brutal, however. The air crackled with the static of fear.

"No, God, please…" A young human suddenly rose from his seat and rushed through the bus. He stumbled, and staggered and bumped against a female marble-head. He recoiled, gibbering in terror and hurled himself to the front.

"Let me off, you bastards. *Let me off.*"

The driver ignored him. The man pounded at the door. It remained closed. The young man slid down to the floor, sitting with his back to the door, arms tight about himself. He wept. He shook his head and choked out great gasping sobs. He had messy, unnaturally black hair, tattoos and piercings. If he was supposed to be tough, he wasn't making a good job of it.

"What's the matter with you?" demanded a woman from the back. She was on her feet, striding down the aisle. She stopped and shouted at the marble-head passengers. "Let him off. Can't you see he's upset? Let. Him. Off."

One of the marble-heads *oooo*-ed to her, which seemed to incense her even more. "Who the hell are you? Why don't you go back to where you fucking came from and leave us alone?"

No response.

"Did you hear me? You fucking monsters, go away. Go *away*," she screamed.

Then she slapped one of them. A young male in a hoodie.

I was on my feet. I couldn't help myself. I wasn't sure if it was sympathy for the marble-head or fear of reprisal, but I rushed along the aisle to where she stood, shrieking her saliva-speckled abuse. As I grabbed at her, the marble-heads opened their mouths and unleashed a different sound to their previous soft coo.

It was a cry. A choir. A soaring, tragic howl of what sounded like grief.

The woman yelped and fell back. I fell back too, arms flailing, scrabbling at the seats and other passengers for support. The woman collided with me and slithered down onto one knee. And all the time that song rang through my head and ripped tears from my eyes.

It stopped.

Silence fell, but for the growl and rattle of the bus.

I made to help the woman to her feet but she shrugged me off angrily, so I returned to my seat.

A lurch and the bus stopped. A hiss. The doors opened and the young man almost fell out. He scrambled free and disappeared. A couple of marble-heads and three of the human passengers got to their feet. The marble-heads made their way carefully to the door. The humans scrambled past, pushing the marble-heads aside in their haste.

We were at a bus stop. The marble-heads were keeping to the rules. *They* were keeping calm and carrying on. *They* were taking over from the humans who seemed, from what I had seen so far, to be losing their grip with terrifying speed.

Two more stops. No incidents. A handful more marble-heads got on the bus, a mother and child, an elderly woman, a teenage couple.

The bus stopped again. I looked up and was startled to see that I was home. It was important not to show panic. The door opened. I took a breath and stepped out.

Robin Road was a quiet little tree-lined avenue of pre-war, bay-windowed semis. A pleasant street inhabited by pleasant people. It was quiet this morning. Not unusual because most of the residents spent their days at work. There were, however, more cars parked than normal, indicating that I wasn't the only one who had headed home. I noticed fresh dents and scratches on some of the auto-paintwork.

The dull background traffic roar was punctuated by car horns and emergency service sirens. Something was going to happen. Something was going to break.

My front door; light-stained oak. I'd bought it from Finches Bespoke Doors and Windows (est 1948) a few months ago. I fumbled the key from my pocket and scrabbled it into the lock. I was shaking. No surprise there. The key turned and the door opened.

"Lisa?" I called out as I stepped into the hall.

And I knew.

Barely able to breathe, I moved through the house to the kitchen-diner. The door was open. I could see the sink unit and, above it, the window with its slatted wooden blind. I stepped through and looked to my right, to where Lisa sat at the dining room table. She was working at her laptop, her back to me. There were papers all about her, some stacked on the floor. She had stayed at home to mark GCSE English assignments.

I tried to say her name.

She turned to look at me.

Her skin was white and veined with grey. Her marble eyes were tiny, featureless black pebbles. Her mouth, when she spoke, was a hole that appeared in the plain featureless surface of the skin.

Then I saw the mask on the floor by her right foot; translucent flesh, long blonde hair.

She got to her feet and moved towards me. This was a monster who had stolen my wife's clothes, wore my wife's perfume and even walked like my wife. She reached out to touch my face with my wife's fingers.

I pushed her away. Violently. She staggered back and fell in the way my wife would have fallen. Her legs gave way. Her arms flew out. She made the same thudding sound as her bottom slammed onto the wooden floor. Then came the heavier crack of her back. She lay there for a moment then lifted her head - the monster's head – to look at me and she said "Oooo".

I fled the house.

Where to? I had family and friends. But…

They were all around us. Amongst us. Everywhere.

I found myself heading into the town centre. Why? Because there were people there? Because I believed that the authorities had taken control? They hadn't, of course. No one appeared to be in control. And the people I craved? They certainly provided no feeling of safety.

The traffic was snarled. People ran or milled around aimlessly. Police officers were trying to establish some sense of order, but no one was listening, especially as half the constables on the street were marble-heads. Glass shattered, looting already. I smelled smoke. The first fire.

I walked because I didn't know what else to do. I still wore my overalls. I tried to make myself as invisible as I could, but there were too many people and too many marble-heads to barge into.

A mob appeared, running along the street. It divided about the cars like the swirling water of a flash flood. Four marble-heads formed the crowd's vanguard. As they came closer, I realised that they were not the pack leaders. They were the quarry.

One of them fell, a young male, by the look of his clothes. He issued a plaintive "Oooo". Then he was swamped by the mob.

I walked on. Not wanting to see what happened next. I thought of Lisa.

I pushed her.

I saw her fall again. I saw her outstretched arms. I saw her legs give way.

I should go back to her.

No. It wasn't Lisa any more. I owed that creature nothing.

The mob was getting closer. The first of its surviving prey raced past me. I felt the shockwave of her passing. I saw the tails of her coat flap the way the tails of anyone's coat would flap if they were running for their lives.

Now I felt the mob. I felt the vibration of its footfalls and the stink of its sweat. I was in its path. They wouldn't stop for me. They were not going to stop for anyone.

A café. People were in there. Proper people. Human people. I tried the door. It was locked. I banged on the glass. A woman in black and wearing an apron, came to the door and unbolted it. I was almost dragged inside. The door was slammed shut behind me.

The mob thundered by.

"What's happening out there?" the woman demanded. She had a husky smoker's voice. "Are they taking over?"

"I…" I shook my head. "My wife is… I don't know what's happening."

"Me too." This was an older man, hunched at a table near the counter, his hands wrapped about a mug of tea, which looked cold and untouched. "My Doreen…"

"It's an invasion. Aliens," said a middle-aged character at another table. He wore a hoodie and trainers, but looked nothing like a teenager and far from cool. He was round-faced, sweating. "It's like that film. You know, with Tom Cruise where the aliens were already here, waiting under the ground. Christ." He sounded as if he was about to cry then regained control. He held out a pudgy hand. "Don."

"Dave." We shook on it.

"Tea?" the husky-voiced woman asked.

I nodded. Nothing sounded better than tea at that moment. The electricity and gas were both on. Everything was working, but for how much longer?

As long as the marble-heads are allowed to carry on running things, while humans thrash around screaming?

"I heard that their ships have already started to appear, over cities, you know, New York and Delhi." Don again.

"They don't seem to have bothered with London," I said. His certainties annoyed me. There were no ships. But surely this *was* an invasion. A deceit perpetrated on the people of Earth.

The tea arrived, along with a bacon sandwich. I sat on one of the café's plastic chairs, rested my arms on one of its melamine-topped tables and stared out of the window. People still ran, or clustered together. Comfort in numbers, I suppose. There was smoke now, drifting, fog-like down the street. Then I noticed the body. Glimpsed, in the road between the cars and vans that did their best to avoid it. Their erratic swerves added to the traffic snarl. There was blood. A glimpse of white flesh, marbled with blue-grey veins. I saw torn tights, one shoe on, the other missing, and a coat. Its tails weren't flapping now.

I stared at the body, transfixed. Out there on an ordinary day in an ordinary street on an ordinary planet.

Someone ran past the café; a young man, eyes wild, laughing. There were boxes under his arms. Loot. Things were getting out of hand quickly. He spun away and dropped a box on the pavement. It was a mobile phone. More looters stumbled past, burdened by their own haul. The phone was crushed underfoot.

I watched, unable to eat or drink and no longer aware of the people in the café. The traffic stopped flowing. A van burned further down the road to my left. People scrambled over, and between, the stationery cars. Some carried goods I doubt they'd purchased.

The café radio blared excitedly about chaos, riots and fighting. The emergency services were unable to cope, not least because half of them had *unmasked*. The word punctuated the news report. Unmasked. The prime minister hadn't been heard from. It was assumed that she was in a COBRA meeting.

The alternative reason for her absence wasn't mentioned.

I watched because I couldn't stop watching.

"The army are going to sort this out," the husky-voiced woman said.

"We don't know that," the old man answered.

"Of course they will. You don't think the government is just going to sit there and do nothing."

I knew it was a lie, but the woman's certainty was oddly comforting. We were going to be rescued, regardless of what the breathless presenters were saying on the radio.

"They knew," Don muttered darkly. "The government, they knew."

Another cup of tea arrived, accompanied by toast this time. We drew together at one table, an unspoken need. The husky-voiced woman was Claire and the old man was Tom. There were two others, a couple who had kept themselves to themselves until now. Stefan and Anna. Stefan's English was good, Anna struggled but was learning fast. Stefan was an intimidating character, but friendly and warm-hearted. I almost liked it in here with these people.

Outside, the world continued to break into pieces.

Lisa was gone now. She/it had lied to me ever since we had met. I owed her/it nothing. Even though she wore Lisa clothes and perfume and fell to the floor the way Lisa would have fallen, if I had ever pushed her.

Which I hadn't, until a few hours ago.

Claire switched the lights on. It wasn't dark yet, although the afternoon was beginning to fade enough to make the interior gloomy. The lamps came on.

I tried to remember if there had been any clue. I first met Lisa in a conventional way, at a pub with some mates. There had been a band, a covers outfit playing the usual, but loud enough to turn every conversation into a shouting competition. A group of young women had come in, laughing and obviously having a good time. I caught the eye of one of them, a blonde in cream blouse and black trousers. She was stunning. She looked back at me across the crowded, smoke-hazed room and I looked at her. Then we both turned away, embarrassed, I suppose. Shy maybe. It was glances after that, until one of my mates, it could have been Unit, elbowed me and told me to 'get in there'.

So, I sauntered over, legs shaking, mouth dry and somehow managed to ask her if she wanted to dance. My timing was perfect because the band slid neatly into *I've Been Waiting For a Girl Like You*, the old Foreigner song (it was a real ale pub for the middle-aged. My mates and I were there because the booze was cheap).

She was the most beautiful woman I had ever seen. She felt light and precious in my arms. I liked her smile and frown and voice. I liked the way she looked straight at me and I came to love her wisdom, kindness and spirit. Corny, I know, but I don't care. There was no clue that night, or on our first date in that Italian restaurant or when I proposed to her on one muddy knee on a rainy afternoon in the Lake District, or when she cried over the news that she, English teacher to the offspring of countless others, could never bear children of her own.

There was no clue or hint or sign that Lisa was anything or anyone but Lisa –

I started as a female marble-head bumped loudly against the café's window. She clung to the glass and looked at me with her tiny, black eyes. There was no expression in her face, yet I could tell that she was afraid. She wore a long cardigan and dark skirt. Her sleeve was torn at her right shoulder. Her blank, face was smudged and dirty. Her breath steamed the glass. I heard her muffled and sorrowful "Oooo."

Suddenly a body slammed into her and she was thrown to the right and down onto the pavement. A gang piled onto her; men and women, some rough looking, others smart, a middle-aged man in a suit, an older man, a woman in a red coat. All of them screaming and kicking and stamping. I saw the marble-head raise her arm. Then I couldn't, see her any more.

Lisa... flying back from me. Hitting the floor...

I was out of the cafe before anyone could shout at me to stop. I grabbed at the nearest of the woman's attackers and hauled him back. He grunted in surprise, swung round and before I could defend myself, drove his fist into my belly. The impact doubled me over. The pain was shocking and reminded me, strangely, of childhood playground scraps. I staggered against the café window, coughing and gasping. The mob backed away from the marble-head and turned their attention towards me.

"Fucking alien lover," the woman in the red coat shrieked. The stocky young man who had hit me the first time, lumbered in.

Pain turned to rage. I'm a big bloke, used to carrying car tyres around. I was angry. I slammed into him and we both crashed down to the pavement. I punched his face, again, again. He struggled. Blood streamed from his nose and the sight of it enraged me even more. I pummelled his ugly, vile face until I was dragged clear. Someone kicked me in the ribs and I once more struggled to breathe. Pain seemed to burst all over me.

I was alone. On my side. The marble-head was only a few feet away. There was a widening pool of blood under her head. Her tiny, blank eyes were fixed on me.

I hauled myself up onto my hands and knees and crawled over to her. I held her hand. There was not much more that I could do. Her hand was warm and human. She gasped then lay still.

As I clambered back onto my feet, unsteady, nauseous and stiffening from pain, I wondered if I was the only one who felt the way I did. I looked around, disorientated by the jammed traffic, the running figures, the smoke, and the marble-heads who now seemed as confused and frightened as I was. Some carried tool bags, briefcases or handbags. One clutched a crying baby to himself. The baby was human.

Glass shattered somewhere. Shouts again, a scream. A shot.

Jesus. A shot.

Lisa...

*

There was a fire in Robin Avenue. For a moment I was convinced… but no, it wasn't my house. I was relieved. Then guilty because it was *someone's* house. Flames spewed from the downstairs windows and from a huge hole that had been eaten into the roof, its ribcage of beams visible amongst the writhing nest of flames. I hurried past, arm over my face in an effort to keep the smoke from my nose and mouth.

There might be people in there…

The heat was terrific. Even if there were people trapped inside, there was nothing I could do. I couldn't get near the place. I had to close my mind to the horror of it. I had to harden myself.

I made it to my front door and fumbled my key from my pocket. Inside. The smoke of the fire was so dense it even tainted the air in here.

"Lisa! It's me."

No reply. I rushed into the kitchen diner. No sign of her. Still shouting, I tried the sitting room and then the stairs. The smoke stink was stronger now. It made me cough. I ran up the steps, quickly out of breath. I crashed into our bedroom and there she was. Lisa, curled on the duvet,

I baulked at the sight of her for a moment. Then remembered the woman outside the café. The widening pool of blood spreading like a crimson halo about her ruined head…

"Lisa." I went over to her.

She flinched away from me.

"I… I'm sorry. I didn't understand…"

Carefully, I climbed onto the bed and reached for her. My hand came to rest on her shoulder. Lisa's shoulder; that familiar shape and feel. This was Lisa. And yet… not Lisa.

She lifted her head to look at me. I could see no thought or emotion in her blank, alien face. Yet I sensed her sadness and her terror.

I pulled her to me. Every instinct cried out for me to push her away. Her head came to rest on my chest. The same weight as my Lisa's head. But the feel of it was *wrong* under my hand; smooth, hairless, softer than it should be.

I forced myself to hold her. I forced myself to kiss the pulsing, alien skin of her denuded scalp. She curled in more tightly to me and in that moment, I understood that, somehow, she really was Lisa.

"Who are you?" I asked, at last. A stupid question because as far as I was aware, the marble-heads spoke no English. I wasn't sure what they spoke, to be honest. Whether the sound they made were words, or a result of telepathy or just a cry of shock or pain.

I let go and drew away, suddenly unable to bear it. The fact that her body felt so normal and familiar and yet she was so utterly alien was too much. She looked up at me from the bed and it was impossible to tell if she was hurt, angry or uncaring.

"I can't…" I said. "Lisa —" It even felt wrong to call her by that name. "I have to know who you are."

Nothing.

I needed to get away from her again, if only to go downstairs and make a coffee. I couldn't look at her any more, or speak. My only concession to her feelings (if she had any) was to not flee from the room, but force myself to exit at a decent pace. Once on the landing, I felt *in*decent relief. What the hell was I supposed to do?

Downstairs, I went into the kitchen, filled and switched-on the kettle.

Lisa.

For the first time for years, I felt like crying. Men don't cry, but I wanted to as I sat at the dining room table and sipped black, unsweetened Nescafé. It was horrible, but I needed horrible. I needed its bitterness and scorching heat.

It was night now, not dark, but a shifting blood red. Houses were on fire. Sounds filtered through, sirens, shouts. The usual theme music for an apocalypse. This was the strangest world-ending I had ever seen. Not that I'd seen any other than on television or at the cinema.

I drank horrible coffee and burned my mouth and didn't care.

I was tired and I couldn't think right now. I needed to sleep then make some plan in the morning. Although what that plan was, I had no idea. Perhaps there was some sort of government sanctuary, a refugee camp. Or the army were being called in to take control of the situation. Well, half the army. The other half would be marble-heads.

Armed and highly trained marble-heads.

Was there no end to this?

Then I heard glass break and suddenly I stopped thinking.

It sounded as if it was the front, of the house. I was on my feet and into the hall. I was unarmed and alone. I heard voices in the living room. Christ. I rushed the stairs and charged the landing. The living room door crashed open just as I reached the top few steps. I glanced back to see a big character wielding an iron pipe. He was on the stairs. I made it to the landing and spun round, aware now of two other intruders who must have followed him in through the broken window. One was a woman. That was all I registered, because my immediate problem was now right in front of me, red-faced and half-mad by the look of him.

I kicked out.

I've never had one martial arts lesson in my life, but that kick was perfect. His face was level with my work boot. I felt the shock of impact. I felt things crunch and give way. Then I heard his yell and the awful percussion of a human body tumbling downstairs. Not only an enemy felled, but an obstacle that hindered his comrades' assault. I didn't stay to watch the struggling and confusion, but hurried to the bedroom and back to the creature that had once been my wife. She was still curled on the bed, where I'd left her. Expressionless she might be, but I knew fear when I saw it.

The light was on, which reminded me that despite Armageddon, the electricity and water and other utilities still worked perfectly. I was convinced now that it was the marble-heads who maintained our civilisation while its creators were trying to burn it down. A fine army of invaders these creatures had turned out to be; unarmed, persecuted and functioning as the human beings they had once been, while the race they sought to subjugate set fire to things and ran riot.

On second thoughts, not such a bad plan after all.

Without a word to Lisa, I grabbed the dressing table from under the bedroom window and hauled it in a rough, clumsy panic over to the door. Bottles of perfume and pots of jewellery crashed to the floor. Talcum powder exploded in a sweet-smelling plume as a flower-decorated tub fell to its doom. I jammed the table against the door as tightly as I could.

A moment later, something, or someone, crashed against the door from the other side. I saw the door shudder and the dressing table slide a few inches across the wooden floor. I grasped its front edge and prepared to hold it in place. The pounding and shouting grew worse. I sensed someone beside me, glanced round and saw that it was Lisa.

I smelled not only her fear, but a hint of her perfume. An odd mix that confused me. I was repulsed and afraid of her, yet she *was* Lisa.

The pounding intensified. I was scared now. A level of fear I had never experienced before. It was intense and disorientating. It turned the real unreal. It sang through my head in great pulses of blood with each labouring heartbeat. I was about to die, yet my mind denied it. Not now, or here. I was supposed to be alive.

We couldn't hold them back for much longer. They were about to break in and when they did there would be Hell to pay. I couldn't imagine the horror of their violence. Oh, I've was in a pub fight or two in my younger days and I'm not afraid of a scrap, but this was different. This was desperate, hate and terror-driven violence that wouldn't be sated by a black-eye or bleeding nose. This violence demanded serious injury and even death.

The pounding rose to a crescendo. The dressing table bucked like an unbroken horse at a rodeo. The bottles and jars that had survived my panicked drag across the room bounced onto the floor. The air was soon thick with a cloying scent of perfume and spilled creams and lotions. I strained into a final effort. Lisa too. She trembled, her formless alien head lowered.

Wood cracked. Paint and splinters burst from a wound in the door.

This was it.

The end.

A horrible, painful, brutal end.

It stopped.

There were whispers. I waited, panting hard. Lisa uttered a soft *Oooo*. Then came the sound of people scuttling downstairs. They sounded excited. I'm sure I heard one of them laugh.

Gingerly, I withdrew from the dressing table and stepped back. If they had played the old-pretend-to-retreat-then-turn-back manoeuvre, we were done for. Lisa stayed where she was, hunched over the dressing table, ready to throw her weight back into the battle if necessary.

We waited. The table didn't move. There was no surprise attack.

I wanted to say something comforting to the being who dressed, smelled and acted like my wife, but I didn't know what to say. I didn't know if she even understood me. I didn't know how simply removing a mask could rob her of language... So we stood there, pointlessly staring at the battered dressing table and the fractured door beyond.

I began to wonder if our attackers had given up and moved on. I allowed myself a little hope.

Until I smelled smoke.

Far from unusual today, but this was too strong and pungent to be from outside. This smoke-smell had an urgency about it. This smoke was close. Intimate.

No, surely not –

The smell intensified.

"Get back," I shouted. "Get away from the door."

Lisa did as I asked. The smell was growing stronger by the second.

I grabbed a dressing gown and put it over my head, with no idea if it would protect me, then wrenched the table back a few feet and carefully opened the door. I saw no flames, but the landing was misted by a thick haze.

There were crackling sounds. A rise in temperature. Fire was eating at my home. *Our* home. I moved out onto the landing. The smoke burned my throat and stung my eyes. I arrived at the top of the stairs and peered down to see the unguarded front door. Still no sign of any flames, but I knew that it was only a matter of time.

"Lisa," I called back into the bedroom. "We can get out if we're quick."

God knew what waited for us outside, but we couldn't stay in here. I slumped against the wall and crouched down onto my haunches. Weren't you supposed to stay near the floor? I discarded the dressing gown, which had become an encumbrance. It was getting hard to breathe. It was getting hard to see, as well.

Lisa appeared, a vague shape that crawled out of the fire-scented fog on her hands and knees. I set off down the stairs, crawling on my belly over the steps. The edges of the treads punched and burned my already sore stomach. The keeping-close-to-the-floor advice didn't seem to make much difference. The smoke was a black oily blanket that clogged my nose and scoured my eyes. I trusted that Lisa was behind me. I couldn't turn around to check. I had to keep moving.

There was a loud bang, somewhere ahead of me. Light flared into the gloom. And heat, brutal, skin-blistering heat that ripped animal terror out of my soul.

Fire.

Bringer of destruction and unspeakable pain. I saw that the living room door had been replaced by a twisting dance of bright orange flame. I scrambled to my feet, tried to hold my breath and threw myself downwards in a half tumble. I hit the front door, pushed myself back and wrestled with the handle, all the while, trying to ignore the searing heat that roiled out of the living room to my left. Other things burned now as the flames groped their way into the hallway.

The handle was hot. It burned my hand. I didn't care. The animal had taken over, screaming at me to get out.

I had to breathe.

One big deep breath, that was all I wanted.

I felt my skin blister. I could barely see. There was nothing but darkness and flickering, restless light. I felt a body fall against my back. I felt hand claw at me. I felt myself fade and burn. There was pain. There was suffocation.

Then the door opened and I staggered back, momentarily throwing whoever it was behind me into a tangle of arms and feet. I didn't care. It was self at that moment. Me. My lungs. My skin. My life.

Out.

Where there was oxygen. I staggered down the short path and into the road. I was outside. I was in pain from the scorching flames. I was gasping for breath and wanting to vomit my lungs onto the tarmac.

I stood, doubled over, hands on knees, panting hard.

Lisa.

She, the alien, was there, a few yards to my right. On her knees.

Behind us, the house burned. I heard crashing noises and glass shatter. It didn't matter. We were alive. We were breathing and the air held currents of coolness that snaked through the heat.

A nearby garden fence collapsed. Figures poured into the night-dark, smoke-fogged street. They were splashed orange by the fire. I saw their vile, hate-torn faces. I saw the weapons they carried, lengths of pipe, knives, lengths of wood. I saw old and young, men and women, smartly dressed and scruffy.

They formed an arc around us. We'd been smoked out. The ambush had been sprung.

I wanted them to get on with it. I was finished and frightened and broken.

Nothing happened. I could see their desire to launch themselves at us. I could see their loathing and fear, but there was hesitation. These were ordinary people, unused to violence. Setting fire to a house was impersonal. You were not looking anyone in the eye.

I had the advantage. Attack is the best defence.

I yelled at Lisa to get away then charged the mob. It felt like a good idea at the time. As I slammed into a man in a roll-neck jumper, I felt an explosion of pain erupt through my side and chest. An iron bar, wielded by a teenage girl with bunches that looked like Micky Mouse ears. Gasping for breath, I collapsed into a hell of kicking and pounding. I tried to fold myself into a protective foetus-curl. They were going to kill me. It hurt. Christ, how it hurt. Worse, they must be doing this to Lisa. God, I tried to save her. I tried -

The beating eased. The feet shuffled and stumbled out of my line of vision. Did they think I was dead? Were they gripped by a sudden crisis of conscience? Or had they stepped aside to allow my executioner access? What was it to be? Blunt instrument to the head? A cut throat? A bullet?

A sound filtered into the odd and sudden silence.

That choir sound I had heard on the bus. From close, Lisa perhaps, and answered from all around and from the far distance. The sound grew in volume. It drew goose bumps from my aching, bruised flesh. It was so plaintive it almost made me cry.

I struggled up onto my knees and saw, in the shifting orange light, the humans exchange uncertain glances. Perhaps this was the signal. The final hammer blow.

Lisa stepped forward and the mob cowered back. I noted that she carried something, which she lifted to her face. It was her skin-and-hair human mask. She reached up and drew it over her marbled scalp. There was no tugging or adjustments. The mask fitted smoothly and perfectly.

Lisa was back.

Yet not Lisa.

The mob looked about them and suddenly there were only humans. Confusion rippled outwards and broke the mob apart. Some of its members shambled off. Many simply stood, stripped of purpose and unable to find an enemy.

Or friend.

I didn't rush into the arms of my wife because I no longer knew if she was my wife. I might go to her, eventually, but not yet. Instead, I wandered away, as confused as those who had tried to kill us a moment ago. Burned, bruised and aching, I wandered into the shattered, smoke-choked streets of the town and stared fearfully at everyone I passed, just as they stared fearfully back at me.

Buildings and vehicles still burn. The dead and wounded still lie where they fell. They are the only ones whose identities we can be sure of. You see, we can no longer tell who are our own and who are strangers. The world stands still and it's doubtful that it will ever restart.

WHAT IT IS

I

And then we were in her bedsit, a place that was a thousand times more untidy than even my own flat. But that didn't matter, not at that moment. That moment was a sweat-slicked, wet moment, a hot-breath, biting and scratching moment. A wild fuck moment.

Skin, the girl I rutted in her cramped lair of discarded clothes and unwashed crockery, had told me nothing, other than that she sang in a punk band called The Shout.

Afterwards she knelt on the bed and looked down at me and said. "Do you always shag the people you interview?"

"Hardly ever."

Never in fact. I was freelance, part time (my real job involved a warehouse and fork lift trucks) and wrote for a struggling new music rag called *Noise*. It didn't bring me into contact with many Big Names. Well, not often. I had been told to piss-off by more than one Big Name at the stage door. Does that count?

But perhaps it was comeuppance time, because back then, in the tail end of that long hot summer of 1976, people had stopped listening to the pomp and strut of those Big Names. People were starting to tell *them* to piss-off.

"Your clothes are down there," Skin said.

"I don't want them."

"Going home naked are you?"

"I thought I'd stay here a bit longer."

She got off the bed and went to the tiny little fridge. She pulled out a couple of beers and threw one to me.

"Anything softer?"

"What?"

"Squash, Coke, with cola, not, you know…"

"Got water, or some coffee, no milk."

"Water's okay." I needed coffee, but I didn't want her distracted by the mundane.

She went to the sink, rinsed a mug and filled it. She was naked, tall, skinny, pale-fleshed. Her hair was dyed platinum, her make-up vivid pink rather than black, which was de rigueur for the new punk damsel. There was a cross-hatch of time-whitened scars on her left forearm.

"Aren't you going to ask?" I said when she handed me the mug.

"Ask what?"

"Why I don't want beer?"

She shrugged.

Her absence of curiosity irritated me, odd, because normally I was sick of explaining myself.

"Stay if you want," she said.

She sat on the bed. I sat against the pillow. There was no bed head, just the wall and its covering of vile wallpaper. I touched her face.

"Pink punk." I muttered. I liked the phrase. I'd use it in my next article.

"What's Pink Punk?"

"You are."

"Fuck you." She wasn't joking. "Punk isn't pink or black or fucking green. It's what it is."

"Pure, yeah." Was it? Christ knows, but I didn't want to see those angry eyes again. I raised my mug in a toast; "Three chords, proud and straight. No pomp, no pretension."

"Is that all you think it is?"

"Well no…" Wrong again, and panicked. One fucking session and I was frightened of losing her. "So what is it?"

"What it *is*." She sniffed, contemptuous. "I'm hungry."

We found a late night café. Skin sported a surprisingly conventional outfit for our adventure in fine dining; jeans, tee shirt and cardigan. "So?" she said when I was stupid enough to comment. "Am I supposed to wear a fucking bin liner all the time?"

The food was greasy, the tea, strong. It was the best meal I've ever had.

Afterwards, we went back to her bedsit. I didn't leave it for another three days, except to go to the day job. I was supposed to write a review for *Noise*, but I didn't go out to see any bands, and besides the typewriter was in my flat. Perhaps that was a sign, time to jack it in. Writing had become a way to fill the empty spaces. Skin filled them now.

Skin was usually at home. There was a television, which she watched most of the time.

"When do you rehearse?" I asked her on the third night.

"We don't."

"But –"

"We just play."

II

I'd never actually seen Skin's band. The interview had been a favour for a badly hung-over colleague. The Shout's next gig was on the Saturday night after we met. The fourth day. I'd never been the boyfriend in the audience before. I had fantasies of secret glances, of lyrics given new meaning by the intensity of our love.

"Where is it?" I asked. We were taking, an afternoon stroll-and-smoke in the local rec.

"Where's what?"

"The gig."

No, I didn't know where it was and she hadn't told me there *was* a gig until this morning.

"Hammer and Nails."

"Where's that?"

"Near St Paul's Cathedral somewhere."

"I hope you know where *somewhere* is or we're going to get lost."

"What do you mean *we*?"

"Don't you want me to see you play?"

She shrugged.

"Fuck's sake. I'm your..." Her what exactly? "I want to see your band."

"We're at the Hammer and Nails, on at nine." She turned to walk away.

I grabbed her arm. "Don't you care if I come?"

"It's nothing to do with me."

"What is it to do with?"

"What it is."

"I'm sick of your riddles –"

"I'm sick of your questions. I'll see you later."

"What questions? I never ask you any questions because you never want to answer them."

She walked away and tossed a weary "Fuck you" over her shoulder.

"Bitch!"

She didn't look back.

My flat. Fifteen floors up the flank of a 1960s tower block, with a big expanse of sitting room window that gave stunning views of the other identical towers on the estate. For all its faults, it felt infinitely spacious after being coped up in Skin's bedsit. I could breathe here. I sat on the floor and stared at my music collection; countless LPs, spines outwards in their second-hand, wood-effect shelf unit. I selected one, at random; *Made in Japan*; Deep Purple live.

I slid the first of the album's two big black vinyl discs from its bronze sleeve and laid it carefully on my hi-fi turntable. A few moments later Jon Lord was leading the way into *Highway Star*. I closed my eyes and let the rock-roar enfold me. There was momentary comfort here. Realities shut out, lids closed. Gillan's scream, Blackmore's virtuosity.

Punk didn't belong to me.

Skin didn't belong to me.

I opened my eyes, shattered by the thought, just as *Child in Time* moved abruptly from quiet-and-menacing to loud-and-terrifying.

The music was suddenly bloated and self-regarding, the flat dusty, tatty and empty; a stale den for a twenty-five year-old teenager who should have grown-up when he did possess the accoutrements of adulthood; a wife, a child and a career.

I did a good job of chasing them all away. I was a serious writer then, a journalist, newly moved from fete-and-wedding local rags to the lower ranks of the *Evening Standard,* as well as some non de plume moonlighting for the music heavies such as *NME* and *Sounds.* I chased them away while fighting in bars, throwing-up in the street, or at best, sleeping it off while exiled to the sofa.

I didn't hit Sarah, or our child. Never. Wouldn't. Couldn't. But I was the maggot that rotted our marriage from the inside. The useless toe-rag who loved a drink, was *entitled* to a drink and was going to bloody well have a drink because He Worked Hard And Deserved It.

I don't know where Sarah escaped to. She had never contacted me since she walked out. My son was two now. They were better off without me.

Child in Time finished, the crowd cheered. Then the turntable arm lifted, silence.

I hated silence. It was the soundtrack of solitude.

III

The Hammer and Nails function room was upstairs. Its ceiling was low, its walls already closing in. The place was packed, everyone in newly-minted punk uniform and tanking-up as fast as their throats and bellies would allow. A scuffle broke out, a punch was thrown. It came to nothing, just the usual dynamics of a tribe waiting for its music.

The performance area, more rostrum than stage, was already kitted out with amps and mikes. I had seen Skin in the bar downstairs, surrounded by a bunch of male punks. They were laughing, having a party. I stayed out of it. I was nervous for Skin. She, on the other hand, hadn't seemed at all anxious.

A stir in the crowd, and then a procession pushed through, stage-bound. I glimpsed Skin, walking beside a huge guy with a shaved head and fearsome looking Mohican. The big guy stripped to the waist then sat down behind the drumkit. A tall, lanky streak of piss plugged in a bass. Beside him, a slight-built, sullen-looking character with sticky, messed-up hair tuned his Strat. Skin said something. There were nods all round. She spun about, grabbed the mike in both hands and screamed. The sound ripped through the room and bent my eardrums inwards until they hurt. There was an answering howl.

The band erupted into life. The crowd surged, swirled, pogoed, more mob than audience. I clung to my Coke bottle. The music was loud, unrelenting, a solid wall of blazing white. Song merged into song, each one too loud to reveal any melodic landscape it might have possessed. It was effect. It was energy, sweat and noise, the soundtrack to a half-lit sub-world of violent, staccato movement and barely-contained aggression.

Afterwards, the band went back downstairs to continue their party. Ears ringing, consumed by an ill-defined sense of dread, I followed. Once down in the bar, I stood on the edge and watched Skin get drunk. Someone, I think it was the bass player, asked me who the fuck I was. Skin said nothing, just carried on flirting with some fat little punk who had more metalwork in his face than Sabbath's Iron Man.

I walked out, went back to the bedsitter and waited outside.

I was still waiting when she came home.

"Didn't you want me there?" I said.

She shrugged as she unlocked the front door. "Up to you."

"I don't want it to be up to me."

"I'm not your mother." This was tossed down to me as we ascended the narrow, ill-lit staircase.

"I just want you to… I don't know… to let me in."

"Let you into what?"

"Your life, you're self. *You.*"

She shook her head. "No one goes there. *I* don't go there."

"I don't know you –"

"Yes you do. I'm here. This is it." Into the bedsitter now, light on, her jacket off, thrown towards the bed but ending up on the floor.

"No one is just what you see."

"Well find someone else who *will* let you in, or whatever it is you want."

"I don't want anyone else." I grabbed at her, tried to pull her to myself.

"Fuck off…"

She struggled and managed to squirm out of my grasp. In one fluid motion she snatched up a knife from the pile of dirty cutlery in the tiny sink. It was a sharp, short-bladed thing, crusted with food. She spun round to face me and slashed the knife across her left forearm. The cut bubbled, thickened and leaked blood.

"For Christ's sake Skin –"

"See it do you?" she yelled. "What's inside? There's nothing, fucking nothing!"

Blood ran down her arm, dripped onto the threadbare carpet.

She backed away and stood in the middle of the room. Her injured arm hung by her side, almost unheeded. "Nothing…" She bowed her head. It took me several seconds to realise that she was crying.

I went to her and this time she let me hold her.

The next day, Sunday, neither of us mentioned what had happened. The cut wasn't serious, easily remedied by a plaster. I cleaned the bedsit. Skin watched me. Bemused, I think. Perhaps it was scorn. I didn't care. I cleaned up, took the sheets and our clothes to the launderette. I fetched my typewriter and some more clothes from my flat then spent the afternoon typing my column; 'Punk; What is it? What it is'.

Skin sat on the bed and wrote a song. She slept, stared out of the window, drank beer, watched me, then watched television; a Western, the news, "Songs of Praise". I moulded myself around the quietness of her existence. I wanted to be here. I didn't want to be alone. The day exhausted me.

IV

A few days later I came home from my job in the warehouse to find the bedsit empty. No sign of Skin. No note, no message, just the crumpled bed, mouldering discarded clothes and a sink full of dirty mugs. Things had settled down, almost into a routine. Skin hadn't asked me to stay, but she hadn't asked me to leave either. So here I was.

Only tonight, here she wasn't.

Even living a life of *what it is* required food, toothpaste and toilet rolls, even Skin needed to go to the corner shop every now and then. I sighed, disappointed to be alone, and filled the kettle. While it heated, I switched on the television and cleared up Skin's mess-of-the-day. *Blue Peter* was coming to an end, Noakes, Judd and Purves, on the sofa, saying good night. A little shock of nostalgia made me stop. I wanted to be a kid again, no worries, except getting my homework done so I could play.

Nostalgia faded. My disappointment turned to irritation. How could Skin live like this? I wasn't exactly Mr Clean-and-Tidy but, compared to her, I was the Jack Lemmon half of *The Odd Couple*.

The kettle boiled. I made coffee, using the last of the milk in the process. Hopefully Skin would bring a replacement from her shopping expedition. I sat down and waited for the News.

It came and went. I sat through *Nationwide*, not paying it much attention. I grew restless. Still no sign of Skin. I stood and went to the fridge in search of food. Cheese, bread, perhaps I should walk to the café. But I wanted to be here when Skin got home. I made a sandwich. I tried to watch *Top of the Pops*, but all it did was add to my irritation. Mimed crap, fronted by DJs who were too ancient for the job. Dear God, when were they going to put that bloody programme out of its misery?

I was up again, wandering to the fridge. Door open. A tub of marge, a half-used tin of evaporated milk, bacon, a few eggs and four bottles of Newcastle Brown. I slammed the door shut.

I deserved it, though, didn't I? How did that song go? *The poor sod is entitled to a drink and is going to bloody well have a drink he because He Works Hard And Deserves It.* Yeah, that was the one.

Off with the television, on with the radio. No, too lonely, too depressing. Cassette player then. A rage of noise. Someone telling me he was the Anti-Christ. Suddenly punk is pissing me off. What the hell was so special about rock and roll played at twice the speed by people who couldn't play it in the first place?

Television back on.

Fridge.

Come on, a little reward for your heartache…

Fuck it, a walk, the café. Skin had lost her chance of a Hollywood homecoming. I had to get out of there.

She wasn't there when I came back to the bedsit three hours later. She wasn't there until one in the morning.

She was gone too long.

I didn't say it. I didn't ask the question. How could I? What moral high ground did I hold now? I was sitting on the bed, television off, no music, no radio. Alone with the dazed grind of my failure. I watched her throw her jacket onto the floor then go to the fridge.

There were, of course, no bottles left. I think I chuckled, giggled maybe.

She sat on the bed, by my feet. She smelled of sweat, cigarettes and stale alcohol and was wearing her stage costume; torn sweater and ripped jeans.

She stared at me, a little puzzled perhaps, but with no recrimination. I reached out to touch her, nervous of rejection, the movement, clumsy. She took my hand and pressed it to her lips and licked my fingers. I grabbed at her and threw her down beside me. I ground my mouth hard against hers and tasted beer, tobacco and the scorching heat of her breath. I fumbled and tore at her clothes and she at mine. And, for a moment, everything was Skin again.

V

For the moment.

The next evening, after work, I went back to my own flat. How could I not? I made a shopping detour on the way. Once indoors I placed my purchase on the kitchen worktop. It was in a plain brown paper bag. I stood as far away from the thing as was possible within the cramped confines of the room. Then I forced myself to turn my back on it and fill the kettle.

Buying the scotch was as much a self-inflicted wound as those caused by Skin's knife.

Nursing a freshly-filled coffee mug between my hands, I walked past the bottle and into the sitting room. I selected an LP. *Watcher of the Skies* hammered through the flat's stale air.

You couldn't get further from punk than Genesis.

I sat on the floor, drowned by the music, *my* music, drinking strong cheap coffee and fighting the urge to run into the kitchen to snatch the bottle from the worktop.

If I did, the tenuous umbilical that joined me to Skin would snap.

And if that happened, I would bleed to death.

"Crone?" I said into the phone's sticky, grubby mouthpiece once the coin had silenced the pips.

"Fuck's sake, Baz, it's two in the morning." Cronin was a friend from my serious music press days, Scottish, soft accent, hard-nosed attitude. He managed bands, successful ones.

"The Shout, one hell of a band." I talked fast, no more ten pence pieces.

"Yeah, them and a thousand others."

"They're at the Hammer and Nails, tomorrow... no, no, it's tonight. Please come, for me, please Crone..." The pips sounded. The line went dead.

I hung up and stumbled out of the phone box. I didn't want to go home, so I walked, miraculously, still sober. Cronin would come to the gig and sign-up The Shout. And I would have made my grand gesture, like Romeo shouting love poems up to Juliet's balcony. Doors would open, literal ones and emotional ones.

He had to sign them. Christ, he had to.

VI

Time always passes, no matter how slow and torturous its passage might be. I abandoned any thought of work. Not a problem, though, the union would make sure I kept my job. I returned to my flat, made coffee and placed *Houses of the Holy* on the turntable. The day would be measured by the forty-minute segments denoted by each album in my collection, played for the last time then snapped over my knee. Each forty-minute slice was a battle through which I only had to stay dry from Track One to the end.

VII

Lights down. The compere for the evening took to the mic. He shouted something incomprehensible. The crowd howled back at him. Someone threw a bottle which shattered at his feet.

No sign of Cronin.

The band once more made their way through the tight-packed crowd like ring-bound boxers. I strained to see Skin, caught a glimpse. She was laughing, hand on the drummer's shoulder. He spoke to her, mouth close to her ear. Panic drove me into the press, trying to tear my way through, to show her I was here.

Someone hit me, not hard, but enough to throw me back. The crowd seemed to give beneath the impact of my body, then pushed me forward and back onto my feet. Hands grabbed at me, pushed, shoved. I fought back, wild in my anger and fear.

"This is all that matters," Skin yelled. She never usually talked to the crowd. They roared back at her and I was forgotten, flotsam, driven forward by the band-wards surge. A whine of feedback then it started, that relentless wall of sound, distortion, energy and Skin's screeched vocals.

Cronin you bastard, where are you…

When it was over the band simply unplugged and left the stage, No goodbye-and-thank-you, no love-you-all, it was done.

I swam through the crowd, trying intercept Skin.

Someone else beat me to it; big man, out-of-date leather jacket, receding hairline, bulldog jowls.

Cronin put his arm about Skin's shoulders and led her towards the stairs.

VIII

Her light was on but she wouldn't answer her buzzer. So I used the spare key. Both doors opened. No chain, thank Christ. I went in.

Skin was sitting on the bed, still dressed in her stage gear: torn sweater and jeans.

"Cronin, I told him about you," I tried not to sound breathless.

"Fuck you."

"Jesus Skin, didn't he want —"

"He was all over me." She looked up, eyes as dead as her voice. "He said he wanted me, and Sledge, but not the others."

Sledge, I had discovered a few days ago, was her drummer.

"That's the business, Skin. It's hard but —"

"Sledge is joining one of Cronin's other signings."

"What about you?"

"Cronin'll put a band together for me, session musicians. What the fuck do session musicians know about punk?"

"They're pros, Skin, they can play anything."

"No they can't, they fuckin can't! He's killed The Shout, you bastard. They walked out on me when they heard."

"Something dies, something's born." Very fucking profound.

"The Shout was mine." She had the knife. I hadn't noticed it until that moment. She drew it across her arm as she spoke, unflinching, as if unaware of its bite.

That scared me. "Okay. Okay, I'm sorry. Skin, don't, we can make this right, we can get your band back. Cronin's my mate, I'll phone hum… listen to me."

A second cut. Blood ran.

"Fuck you."

"You ungrateful bitch. I got you what anyone else in the bloody world would die for and you throw it back in my face!"

"I had what I wanted." She sawed the blade over her flesh in time to her words.

"You've got something better."

"How do you know? How of you fucking know? Who are you anyway? I wish you'd just leave me alone"

"Skin, please, I love —"

Blood fountained.

Jesus, she had hit something vital.

Black-red juice squirted in pulsing gouts across the room. I grabbed her and rammed a handful of bed sheet over the wound. The sheet was instantly transformed into a sodden, red mass. Skin's face whitened, she fell back. I shouted her name, sobbed her name.

Then just sobbed.

For her, for me, Christ knows.

STRINGS

The Tiger Lillies are a real band whose songs are the inspiration for this story. It is to them, that Strings *is dedicated.*

There was a promise of something indulgent, exciting, mysterious even, in the envelope's soft brushed surface and rich red hue. An exoticism heightened by the neat, cursive handwriting which spelled out Thomas Monroe's name and address on its front. There was no stamp, adhesive or franked, which was odd. Neither had there been a request for payment of the postage by its deliverer; odder still in these days of no-money-no-service.

Monroe knew that its fascination would be short-lived. The envelope was sure to contain junk mail. Nevertheless, he opened it carefully. It was that sort of envelope, one you didn't want to tear apart with reckless abandon.

Inside was a smooth, creamy-white card. Its legend was also handwritten.

Dear Mr Thomas Monroe
You are invited, gratis, to an evening of burlesque cabaret at the Theatre de la Nuit. This show plays for a short season only and features some of the most unique artistes in this world and any other. The entertainment commences at the hour of nine of the clock. Please do not be tardy, as entry is not possible once the performance has begun. A table for one has been reserved in your name, and complimentary champagne will be served.
   Yours sincerely
      Madame Morte, Proprietor

There would, of course, be a catch. There always was. He examined the card, no clue, no corporate logo. Nothing. He dropped it onto the table beside his plate of half-eaten breakfast.

"Anything interesting?" Nina asked him.

Monroe looked up. His wife sat opposite him at the dining room table. She was dressed for work: smart white blouse, neat black cardigan, hair bobbed and suspiciously blonde. Monroe was heading into early middle-age with resigned grace. Nina was fighting back.

Why Nina? What's the point? We're done. Time to step aside to let the new wave of beautiful young things take over...

"Junk mail," he said then glanced at his phone and checked the time. "I'd better be going."

There was still plenty of time, but he needed to get out.

More to the point, he needed to get away from Nina, who said, "Me too," and got to her feet.

She kissed him on the lips, the contact warm and moist and loving. "Later," she whispered and touched his cheek. She headed for the door. Monroe knew he should be happy, euphoric even, that his wife of twenty-one years would breathe a perfume-scented promise into his ear before leaving for work and be waiting for him in their bedroom when he came home. Such a promise was, if the male conversation he heard at work was to be believed, as rare as a dodo egg.

So why wasn't he euphoric? Why did the thought make him tired, irritated even?

Nina was generous, warm, as attractive a woman as anyone could hope for. And yet...

He rode the tube, propped in position by the hordes of dead-eyed commuters, then hurried along seething rain-washed streets, past canyon walls of glass and steel, mind-numbed by the relentless hiss and roar of traffic. He entered his allotted monolith, rode the crowded lift to his floor and slumped at his desk in his 'pen'. He switched on his computer, and prepared to make the world a better place by... what? What exactly was he contributing? What were any of them contributing in this sterile, bright-lit, slave galley? Projects to be run, reports written. And if they weren't? Would the world stop turning, society collapse, the universe cease to expand?

There was a picture of Nina on his desk. In the photograph, she wore a summer frock and big broad-brimmed straw hat. She smiled her sparkling and delicious smile, the smile that he had fallen in love with.

So why didn't he feel that way now? What was she doing wrong? She held him and murmured to him and kissed him and touched him when he needed to be touched and yielded to him when he needed relief.

Nina yearned, he knew, for children. It was a quiet yearning, seldom spoken and never worn on her sleeve. Despite her career and wide circle of friends, she was made lonely and saddened by their lack. Children disinterested Monroe. He saw them as a problem, a thorn-in-the-flesh that would ruin their easy life, their freedom...

Their happiness?

Is that what they had? Happiness?

He would give in eventually, although it would have to be soon if they were to beat the biological stopwatch to its final sixty-second sweep, he knew he would. For Nina, it would be the final piece in her jigsaw of contentment.

Monroe took off his coat, reached into the pocket for his phone and found the envelope. He had no recollection of putting it in his pocket. The last he remembered of it, he was going to file the thing in the recycle bin under the kitchen sink.

He frowned, drew out the card and lay it on the desk by his computer. Then went to make his first work coffee.

"I'm really sorry Nina, a new project... urgent. I have to stay late."

A sigh, followed by a reluctant; "I understand." Nina chuckled over the phone and offered a second, comically dramatic sigh. "Here I am sprawled across the bed, all lipstick, stockings and high heels, and you've got to work... what's a poor girl to do?"

"Stay exactly where you are, don't you dare move an inch." Monroe hoped his fake lust was convincing.

She chuckled again. "Oh, you're such a brute."

Guilt sliced through his irritation. He didn't want to hurt her. She didn't deserve that.

Despite the address on the card, the Theatre de la Nuit was hard to locate, even for a Knowledge-possessed cabbie. When the car swung into the road specified, Monroe's heart sank. It was a dead street of boarded-up windows and mindless graffiti, ill-served and shadow-strewn by the few of its street lamps that actually worked. He had been conned, made a fool of, or worse, led into a trap by a gang of muggers.

Then he saw a glow that tore open the derelict heart of the place and knew that it was real and that he had arrived.

The theatre was a palace of restlessly dancing light and shade, of intimacy and grandeur, a confusing pallet of fractured impression. Its foyer and grand staircase thronged with the evening's audience, many of whom were imposing in expensive fur and evening-wear. Monroe felt shabby and stale in his work-worn office suit. Embarrassed, he headed for the auditorium and his table-for-one.

Which turned out to be in a prime position, close and central to the stage. The table was small and decorated with red cloth, gently flickering candle and, as promised, a complimentary glass of champagne. The corners and boundaries of the theatre were hidden in shadow, which created an impression of great size, of titanic chandeliers, of balconies, private boxes, fluted columns and gold leaf. The stage itself was concealed behind immense scarlet curtains. An orchestra tuned up, unseen in their pit. The audience talked and laughed and the atmosphere grew tight with anticipation.

The curtain twitched and a figure emerged: tall, elegant in white bow tie and tails. His cheekbones were high and razor sharp, his lips curved into what looked to be an everlasting sneer of disapproval. His manner was languid. He held a cigarette between slender fingers.

A cigarette? In a public place?

Oddly refreshing, an act of defiance Monroe approved of.

"Good evening," the man drawled, "and welcome to the Theatre de la Nuit's Dark Burlesque. For this enchanted evening, I am your interlocutor, your host and your friend."

There was applause, enthusiastic enough for Monroe to believe that most of the audience were regulars who understood the rules and etiquette of this place. Strictures, he sensed, that were complex and immutable.

"And so, to the first of this evening's entertainments." The Interlocutor smiled faintly and peered out at the audience, as if gauging their fitness to receive his theatrical bounty. "A musical ensemble of a most delightfully wicked kind. The Tiger Lillies."

A cheer. The curtain swept open to reveal a trio, three men, each daubed with the kind of clown make-up used only in the circus of a nightmare. There was a double bass, a drumkit and, at the centre, an accordion player who set the group into life with a tango rhythm against which he sang in a startling bel canto voice. It was a song of gin and sin, of prostitutes, pimps and thieves, all flavoured with a strange sense of tragedy. Monroe was deliciously appalled as the set reached into the darker parts of his soul and found union.

Next there was an acrobat, a woman who, it seemed, had little in the way of bone or joint. She was followed by a magician and his assistant, who, chained and hooded, was lowered head first into a glass tank of what her master had claimed to be sulphuric acid; a claim apparently proven as the woman's flesh reddened, then blistered, erupted and melted. There were cries from the auditorium, Monroe surged to his feet, horrified, feeling sick –

She was hoisted out.

Whole, unblemished.

Smiling her impeccable, white-enamel smile.

A crash of symbol, a roll of drum then The Interlocutor glided, once more, from the shadows.

"Ladies, gentlemen, and all between and beyond," he purred. "For you delectation and delight and for your adoration, the beautiful, the tragic, Liana!"

He moved aside, arm extended into the well of darkness revealed by the swiftly parting curtains. A darkness, pregnant with possibilities, and that seemed to hold the audience in a hush so taut Monroe feared some communal vessel would burst and haemorrhage in a flood of violent, hair-tearing emotion.

The darkness was sliced apart by a single red down-light.

Lania.

For a moment, Monroe couldn't understand what he saw. Lania stood alone, head bowed, arms crossed over her breasts in the manner of a formal corpse. She wore a dress that reminded him of gypsies and of flamenco, and it was as black as the hair that tumbled, lushly, about her face and shoulders. When her head snapped up and she spread her arms wide and high, crucifix-style, Monroe's bewilderment increased. The movement was... wrong. There was an odd jerkiness to it, something mechanical.

And her face.

It was beautiful, yet exaggerated, her dark, dark eyes, her rich, ruby lips, all too large –

here I am sprawled across the bed, all lipstick, stockings and high heels, and you've got to work... what's a poor girl to do?

– and frozen into an expression of sadness and loss that gave her an erotically-charged vulnerability. As she began her dance, and even before he glimpsed the silvery threads linking her to the impenetrable shadow above the glare of stage lighting, Monroe understood that Lania was a life-size marionette. A thing of wood, steel and paint.

The music to which she danced was provided by the Tiger Lillies, and began as a lament, pierced by an accompanying violin, and punctuated with the anguished respiration of an accordion.

Her dance grew in intensity as the music accelerated towards some far-off climax. Her dance was sinuous movement, feline, serpentine. It became furious, pirouettes so fast her body blurred into a grey tornado of outstretched arms and swirled hair, she stalked and leapt, tumbling impossibly as she threw herself –

herself? she could do nothing herself, she was the plaything of her puppeteer

– to the floor, where she crawled and writhed then arched her body and clawed at some imaginary lover.

What's a poor girl to do Tom?

As each moment passed, Monroe fell deeper into the illusion until all mechanical artifice had faded and Lania became a thing of fragile, tormented flesh. The performance unsettled him, drew tears into his eyes and, more disturbing still, electric shocks of desire through his nerves.

It ended, as it began, Lania at the front of the stage, head thrown back, arms pinioned to some imaginary cross. She bowed, the action graceful.

Then, when she once more lifted her head, Monroe was sure that he was the focus of her frozen, paint-on-wood stare. The stare was filled with longing, sadness. The stare was a plea.

What's a poor girl to do? Tom? Tom, are you listening to me? Tom?

As the auditorium resounded to the deafening storm of cheers and applause and the synchronised surge of bodies coming to a standing ovation, Lania stepped gracefully back to allow the curtains to sweep shut.

And, in the last seconds, as the gap was about to close, Monroe saw her jerked roughly and carelessly backwards into the shadow and there was a moment, a ridiculous and mad moment, in which he was sure he saw pain and humiliation.

The dance ends and she stands, crucified on her invisible gibbet, at the front of the stage as the audience roar in delight. Monroe is there, hands sore from clapping, throat torn by cheering. This time, though, his euphoria turns to panic. The curtains are closing. He has to get to her, before that moment, before that final, terrible, jolt that wrenches her away from him and into the darkness.

He claws his way through the crowd, hemmed in, desperate, barely able to breathe. Fighting off hands that grasp at him and tear at his clothes, that uncurl, tentacle-like from the orchestra pit, he climbs onto the stage and hurls himself through the momentary sliver of black between the onrushing curtains.

She stands, face a mask of desolation. He cries out her name and lunges towards her. He feels her hands, wooden, unyielding, yet warm. He feels her fingers close about his.

The he hears the heartbeat. A deep rhythm that pulses from the deeper darkness above them. It grows louder, thrums through his skull, through his flesh. The sound of it cracks bone, shreds nerves. Weakens his grip.

Until

Lania is wrenched away from him in a tortured clatter of wood and rustling taffeta.

He cries out her name –

"Huh… Whuh… Wha' did you say?" Nina mumbled sleepily.

Monroe, suddenly awake in the bed beside her, realised that he must have voiced his dream shout.

"Nothing," he sighed, feigning weariness. He reached for his wife and she settled into his arms, a warm, comfortable shape. There was no lipstick, stockings or heels. They had been swapped for shapeless tee shirt and pyjama bottoms long before he came home.

After all, what was a poor girl to do when the clock struck midnight and her lover was nowhere to be found?

Monroe looked at his wife, who sat opposite him at the dining room table, finishing her last cup of breakfast coffee. She was dressed for work: smart white blouse, cardigan, soft and green this morning, hair bobbed and suspiciously blonde.

Monroe glanced at his phone, checked the time. "I'd better be going."

There was still plenty of time, but he needed to get out of here.

He needed to get away from Nina, who said, "Me too," and got to her feet.

She kissed him on the lips, the contact warm and moist and loving. "Later?" she whispered. It was a question this time.

"I don't know… this project… It's only for a couple more days." His response startled him. There was no dark red envelope today, no second invitation to the Theatre de la Nuit. So why did he need two more days?

He rode the tube, propped in position by the hordes of dead-eyed commuters, then hurried along seething, rain-washed streets, past canyon walls of glass and steel, mind-numbed by the relentless hiss and roar of traffic. He entered his allotted monolith, rode the crowded lift to his floor and slumped at his desk in his 'pen'. He switched on his computer and prepared to work.

A meeting was called. In one of the goldfish bowl conference rooms, the oh-so-young, departmental manager fed them a generic spiel littered with the very latest in management phrasing. In return, the assembled underlings demonstrated their own of cliché-awareness. Monroe became aware that he had been asked a question.

"I'm sorry?"

"The Grown-Up-Dot-Joined-Thinking Plan, have you finished it yet?"

"Uh, almost –"

A moment, redolent with carefully manicured, managerial annoyance.

"It should have been delivered to the review team two days ago, Tom."

Mister Monroe to you, sonny. Show some respect for your elders and betters you acne-ridden whelp.

"I know but –"

"Tom, Gup-Deejay-Peetee is a keystone project. There's no milestone-manoeuvrability here. We need that plan."

"I know –"

"I think you and I need some personalised face-to-face. There are obviously issues here."

Class was dismissed, Monroe asked to stay behind.

"What's going on, Tom?" Voice and body-language carefully adjusted to the matey setting, hand on the shoulder, skilfully composed expression of concern.

"Nothing that's any of your bloody business," Monroe wanted to say.

"You know, lost focus I suppose. I'll have it done by the end of play," he said instead.

"On my desk by four-thirty."

"Yes, yes, of course."

This time, he brought flowers. He didn't know why and he didn't think too deeply about it, either.

Despite his lack of neck, the Theatre de la Nuit's doorman cut a remarkably majestic figure in dark suit and bow tie. He frowned and asked Monroe for his invitation.

"I must have left it at home."

"Sorry sir," said the doorman and sounded as if he meant it.

"But, I really must go in –"

159

"Not wivvout a invitation sir."

"I'll buy a ticket. How much? It doesn't matter."

"Sir, I regret that you can't purchase –"

A second doorman appeared, as large and brutish as his colleague. There was a whispered exchange. The first man frowned, shrugged and said. "It happears that Madame du Morte 'as taken a personal interest in you. She says that you can go in, if you feel that it's the right fing for you to do."

It was. He needed this. He had extinguished the miserable embers of his dignity today, in an effort to keep his job. He deserved this one indulgence.

He was shown to the same table.

Tonight's cabaret was again introduced by the gaunt-faced Interlocutor, but it was a different show, and Monroe's heart sank. The Tiger Lillies opened proceedings as before, with witty ditties about madness and murder, but the acts that followed were not the acts from the previous night. There was a juggler who threw and caught so fast it seemed as if the white balls he used were transformed into human skulls, there was a set of twins, one male, the other female, who tumbled and cavorted but, at times, appeared to merge one with the other and form a single, androgynous creature. There was a fire-eater who blew flame from his nose, ears and eyes.

Then, as Monroe's mood reached its nadir and he began to contemplate leaving, The Interlocutor appeared one last time. He drawled a single name.

Lania.

The dance was the same, but somehow more frenetic as it neared its climax. Monroe was, once again, transfixed, and so nervous he could barely breathe. A voice yammered at him from some tiny niche at the back of his skull, to remind him that Lania was mere artifice. But the blood roar of his fascination was too loud, too red, for him to hear.

Again, she accepted her adoration in that crucifixion-pose.

Again the big, unblinking eyes locked with Monroe's.

Again, in those seconds before the curtains collided, she was yanked backwards, with what looked like deliberate cruelty.

*

"A little unusual, I must say, but I can't see no reason why not. I'll 'ave to stay wiv yer, of course."

"Yes, I understand." Monroe's mouth was too dry for sensible speech. He was also startled by the ease with which his wish was granted by the doorman at the theatre's stage entrance.

"Right-o then. Follow me."

The doorman led Monroe into the maze of passageways that fed the machineries of performance like veins routing blood to the brain. There were scene shifters and chorus girls, people with clipboards and headphones and others carrying coils of cable. The place was all rush and hurry. Monroe recognised some of the evening's artistes, out of make-up, and, no doubt, headed for whatever hostelries might still be open at this hour.

They arrived at a door decorated with a small, painted star. Under the star was a name, printed on a card. Monroe was surprised to see that the card's legend was 'Lania', and not the unfamiliar name of her, as yet unseen, puppeteer.

The doorman swivelled his muscular bulk to face Monroe. "The flowers... You do, understand that Lania's a puppitt. She ain't 'ooman, sir."

Monroe nodded, power of speech finally dissipated by his tension. This was something he *had* to do, an act of madness to be purged from his system before he returned to the grim uncertainties of the real world.

"All right then, you can go in, but you mustn't touch. I'll wait 'ere."

He opened the door, without knocking. Monroe took a steadying breath and went in, prepared to gush some lame explanation to Lania's owner and operator. Hopefully the man, or woman, would laugh, accept the flowers on the marionette's behalf and the whole thing would become a huge, amiable joke.

The room was as he had imagined such places to be. Small, with a chair, a dresser and a mirror edged with light bulbs.

There was no puppeteer.

Only Lania.

Who sat slumped in the chair, facing the mirror.

She was slack and devoid of life, a careless mess of dead limbs and tangled strings, obviously dumped there by her heedless owner.

Monroe placed the flowers, awkwardly on the dressing table. The doll merely sat. No heartbeat or breath stirred her chest. She still wore the drees. Her hair was lustrous and realistic. Her perfect head was tipped to one side on a neck that could not support it.

Her face was blank, yet not blank.

Monroe could see the grain. The texture.

Touch her.

The thought was a blow, a shock.

Touch her.

No, she... it... was not his to touch.

He moved closer and stared at the reflection of her face in the mirror. Her eyes were bleak, unblinking wells of blue. Monroe saw desolation and loneliness in those eyes.

He touched her.

And felt the lustrous texture of her hair. He touched her face. Its flesh was rough wood. There was no flicker of movement, no pulse or blood-warmth.

His fingers moved slowly, gently, over her lips -

Suddenly appalled at what he was doing, Monroe fled the room. He ran, not knowing which way to go.

A huge hand closed over his arm and yanked him to a halt. He yelped in terror and shock.

"Sir, sir, are you all right?" asked the doorman, breathless from pursuit.

Nina was waiting for him in the sitting room. She looked a little haggard. She was still dressed in her work clothes, though her shoes had been replaced by slippers. She held the soft green cardigan about herself as if for comfort. Monroe was both irritated and relieved to see her.

"I couldn't sleep," she said. "I'm worried about you, Tom."

"Worried?" Monroe's voice was tremulous. He didn't want this conversation. He needed to hide, in the dark, in his own sleep.

"You look tired, pale. This project..."

"Almost finished," Monroe answered without thought.

"How much longer? I miss you."

Please don't. Because I seldom miss you these days, I prefer to be alone, away from you. I'm suffocated, bored, irritated...

"One more night."

One more night? Why did there have to be one more night? Surely it was over, this madness.

"One more night," she said, and it sounded like a warning, an ultimatum. Then she stood, crossed to him and kissed him, open-mouthed and hot with tongue.

In the moments before he came, upstairs, in the superheated bedroom dark, he felt her flesh turn hard and grainy, and her hair transform into a nest of razor-thin, steel strings.

"But I have to."

"No one 'as to," said the doorman.

"You let me in last night."

"Last night was last night, sir."

"I need to come in. I need to see the show. Please!"

"No, sorry sir."

Monroe was exhausted from dream-sodden sleep, and from a day that had been a lie from the moment he had dressed for work and kissed a radiant Nina goodbye. After work, he had killed time wandering the streets. Cold, lonely, aimless and increasingly afraid.

And now this.

"I'll pay –"

"Please go away, sir." The doorman's tone was no longer polite.

Monroe pulled his coat about himself and set off into the dark. Rain stung his face. He shivered and, for a moment, wanted nothing more than to go home. But suddenly he was outside the stage door, with little memory of getting there. The door was, inexplicably, unguarded. No security. No watchful eye and, as far as he could tell, no CCTV.

He promised himself one attempt. If he failed, he would retreat and try to forget about this. If not...

He had no plan for afterwards.

The door was bound to be locked.

It wasn't.

Scarcely believing his luck, Monroe slid inside. The passageway was deserted. He saw a drum of electrical flex and knew what to do. He took off his coat, jacket and tie, and shoved them into one of the passageway's many darkened alcoves. Then he rolled up his shirt sleeves, hoisted the drum of flex under his arm and set off into the maze.

It wasn't long before he encountered the first clutch of dancing girls, resplendent in feathers and glitter. Then a pair of technicians, a woman with a clipboard, who was talking rapidly into a radio. More artistes: an elderly man with a ventriloquist's dummy, a stocky woman in a leotard, carrying a dumbbell as if it was a paper bag, a tall, slender, lugubrious-looking man in an evening suit who had to be a magician. Monroe fought to avoid eye-contact and maintain an expression of out-of-my-way busy-ness.

He moved deeper into the labyrinth, always selecting the busiest corridors, hoping it would lead him to the stage.

He heard music. He saw the magician again, shown up a set of stairs by the woman with the clipboard. Monroe followed and found himself in the wings, stage right. He was out of breath, and unnerved by the fact that he had made it this far without challenge or failure.

The magician's act climaxed in a flurry of white doves that soared upwards and vanished. He took his bow. The curtains closed to muffle the last of the applause, and the Interlocutor's next announcement.

Monroe could already feel her presence. She was a dark shape in the dark that transformed his heartbeat into a series of sledgehammer blows.

The curtains opened to a wall of blackness, all view of the audience blanked by the glare of stage-lights.

On came the red downlight.

Lania stood, proud and elegant. Monroe's breath caught, his mouth dried.

The music ached into life. And her dance began, building towards that last, mad-dervish pirouette. The strings jerked like the strands of a fly-trapped web.

The music reached its crescendo. And stopped dead, freezing Lania into her crucifixion. The red spot returned and as the audience broke into cheering and applause, Lania, bowed then backed slowly from the front of the stage.

A heartbeat.

Monroe's own, loud in his ears.

The curtains rushed in.

And Monroe rushed out, the cutters, taken from his tool box that morning, were in his hand. There were cries of protest. Ignoring them, he caught Lania as she was yanked back, held her tight and snipped at the wires. The heartbeat grew louder and louder, pressure waves hammered down from above and beat at his skull. He didn't look up.

Snip.

Snip.

Snip...

The last of the strings snaked free, and, carrying Lania in his arms, Monroe ran. He barged past performers and technicians, who all seemed too startled to stop him. But something followed. It boiled out of the darkened stage, along the endless passageways. Its heartbeats thrummed through the air in rhythmic shockwaves.

Monroe stumbled on, out of breath, chest on fire.

The exit.

He lurched towards the door, crashed through and out into the street. Panting, he fell to his knees, beneath a lone streetlamp. He clutched Lania to himself, trying to shield her from the icy rain. She clattered in his arms, a loose-jointed thing. Her strings hung about her and trailed in the puddle-ridden tarmac.

Monroe looked into her face. She stared back and there was softness in those sightless blue-eyes. He kissed the painted, pursed lips, and tasted their wooden sweetness and their heat.

He had to get her to a safe place. There was little time. The road shuddered under the beats of that monstrous heart. Monroe stood and a foot clattered onto the road, a hand, a leg. Lania was shattering in his grasp. He tried frantically to gather her parts together, to nurse them in his arms, but she was crumbling fast as her ancient joints and mechanisms failed. He scrabbled at the fragments strewn across the wet tarmac, until his clothes were sodden and his fingers bloody.

Exhausted, sobbing, Monroe finally let her go.

He lurched to his feet and, as he stumbled away, glanced back at the theatre, but saw nothing, except the rain that scoured the ill-lit alleyway. Then he heard the heartbeat and felt pain in his own chest and it was as if it was being strangled by coils of steel string.

THE LISTENERS

"Let us in, please, let us in!"

There was someone behind that faded blue door, trying to conceal their presence. Their silence was a messy, incomplete thing, different from real silence.

"For Christ's sake, open the door!"

"Paul, stop it," Judith pulled at his shoulder, crying, angry, frightened. "You'll bring them here."

You'll bring them here? This was *his* fault?

Paul swung round. Judith recoiled, her hand flying from his shoulder as if stung.

"Where do we go, Jude? What do we do? Tell me." He grabbed her arms, too roughly, an attempt to calm her. Her dark hair was awry, her face, a mottled map of ashen-white and crying-red. Her eyes burned though, with rage and contempt.

"There's no one here," Judith said. "We have to try the other doors."

Paul released her, swung round and hammered at the blue door again. His fist hurt. Everything hurt.

"Help us. We have a child..."

Their *child*, Sarah, was fifteen years old. She stood apart from them, arms wrapped, protectively, about herself, head bowed, face concealed by the fur-edged hood of her parka. She leaned against the wall between this door and that of the next flat. Sarah had separated herself. Even here, in the midst of this catastrophe, she was acting like the moody teenager she was.

Judith turned her back on her husband, clutching at the low wall of the connecting balcony like a doomed *Titanic* passenger watching the departing lifeboats. Paul wanted her to step back from the wall. If *they* were down there, those things, swarming in the scrubby-grassed, litter-strewn triangle that separated these three ghastly tower blocks, they would see her.

Except they couldn't see.

They listened.

That was why there was silence, why the city was empty and absolutely quiet.

"Please, in the name of Christ help us!" Paul's fist bled. His voice was hoarse.

Judith uttered a brief scream. Startled, Paul turned. She was looking down, over the edge. "They're coming up the walls!"

Paul rushed to the balcony, his right arm pressed against the soft quilt of Judith's coat. He could feel her trembling, hear her ragged breath. He wanted to hold her.

Movement. Nothing. He couldn't be sure. There were too many shadows, too much emptiness, silence; a white, howling tornado of blank noise.

But they were coming, squirming, up walls, over windows, pouring into the balconies below. Now he could hear them, their whispers and rustle and wet breath and the scratch of their claws—

Paul spun round as the blue door was flung open to reveal a broad, muscular man, whose big right hand was curled about an iron pipe. He was heavily tattooed; neck, cheeks and arms. There was stubble on his jaw, a fuzz of regrown hair on his shaved scalp. He wore an unseasonal tee-shirt, plus camouflaged combat trousers and boots. He glared at Paul for a long moment. Then growled "You'd better get in here," and stepped aside.

"I couldn't leave them out, there could I?" the big man shouted at the slim, thin-faced woman who blocked their way. She had short, dark hair, tattoos of her own, and a baby in her arms.

Paul, Judith and Sarah were trapped behind the man, just inside the flat, crammed between him and the door as the argument raged.

"Stupid bastard. We haven't got no food or water, Carl," the woman snapped. "We don't even know who they are."

The big man's name was Carl, then.

"The bloke can come with me when we go out for supplies, someone to watch my back."

Bloke? "I'm Paul." He was ignored. "Look, we don't want to cause you any —"

"You can trust him can you?" the woman demanded. "And what's wrong with Justin?"

"There's nothing wrong with Justin, but three of us will be better than two. We can get more stuff."

"We'll *need* more stuff."

"They were desperate Aims, what was I supposed to do?"

Aims was Carl-speak for Amy, presumably.

"Listen!" Judith shouted, struggling to make herself heard above the argument.

"What is it?" Paul asked her. He was forced to shout.

"It's them. Paul, listen, it's them."

He put his ear against the door and heard the familiar ocean-wave hiss of his own blood. Then...

"Quiet," he said.

Still no one listened.

"Shut up! Bloody shut up!"

Silence fell, immediate, startled. Its soundtrack was breath and baby-murmur.

"I don't hear nothing." Anxiety had replaced Amy's anger.

Her baby's murmurs grew louder, mounting towards a full-throated cry.

Something crashed against the outside of the door. Crying out in shock, Paul leapt back, and collided with Judith, who, in turn stumbled against Carl. Everyone shouted and screamed. Everyone writhed and struggled to force their way into the flat proper. Paul dropped to his knees, hands over his ears as the world turned grey and the wet, mocking voices babbled. As the pounding and squealing spiraled in and filled the entire universe and all self-control broke down in the flat.

Someone sobbed, Sarah. He couldn't get to her because Judith was in the way, her arms already wrapped about the girl. Amy's baby cried too, loud grating wails that went on and bloody on.

At any moment the door would crash inwards and hell would boil through, an unimaginable hell of claws and teeth and pain and raw, primal terror —

The assault ended. Abruptly.

They hid in the lounge. Paul, Judith, Sarah and their reluctant hosts. There was a middle-aged woman sitting on the sofa when they entered the room. She looked up and smiled warmly. She was well dressed, and said hello to them in a strong West Indian accent.

"Angela," she said and held out her hand. Paul shook her hand first, followed by Judith. "I'm the next door neighbour. Carl and Amy took me in. I live alone. I was frightened."

"It's the least we could do for you love," Amy said. "You've always been good to us." She glanced at Paul and Judith and there was a sharp edge to that bland-sounding comment. Angela had done things for them, was what Amy was really saying. What are you two going to do?

The baby cried. Its face was purple with rage, its tiny fists clenched. It stank. Someone needed to change its nappy. The room's big window and its view of the Emerson and Lake tower blocks were hidden behind a heavy, blue curtain. Paul leaned against the wall, arms folded. Judith and Sarah were huddled together on the floor beside a huge television, which was switched off and would probably never be switched on again.

It was Carl who finally spoke. "Why were you out there?"

"Good question," Judith said, her tone sour. She had wanted to stay in their four-bed, three-bathroom, suburban fortress and wait for the rescue she was sure was on its way. All systems may have failed; power, internet, television. People had disappeared and something terrible had taken the night, but surely the government would have contingency plans. COBRA would meet, the army mobilize.

"We needed to know what was happening," Paul said, which was true, to a point.

"Did we?" Judith snapped. "Really?"

A moment of awkward silence. Judith glared at Paul. He decided not to respond. They were trapped in here. A fight was not a good idea at this moment.

"Well, you know now," Carl said.

"It's the beginnings of the Tribulation," Angela said.

"I'm sorry?" Paul asked.

"The end times are here. The Rapture must have happened already." Her voice broke, she shook her head, as if puzzled. "I've been left behind. I thought I was saved. I tried to be faithful. I really did…" She began to cry. "I love Jesus…"

"Awww, don't cry love," Amy said and perched herself on the sofa, her arm about Angela's shoulders. "I'm sure He'll come for you. You're a good person."

Paul noticed a teenage boy sitting on the floor at the far end of the room. Presumably, the Justin that Amy had mentioned earlier. He leaned against the wall under the window, his hood up, staring at no one or anything in particular, though Paul had already seen his furtive glances towards Sarah

Stare all you like, she's out of your league.

Sarah glanced back at the boy, sneered and looked away. Good for her.

"Me and Justin are going out to and scavenge later," Carl said, "before we all starve to death."

"I'll come with you," Paul said, and regretted it immediately. He didn't want to stay here any longer than necessary, or get involved with these people. There had to be shelters, some official sanctuary.

Even so, they needed to rest. Judith was exhausted, Sarah, pale and wretched with shock…

…They had been under siege in their own suburban house for two days, from the moment everything had failed and the assaults began; doors pounded, glass broken, things glimpsed in the dark outside.

"Spiders," whimpered Sarah.

"Rats," whispered Judith.

Something that pours and swirls, gibbers and drips poison into our ears, thought Paul.

They can't find you if they can't hear you, they all agreed.

Listeners.

Judith had demanded that they board-up the broken windows, lock themselves in and wait for the police, the army, the rescue services, because they *were* coming, they *had* to be coming. But Paul had dragged them out while it was still dark and frost-rimed, unable to control his spiralling claustrophobia, unable to stand the walls and locked doors and fear of another attack. They drove. Through streets of shutdown houses, empty shops, broken windows and burning buildings, until the snarl of abandoned cars choked off their progress.

Then they ran. Under a lowering sky that was the colour of rust, lit by a sun that was too large and too pale to be their own. Centre-wards, driven by the belief that it would be there that control had been restored. They ran, joining, then leaving, small knots of similarly terrified refugees, knowing that they were being pursued and that the Listeners were closing in. The day drained towards night. In need of refuge, any refuge, they pounded doors until this one had been opened to them...

The baby cried. Amy shushed and rocked and patted its back, but nothing would calm it down

"Your baby's hungry," Judith said. It was impossible to tell whether she was being friendly, helpful, or impatient.

"Nothing to give her," Amy replied, openly hostile now.

Her baby cried, on and on, incessant, loud, desperate. The sound drew in the walls, echoed as if from the end of a long tunnel. The light in the room had changed. The dull grey of the dying winter afternoon had turned dirty ochre, as if the air itself was stained. The electric wall lights buzzed and flickered into brief, staccato life. No one seemed to notice. Paul tried not to look at them, their stroboscopic bursts were a dripping tap, unpredictable, nerve-shredding and all-consuming.

It was as if the world itself was bending out of shape and tearing at the edges.

Then Judith was up, fists clenched and shouting. "Shut it up, shut that bloody baby up! Shut it up!"

Amy shrank back, face twisted into a mix of hate and fear. Paul and Carl were on their feet simultaneously.

"Take it out," Judith screamed. "Take it into the bedroom, anywhere, just make it shut up!"

172

"Fuck off, she's my baby and it's my flat," Amy yelled back. She was standing face-to-face with Judith. Paul made to force himself between them, but Carl got there first.

"Back off," he growled at Judith. She flinched, intimidated.

"Leave her alone," Paul snapped at Carl, who turned to glare at him.

"She doesn't talk to my Aims like that." Carl's voice thrummed with barely concealed threat.

Angela was on her feet now. "Don't, please, if we turn on each other, the devil has won."

"All right all right, we're all tense, and scared. We need to calm down." Paul dug deep into his management training. It all seemed very feeble now in this, the real world. "Angela's right," he said. "We mustn't fight among ourselves."

An uneasy calm fell, a surface calm.

Judith sat down. She propped her elbow on the arm of the chair and rested her forehead in her hand. The hand trembled.

"We need baby food," Amy sounded panicky now, worn ragged by the infant's cries and shaken by Judith's outburst.

"Let me take her for a bit," Sarah said.

Amy started and looked round. Paul, too, was surprised to hear such concern in his teenage daughter's voice.

"You need a break," Sarah continued. She stood.

"It's all right, love."

"Please, for a few minutes," Sarah said.

"Yeah, Mum, give her to us," Justin added. He got up and moved across to stand beside Sarah.

Us?

Paul baulked at the word. The two of them, his beautiful, raven-haired, hazel-eyed daughter and that rat-faced loser were *us?*

Amy shrugged and, sniffing back tears, handed the baby to Sarah. She was awkward at first then managed to shift the child into a more comfortable position in her arms. She rocked her and sang to her. This was too ironic for words, Paul decided. His teenage daughter, baby in arms, in the middle of this council estate, with that scrawny good-for-nothing looking over her shoulder and sharing the moment, looking for all the world like the kind of too-young parents you found in these bloody places.

Judith also watched, a ghost of a smile on her lips.

The baby cried for a few more moments then stared up at Sarah and settled, still tetchy but no longer howling. Sarah returned to her patch of floor by the television. Justin, thank God, went back to his own place under the window.

"She's a natural." Carl said. He lit up, handed the cigarette pack to Amy then offered one to Justin.

"Sorry," he said to Paul and the others "It's our last pack."

"It's okay," Paul said. "We don't smoke anyway."

Justin caught Sarah's eye again and, this time, held out his half-smoked cigarette to her. Paul snorted, she wouldn't - but she did. She crawled over to him, baby tucked skilfully under her arm, accepted the cigarette and drew in smoke like a veteran, eyes half-closed as the nicotine hit.

Judith looked at Paul.

"Sarah."

"It's all right," Amy said. "We all need a bit of comfort,"

"She's our daughter," Judith snapped. "We decide what's all right." Judith turned her attention on Sarah. "Stop it, now. Do you hear me?"

"Piss off," Sarah grunted and took a long, happy drag at Justin's cigarette.

Paul was across the room in a moment. "Don't you ever talk to your mother —" He snatched at the cigarette. Startled, Sarah flinched back, swinging the hand out of Paul's reach.

"Leave me alone."

Disturbed by the tussle, the baby resumed its crying.

Paul grabbed her wrist. "Give it to me, now, give it to me."

"I'm not a child, let go. Let me go!"

The lights flickered and sparked.

Enraged, all Paul could see was her anger, and her defiance of all they had tried to teach her. Before he could give the action thought, driven by pure instinct, he whipped up his hand to slap her face.

"No!" It was Carl, suddenly there, between Paul and his daughter; big, implacable, terrifying, yet there was anguish on his face. "Don't do that, mate," he said quietly. "Not to your own kid."

Slowly, appalled at what he had been about to do, Paul lowered his hand.

And the Listeners came back.

Everything froze; Carl standing between Paul and Sarah, Justin open mouthed, Judith on her feet, Amy half-risen –

As

Something slammed against the flat's window. Voices flooded Paul's head, clamouring, mocking, growing louder and louder. The window shuddered as something battered at the glass behind the curtain, which was not possible. Surely there was a sheer drop out there. The hammering grew faster and faster until it was a staccato rattle.

Followed by an explosion of glass.

People screamed. Angela was on her knees, face and arms raised as tears poured down her cheeks. Justin dived floor-wards, taking Sarah with him. Paul staggered back and dropped onto his bottom. The curtain billowed crazily. The baby screeched.

Carl surged past, iron bar once more in his fist, shouting. "Come on you fuckers!"

Justin lifted his head, looked round, still protecting Sarah, who lay in the cage formed of his arms and knees, and was, in turn, shielding the baby.

Carl ripped aside the curtains.

Paul tensed, ready for –

- a rectangle of wet, cold, brown sky. Rain lashed in, driven by gusts of icy wind.

"Christ," Carl muttered. He crouched down and put his hand on Justin's shoulder. "You all right, mate?"

Justin nodded, wearily. He drew back and Sarah crawled free. Amy recovered the baby from Sarah. It had quietened, no doubt exhausted from its crying and weakened by hunger

"What about you, love?" Carl asked her.

"Yeah," Amy said. She held the baby tight, kissing it and murmuring and crying.

Paul went to his own daughter. "I… I'm sorry," he said. "I…"

Sarah turned away. Justin helped her up onto the sofa and, casually, confidently, put his arm about her shoulders. Paul didn't like that. Not at all. He didn't like his daughter being touched by a lowlife piece of council estate scum like Justin.

Paul stood in the middle of the room, alone, desolate. It was as if everyone drew back from him. Paul the Unclean. He looked round, at his wife. "Jude, please…"

"I hate you," she said, voice low.

The curtains billowed, rain came in. The light faded into night.

"We need those supplies," Carl growled.

"You can't go out there," Amy said to him. Her eyes were wide with fear. She sounded distraught. "I won't let you."

"I have to," he said. "We'll starve in here if I don't."

"No Carl –"

"I'll go," Paul said.

Silence fell, like a hammer blow. Was that relief in Amy's eyes? And why hadn't Judith fallen into his arms to weep and beg him to stay, instead of glaring at him as if he had just said the most ridiculous thing in the world?

Why wouldn't Sarah, his own daughter, even look at him?

"It's too dangerous, mate," Carl said. Was Carl really his only ally now?

"I'm going," Paul said, beginning to lose his certainty. "You stay here, look after everyone. Cover up that window, in case they come back."

"You don't even know where the store is."

"You'd better tell me then, hadn't you."

The fire door creaked as he pushed it open. Paul froze, his mind filled with images of blind, loping, hungry shapes, drawn by the sound, converging on the tower block, pouring up the stairs…

His descent was slow. His legs were stiff, his back ached with tension. And fear, real fear. He thought he knew what fear was, but it had been a philosophical construct. The frightened animal asleep inside the cage of his soul, barred-in by complacency, logic, and self-delusion over his own imagined courage.

Now the animal was awake and trembling.

Each turn of the fire escape led into a darkness deeper than the one before. Most of the lights were broken, but some worked. Which meant that somewhere, somehow, electricity was being generated, although the light was wrong, too dim and rusty, almost a living thing writhing within each glass bulb.

Another landing, its edges and corners inked by shadow. It was cold and urine-scented. There was litter and graffiti. Next flight. Each step took him further from his family. *His* family? Were they *his* family now? Hadn't Carl adopted them, or rather stolen them? Big, scary-but-gentle Carl, the antithesis of everything he and Judith stood for, the sort of father Paul had fought hard not to be. Yet Carl was the patriarch now. Paul began to doubt that this act of atonement would win his wife and daughter back.

Outside, a few tenacious streetlamps illuminated the scrubby grass of the communal area with their unwholesome, stroboscopic flicker. There were cars, abandoned, doors open. Some had broken glass, one looked to have been burned. Others, however, were untouched. Perhaps he should take one, drive to the shop. There were probably keys in their ignitions.

No, he didn't know the area, he would get lost. If *they* came for him, he would be trapped. And they would come, because cars had engines and engines made noise.

He wanted to go back, to hammer at the faded blue door and beg to be taken in. He would weep and his wife and daughter would forgive him and tell him he had been brave, and that what he had attempted was humanly impossible -

He walked on through the narrow alley between Emerson and Lake, and into an underpass. There was still light in the tunnel, uncertain but sufficient. His footsteps mingled with others. He spun round, no one. An echo, nothing more.

There *were* others out here. Glimpsed, scuttling away from him, as he scuttled away from them. But most of all there was silence. Paul wanted noise. Any noise, a shout, a scream, anything but this utter, raw silence.

Asda.

Familiar, though not a place he and Judith ever shopped at. It was in darkness, plate-glass windows broken, doors hanging off their runners. Its entrance was a yawning, empty mouth.

Inside, he moved cautiously over floors littered with broken cartons, bottles and food. Small animals scuttled away at his approach; rats.

There were tinned and sealed foodstuffs scattered along the shelves. There would be nothing to cook them with, but cold food was food and his own burgeoning hunger had already overcome his ingrained revulsion to convenience meals. He grabbed one of the many abandoned trolleys and a handful of bags from the tills and filled as many as he could; beans, soup, tinned fruit, vegetables and meat, bottles of water. He moved to the baby care aisles and filled another bag with powdered milk tins, and as many nappies as he could handle.

He crept along the lanes, pleased with himself. Paul the hunter-gatherer. He chuckled and for a moment, forgot -

His nerve failed, suddenly, catastrophically. The dark, the emptiness of the place, the sounds and shadows...

And something else.

He ran, shoving the trolley ahead of him, careered through debris, bumped into shelves, the door frame.

Coming.

He didn't look back. He didn't want to see them. If they took him, he wanted it to be sudden and quick. He heard them though. Christ, he could hear them, pouring, towards him along the pathway, running down its steep sides, a swarm, a horde, a herd, a pack...

He made it to the Palmer Tower and rammed the trolley through the doors to the small lobby at the bottom of the fire escape. He stopped and held his breath. Silence, his only defence. He waited. Nothing. They were out there, of course, somewhere, milling around, confused, their prey vanished into the quiet.

Carefully, he scooped an armful of supplies from the trolley and mounted the stairs. He was out of breath, but there could be no gasping or wheezing.

He stumbled out onto the fourth-floor balcony, and hurried to the faded blue door. He felt sick, his head throbbed. The night was wrong, red-tinged, as if the moon bled. The bulkhead lamps on the balcony flashed, buzzed and danced their staccato dance. Paul rapped at the wood.

No answer.

He knocked again. Still no reply. Only the messy, incomplete silence of the hidden.

"Judith, Judith? Carl?"

The silence went on.

His knock became a frantic hammer. He dropped the bags, battered the door with both fists, shrieked and raged.

"Judith! Open the door! I'm sorry, please..."

No answer, no sound, apart from his own voice.

Oh Christ, his voice, a beacon in the dark –

And then there was no silence at all.

HEAVIES

Saffron has never talked to a heavy before. Spoken to, yes, but never *talked* to. Come to that, she'd never met one working solitary and unsupervised, either. This one is something of an urban myth amongst luners. She was beginning to think that he didn't exist. That he was a bogie man used to scare the young to sleep. But here he is, clad in a botanist's white overall, gently lifting and examining the leaves of some new strain of maize bred in the Experimental Hydroponic Dome.

"Wilson?" Saffron feels surprisingly awkward in his presence. Must be his near mythical status, she supposes.

Wilson ignores her. He's a non-descript specimen, just past middle-age. His salt-and-pepper hair is long and tied roughly back. His face is care-lined.

Saffron doesn't find heavies as repulsive as some of her friends and colleagues do. Okay, Wilson's short and there's a lot of flesh on him and his shoulders are too broad and rounded. But heavies are as human as luners, their hulking posture and stockiness the result of a lifetime in six-times gravity. It doesn't make them monsters. The forefathers were heavies, after all.

"Your job," Saffron says. "Special privilege, or punishment?"

"Both," he says at last. He holds her gaze, another rarity among heavies.

"I have some questions," Saffron says.

"I won't answer them."

She's not surprised. "I want your side of the story."

"Why?"

"Because I'm writing our history."

"A propagandist, then."

"I don't want to be. I'm risking punishment breaking in here to talk to you." Saffron shows him her fake pass.

She can see the cogs working. Unlike luners, heavies don't hide their feelings. Luners live communally, but they're still individuals in need of privacy, so they learn to wall themselves in.

"So, you want to know the truth."

"I'm discovering that truth is fluid."

Wilson offers a brief, wry smile.

Saffron says; "It seems there's a big difference between writing user manuals and recording human memories."

"That's insightful for a skinny."

Saffron doesn't rise to the insult.

"Apparently," she says. "I'm one of the finest (which means pedantic and dull) technical writers on the moon. The Committee's decided that a history is needed for future generations. I'm the woman for the job, because they want it to be as dull and safe as possible. You know how it is here. Creative writing, creative *anything*, is seen as non-productive. No spare fat. No waste. Every breath taken must be for the good of the colony."

"Skinny OCD."

"What's that?"

"Obsessive Crater Disorder."

Saffron chuckles. "This will be no user manual. It's messy. Everyone I speak to has a different recollection, a different angle. Then I found out about you, the moon's dirty secret. I was prohibited from speaking to you."

"But you didn't obey orders. What'll they do to you if they find out?"

"I don't know and that scares me. The colony is fiercely self-protective. It has to be. Our own world wants to kill us."

No reply.

"Do you have a first name?"

"I'm Wilson."

"So, will you —"

"I understand unreliable narrative." Wilson concentrates on his work as he speaks. "My world was torn apart by unreliable narratives. By a million variations of 'I'm right and you're wrong, therefore I'll kill you.'" A bitter laugh. "We westerners were *right*, of course. After all, we had democracy, technology, clean drinking water and invisible sewage disposal. We also raped the planet and shit in our own backyard. When the water dried up and the summers got too hot and the crops failed, the *wrong* ones moved against us."

"I know this –"

"You want my story, you get this. You want a tree? You need its roots and the soil it grows in."

Beleaguered, that's how we saw ourselves. The last outposts of civilisation holding out in our city states; Birmingham, Paris, New York, London. The walls were built and the minefields sown. There were no guarantees. *They* had aircraft. *They* had artillery and rockets and drones. Although, it was unclear who *they* were. A thousand gangs and hordes, Christ, even entire populations, were streaming into Europe and the USA to escape from the Sunburn. It was the equatorial areas first, then the tropics, then Southern Europe and South America. The Sunburn was expanding fast.

They fought us and they fought each other. But all of them, the good, the bad and the beautiful, had one thing in common. They wanted to rape us the way we had raped them. And who could blame them?

I'm a Londoner. I worked for the government, as did Sonja, my wife. That's the official government, by the way, not that bunch of fascists in the south of England who called themselves the RBG, the Real British Government.

We lived in Whitehall, in a government workers' flat on the first floor of a mouldering old MOD building that overlooked the River. We had a daughter. She was twelve and her name was Charlotte. She had blonde hair, like her mum. I adored them both.

Sonja and I were both doctors of science, she a chemist, me a botanist. Once London was sealed off there was no need for either, so we worked in the distribution department, organising supply convoys to other government-supporting enclaves. We were forced to deal with the RBG. They protected the convoys. As payment, they helped themselves to a percentage of the food and raw materials in the lorries.

Their considerable arsenal did not prevent the drone strike on Charlotte's school, however.

A school. A fucking school.

We heard it from our office. It shook our windows and broke glass. We left everything and ran, not because we were afraid for ourselves, but because most of us had kids and we knew, instinctively what the target had been.

Sonja's hand was in mine. She held on tight.

Smoke rolled cross the Embankment to fog the dirty old river. There were sirens announcing the arrival of the battered remnants of the emergency services. I coughed on the smoke and burning flesh stench. There was dust, gritty in my mouth. I felt a wave of heat then saw the first bodies, there on the weed-cracked pavement and the pot-holed road and glimpsed through gaps in the smoke. They were torn, half-unwrapped human packages. Police in battered helmets and scuffed breastplates tried to hold us back. But there were too many of us, fuelled by panic and grief.

We stumbled through the smoke and swirling dust, over rubble and glass. One-by-one people dropped to their knees to howl out their grief as they recognised their own among the dead.

Then figures began to emerge from the blazing ruin. They were the living dead, walking slowly, unsteadily, heedless of the heat and smoke and keening of the crowd.

One looked like Charlotte. I daren't hope. Sonja had no doubt,

It was my daughter, soot-smudged, clothes dishevelled and blackened. She was silent, unresponsive, her eyes emptied by a shock so deep I wondered if she would ever come back to me.

That night, in our cramped, damp little excuse for a flat, I told Sonja that we had to get out. I told her how and where we could go. Sonja said no. She said it was too dangerous.

I reminded her that some horde of psychopathic bastards bombed the school. "They got a drone through the mesh and tried to kill our child."

"But they didn't, did they."

"They're coming, Sonja. The walls won't hold them back for much longer."

"And your answer is for us all to climb aboard a death ship to the moon?"

"They're not death ships –"

"Really? Don't you watch the 'casts? Fifty percent failure rate, auto-freighters and shuttles that should have been scrapped long before the Sunburn, breaking up in space or miles off course. They're run by RBG traffickers. They don't give a damn."

"Are things going to get better here?"

Sonja had no answer to that.

"We have enough money." I said.

"What do you mean?"

"I've been saving." Not enough for Mars, but enough for a moon run.

"You've been saving? While we struggled to buy food and clothes and –"

"My sanitation job." Three nights a week on a corpse clearance team, picking up the murdered, street-dead and the dead-at-home. There were no undertakers any more, only the sanitation crews and the ovens in the abandoned hulk of Battersea Power Station. It paid well. There was a shortage of sanitation operatives, but no shortage of dead.

"You've been planning this."

"I suppose... I don't know." I wasn't lying. I had no plan, no fully formed idea, but the possibility of escape had been in my mind for a long time.

"So, you want to give it all to traffickers and hope we actually make it to the moon?" An angry laugh. A shake of the head. "You have that much saved. And you would risk our lives..." Exasperated she sat back and covered her face with her hands.

I repeated the mantra.

They got a drone through the mesh and tried to kill our child.

"I took my family into Hell," Wilson says.

Saffron doesn't have an answer. She has never been in space. She can only imagine it and, even then, the imagery is vague. She sees darkness and knows that there is cold. She has some vague sense of the womb-like comfort of a space craft. Luners seldom travelled. There was some trade with the Martians, but no love was lost between the two colonies. They never visited Earth.

"It was done in shadows." Wilson says. He looks haggard now. He stands over his precious plants, but no longer tends them. "Access to government computers gave me names. There were small hours meetings in dangerous places. Money changed hands. A month later, we were buried under the false floor of a food convoy truck, on our way to the old Gatwick Space Port. Ironic. Sonja and I had spent our working days organising convoys like this.

"We clung to each other and tried to forget we were nailed into a travelling coffin. Charlotte was the bravest of the three of us. She didn't murmur. She held our hands in the pitch dark and whispered that she loved us, over and over again. I wondered who was comforting who. I was close to screaming by the time the lorry reached Gatwick. I could taste the darkness.

"The RBG had the port. They had the technology and the controls. There was a temporary respite when we arrived; the few minutes it took to transfer us and a score of other desperate people from one set of travelling coffins to another."

There was no wonder in this version of space flight. There was an ageing, tarnished-looking auto-freighter glimpsed on the pad as we were hustled into the launch tower lift by a platoon of armed men. Their contempt for us was palpable. It felt like an arrest, as if we were being herded towards a mass execution.

Perhaps that was exactly what it was.

There were forty horizontal couches in the freighter's cramped, tubular hold. The passengers were tightly strapped in.

"You stay on the couches until you get to the moon." The speaker was a shaven-headed hulk dressed in RBG camouflage and Kevla. An automatic rifle was nestled, baby-like, in his enormous arms. "The straps are locked until touchdown." The hatch clanged shut. It was dark but for the dim red glow of a line of security lamps dotted along the low, curved ceiling.

The sobbing and screaming started long before ignition. I reached out to take Sonja's and Charlotte's hands in my own. The dull, bloody light carved fear-lines deep into their faces, which were, no doubt, reflections of my own.

The engines exploded into life.

Then there was vibration, a crushing weight that bore down onto my chest. And there was noise, a white, unrelenting, all-consuming roar that drew blood from my ears and nose. It felt as if my heart would stop. I couldn't breathe. The vibration became a maddened shaking.

Oh, and that noise. Unthinkable, incalculable, screaming *noise*. It rose and rose to a crescendo. Surely, something must give way, something must burst apart -

It stopped, all of it.

Silence replaced the engine-roar.

I felt my body strain again the straps as it tried to float from the couch. There was a falling sensation. I heard people being sick. I heard sobs and cries. Someone gibbered, already driven crazy.

We were in space.

It was incomprehensible.

The ion drive had cut the crossing to the moon down to twelve hours. But each of those hours had to be lived.

The traffickers may have been mercenary and ruthless, but they also possessed a spark of humanity because there were food tubes and water bottles bolted to sides of the couches. Unused to weightlessness, we were clumsy. Water was spilled into shimmering spheres and escaped nutrient paste writhed past our faces like blind mindless snakes. They were soon accompanied by vomit, urine globes and faeces. The hold stank before the first hour had passed. The stench induced more nausea. Someone begged for help, over and over again. I wanted them to stop. To shut up.

I forced myself to swallow the food paste and managed to keep it in my stomach. I tried to talk to Sonja, but she seemed unable to speak. The fear etched into her face at the commencement of the voyage had become raw terror. I held her hand and felt her violent trembling. Her distress was disconcerting. She was always stronger and clearer thinking one. She was the one I normally relied upon in a crisis. Suddenly, *I* had to be strong and it wasn't working.

The temperature increased and the heat became stifling. A new fear rose up like a black wave. There was a malfunction. We were going to bake alive in here. We were on the wrong course, heading for the sun. It grew hotter. Panic rippled through the strapped-down cargo. I realised that I was crushing my wife's and daughter's hands in mine.

It went on. The heat gave way to sudden cold. The air grew foul with the stink of human waste. Metal groaned. Knocking and hammering erupted from somewhere deep in the freighter's mechanisms, then ceased as suddenly as it started.

Sonja was right. This was a death ship –

The engines erupted back into life. The roar and vibration resumed. Gravity returned. We fell, fast. I could feel it; the gut-wrench of rapid descent. We were going to crash. Any moment now, any second, there would be an instant of unspeakable violence and pain. Sonja's hand crushed mine. I think I called out her name over and over again. I can't remember. There was too much noise.

We stopped, abruptly, jerked roughly against the straps. The noise and shaking increased. Then a final drop.

And impact.

Bone-jarring. Shattering.

Silence.

"There was nothing we could do but wait."

Saffron tries to imagine the horror it. Trapped in the dark, temperature dropping, air running out. No suits. No hope. The squalor and stink. Corpses mixed in with their living, the sick and dying. Children cry. People sob and rage.

A few people unstrapped and tried to aid and comfort the injured and distressed. The chaos was made worse by the low gravity. We fumbled and careered into one another and rolled into a broken, disoriented knot of wretched humanity. I saw Charlotte crawl across to a frail-looking, elderly woman, who seemed to be having trouble breathing. Charlotte stayed with her and stroked her hair until she took her last breath. I was proud of my daughter, at that moment. She was the bravest of the three of us.

The skinnys finally arrived three hours after the freighter crash-landed. They came in through the airlock and moved among us, disturbingly tall and graceful in their close-fitting space suits, and anonymous, behind the visors of their helmets.

"You didn't treat us well," Wilson says.

Despite her determined objectivity, Saffron is offended. "I had nothing to do with it. I was a teenager when you earthers started to arrive."

"I don't blame you." Wilson makes a placating gesture. "There were almost three hundred of us seeking asylum here. That's a lot of mouths to feed in a place like this."

"And we did feed you, and clothe you and gave you a home."

"It was the coldness."

"You were given work."

"There's more to life than work. The dormitory dome you put us in, it felt like a prison. There was no privacy. Everything was communal, we ate together, slept together. We were like rats in a laboratory tank."

"What else could we do?"

"Trust us."

Saffron laughs. The very concept of trusting a heavy is so inconceivable that Wilson's comment sounds like a joke. "After what happened?"

"Perhaps it's why it happened."

The refugee camp was a large dome off to one side of the Endeavour Colony joined to, and separated from, the main city by a transparent tube, sealed at either end by an airlock. It was clean and warm. Its beds were converted flight couches recovered from the trafficker's auto-freighters. There was running water, and shower and toilet facilities

Huge windows gave a view of the moon outside. The novelty of the motionless, grey wasteland quickly wore off and its desolation bore in on us. There was no rain or breeze or gale or snow. No fog or dust storm. The sky was always black. The landscape always grey. Nothing happened out there apart from the occasional arrival or departure of the skinny's balloon-wheeled transports. The tracks made by the vehicles remained, forever undisturbed. Those snaking ruts almost drove me crazy. I wanted them to fade. I wanted them to be filled by rain, turned to mud, anything but stay frozen and eternally the fucking same.

Instant death waited on the far side of those windows. Death, only a few millimetres away,

Reduced gravity only added to our troubles. Walking was a clumsy, shambolic bounce. When you fell, you fell slowly in an ungainly tangle of flailing limbs. Once down you scrabbled and kicked like an overturned beetle. Anything thrown, an increasingly common occurrence because tempers were short, the missile hurtled faster and further than expected. A blow from some flying object would cause yet another argument, another fight.

Everything was wrong. Everything was difficult.

Work was shared out. We were given a cycle of shifts. Five days in the filth and stench of the waste recycling plants, five days in the makeshift nursery and school area we set up for ourselves in the dome, and finally, five days tending the crops in the immense hydroponic farms. The latter sounds the better option. It was, but only marginally. The hydroponic units were hot and humid. There were countless insects, the descendants of those who arrived in the early days as frozen eggs. The insects pollinated the plants. The pollinators needed predators to control their numbers and maintain the quality of their genetic stock. Survival of the fittest meant survival of the *fittest*. Many of the insect predators and pollinators stung and bit. One-sixth gravity plus steady heat and humidity meant that the insects grew larger than on earth. The spiders, whose webs adorned the ceiling of the farms, were best not seen at all.

The work was hard and relentless.

The only time we left our dormitory area was to work.

Humans don't fare well when kept like farm animals.

I felt the tension when we arrived. It was an undercurrent. There was hostility from those here already, and suspicion, which meant that we kept ourselves to ourselves for the first couple of weeks.

Sonja was stoic and, as always, got on with things and made the best of the situation. Charlotte adapted surprisingly well and seemed at peace here. I think she felt safe. No one was going to drop bombs on her. No one meant her any harm.

Our initial interaction with a veteran of the place was with a tall, shaven-headed muscular character who looked too much like an RBG thug for comfort. He walked over to the trio of flight couches that represented home for us. It was evening. We were resting and talking with a neighbouring family group. As the veteran approached, I anticipated trouble and was unsure how to react to it.

"Tom Carpenter," the man growled and held out a huge hand. We all shook it and introduced ourselves.

To my relief, he seemed amiable enough, but I quickly sensed that he was a man barely in control of his emotion. His steadiness was carefully erected containment for his rage.

"Welcome to the moon," he said. "It's hard going, but it's a new life."

"A new world," Sonja agreed.

"A bloody dangerous one, but yeah, a new world."

We chatted. He gave advice on living here, the unwritten rules. Everyone pitches in. We are a community. There was a hard edge to that welcoming speech. As if it was a warning rather than a greeting.

We are *a community, so don't step out of line.*

"Sounds good to me," Sonja said.

"Yeah," I said. "Good."

Tom ran a poker school and I was invited in. I was nervous, but the group, a half dozen or so, made me welcome. We played for narcorettes. I began to look forward to poker nights.

"No one's happy," Tom said, suddenly. It was my third or fourth evening with them. It was after lights out. Someone in the group had obtained a couple of torches from somewhere, so we played on.

I didn't have an answer.

"We're looking at ways to improve our situation."

Murmurs of agreement.

"The skinnys think they can keep us cooped up in here, but they can't. We'll go mad. There's already fights and squabbling. Someone is going to get hurt soon if they don't let us out of this dome."

"They will, eventually," I said. Then added, lamely. "They have to, surely."

"You'd think. But it isn't going to happen," Tom said. "Unless we make sure it happens," He looked across at me, his face up-lit by the torch he held. "You in?"

"Yes," I said, unsure if he meant the next game, or whatever *making sure* he was planning. "I'm in."

The fights got worse. There was unrest; resentment. The refugees were breaking into factions who divided the physical space between themselves. There were brief alliances and short, sharp wars denoted by occasional localised brawls. We were among those who kept out of the disputes and, in so doing, became a clique of our own.

I clamped down on my frustration and my claustrophobic hatred of the moon. I loathed all of it; the black sky and empty, dead landscape, the gleaming white domes and cubes that were the colony and, most of all, the over-thin, over-tall, fragile creatures who had dominion over us, whose recent ancestors were human, but were themselves as alien as visitors from the stars. I hated their arrogance and coldness.

Sonja and I clung together, we both worked and at night we learned to make love in a place where there was no privacy, because our marriage depended on it. It was the fingerhold by which we hung over the abyss.

We tried to help when a new batch of refugees arrived. They were bedraggled and filthy and stank before they went to the showers and were given bio-fibre overalls like the rest of us. They told us that things were getting worse on Earth.

They were the last to arrive here.

"Is this any better?" Sonja asked me one night. "We were trapped before. We couldn't leave London, so how different is this?"

"No one wants to kill us here."

"The skinnys don't want us."

"Who can tell what the skinnys want? We do the work they don't want to do. They feed us and give us medical supplies." They also seldom spoke to us. They oversaw us at work, sent doctors to attend to our emergencies, but were always aloof.

Contempt or fear?

So, it ground on. The hydroponics farm with its sweltering, wet heat and biting insects. The recycling plant with its coffin-like filter tubes and all-pervasive stench of human waste. The nursery, the dome's neutral zone, filled with sullen, frightened, introverted children. And the dome itself, a seething slough of arguments, fights, crying, shouting and coughing, a surging, stinking, restless, angry, press of human beings under which I was buried.

That night, *that* night, I dreamed of burning schools.

"*That* night?"

"Things just happen," Wilson says. He returns to his work.

Saffron says nothing. She waits. That's something she has learned. When trying to get at the truth beneath the truth, you wait.

"Perhaps they planned it. Sub-consciously, if not consciously…"

"Planned what?" A little prompt. Let him know you're still listening.

"There is always spark. The match that lights the fire."

I woke to screaming. Someone in terrible pain. The lights were off, the dome bathed in a silver-grey moonglow that turned the drama into a frantic shadow.

A shout. "It's his appendix, It's his fucking appendix." Tom, of course. At the airlock, pounding its plas-glass with his fists. "We need a doctor. Now. *We need a fucking doctor.*"

The light came on in the tunnel which connected us to the main colony. Figures appeared. Skinnys, four, no five of them. They bounded gracefully to the door. Our lights came back on. There was uproar.

The screaming collapsed into pain-wracked sobs.

I made my way towards the centre of the cacophony. Others were streaming in to watch, to help or to add their voices to Tom's shout for assistance. The inner airlock door opened and three skinnys came in. The door slid shut behind them. Two were armed.

193

They towered over us, but they looked fragile and scared. The third carried a bag.

"Where's the patient?" he demanded.

Tom pointed towards the centre of the dome. I couldn't see who it was, there were too many people crowded around. Towering over the rest of us, the doctor set off into the crowd. His bodyguards followed. I broke through and saw that the patient was a teenage boy, about Charlotte's age. He was doubled over into a foetal position on his couch.

The doctor emerged from the crowd. He took a step towards the boy.

A woman, presumably the boy's mother, tried to push the doctor aside to get to her son. One of the armed skinnys pulled her back. She shouted at him angrily. He had *pushed* her. He had *touched* her. How dare he? Skinny bastard.

The skinny looked shocked? He shook his head, his long white hair trailing the motion with disturbing underwater slowness.

The mother's near-hysterical protests were taken up by others

And suddenly there was a fight. The armed skinny dropped his weapon and covered his face. I saw blood.

The scuffle spread. The doctor cried out in fear and was swallowed into the melee. Then re-emerged, held by three of Tom's thugs who bundled him towards the airlock. Swept up by the mob, more thrilled than angry, I followed. I was enjoying the humiliation of our oppressors. I wanted them hurt. I wanted them to suffer. I heard the loud, sharp snap of a bone. The doctor yelped in pain.

The guards, including the injured one, afraid for their delicate moon-born bones, had retreated into tunnel, no shot fired. There were women and children among us.

Tom wrenched the doctor's fractured arm up to force his palm onto the keypad. The dome-side door hissed open. I saw the doctor's broken form hauled inside. The skinnys on the other side backed away.

The tunnel-side door of the airlock opened.

The mob, Tom at its head, surged into the tunnel, a raging torrent of anger hate and mind-dead violence. I clawed and battered my way towards the airlock.

They bombed the fucking school...

The skinnys in the tunnel were lost to my view. All I could see and feel was the mob, charging towards the far airlock. Towards the colony, towards the homes of those who had taken us in. I wanted to go with them. I wanted to smash, tear and burn.

They bombed the school...

I reached the airlock.

I saw the emergency close button.

A fucking school...

I stumbled to a halt, suddenly drained of rage.

A school.

No.

No more of this.

I punched the button and the airlock slammed shut to trap myself and the majority of the refugees in the dome. People piled up behind me and crushed me against the door. There was screaming and pounding, then crying.

I watched as the skinnys fled and closed the far lock behind them. I watched as they purged the tunnel of those who threatened their own. I watched Tom Carpenter and his mob die as the air was dumped from the tunnel and given to an ungrateful moon.

"Your people got me out of the dome fast, before I was beaten to death. Perhaps they should have left me there."

"What about Sonja, and Charlotte?"

"I haven't seen them since."

"It's ten years ago. It's a long time, surely —"

"They've never asked to see me."

"You saved the colony. You probably saved your own people."

A shrug.

"Things are better for them now."

"I'm glad."

"Imperfect, but better."

"So, what's the point of your *true* history?" Wilson asks.

"Perhaps it will speed up the integration programme."

"I don't see how."

Saffron closes her noter. "Someone once said; if you want a tree, you need its roots and the soil it grows in."

SPACE

I

There was too much space, too much nothing, between Nyk and the hatch. The hatch promised dark and tunnels to give him boundaries and walls to give him back the borders of his world.

Walls to touch.

He lay on his belly, palms pressed against the open, wide, floor. His eyes were tight closed. A moment ago he had looked up and seen that the room he was in was vast. There was no sign of its walls. Its distant blue roof was stained by what looked like distant puffs of grey-white steam.

The room was lit by a dazzling, hot illuminator, so bright he could not so much as glance in its direction. Its heat burned into the back of Nyk's head, yet it seemed so far away.

Far.

A terrible word.

Why was he here, in this immense room, this titanic module of nothing, this place full of farness? Was this a punishment? If so, he was sorry. He wanted to shout it out to them, but he could barely draw breath, let alone force words from his throat.

So he lay flat and touched the floor with as much of his body as he could and wondered how long he would be here and tried not to believe that they may never want him back in the complex.

II

The alarm shattered Nyk's sleep with its announcement of a new workday. The light in his womb-module snapped on; bright, stark and cold. Nyk's eyes stung, as always, as he blinked against the sudden wash of light. He twisted his head and latched onto the nutritube. There would be wholefood later, but for now it was a sweet puree that assuaged his wake-up hunger and energised him for his shift.

The womb's hatch swung open and Nyk slid out, feet first, into the main dormitory tunnel. Along the narrow passageway other workers were emerging from their modules. All, like Nyk, were naked and bleary-eyed. Each head was shaved, each face aglow with a healthy pallor.

Nyk joined the flow, his back and shoulders moulded into his habitual slouch. The iron ceiling was low, the iron walls close. The illuminators were set for morning level. Not too bright, high in the orange scale. The workers moved quickly shoulder to shoulder, shoulders against the walls.

And there was Shen, glimpsed ahead of him, visible-gone-visible between the workers that separated her from Nyk. She looked back. Nyk gave her a shy smile, which she returned.

Nyk stayed close to the cold, rough wall and relished its textures and the orange crumbs that scraped and stained his skin. He needed wall. Some workers were content with the brush of shoulders and arms, but arms and shoulders were inconstant, and moved in and out of touch too quickly.

The stream stopped, started again, stopped. People were passing through the shower, always a bottleneck.

When it was his turn, Nyk huddled himself against the smooth shower wall and luxuriated in the power of the spray. He glanced up and saw Shen. He stared at her, breathing hard. His face felt as if it was on fire. Shen looked at him and smiled again then threw back her head. Water ran over her face, spilled down the sides of her bare scalp and traced the curves and lines of her body. Nyk could not stop watching the water, and could not stop wanting to run his fingers over her in the same way. He wanted to feel her.

Then he realised that he was hard, the way he was when watched pleasurevids. He faced the wall, pressed himself against its whiteness and closed his eyes for shame.

Wet bodies slid passed, battered, pushed and pulled at him. He waited, trying to gauge the amount of time it would take for Shen to finish her shower, then opened his eyes and turned back. She was there, in front of him. She stared at him, as if puzzled, or amused. Then she touched his lips with her fingertips, laughed and was gone.

Touched his lips.

Which tingled. He reached up, placed his own fingers on the spot and felt a huge wave of joy surge through him and burst out as laughter. The other workers passing through the shower stared at him. Some grinned, others shook their heads. Some even hurried through as if frightened by his mirth.

III

He had to move. There was nothing here, no food or real heat or real light. Nyk opened his eyes, lifted his head and looked towards the hatch. He took a deep breath, a hard, dry-mouthed swallow and began to crawl. His belly scraped over the rough floor, which tore at his skin and made it raw. It wasn't iron but smooth and grey. Something like green hair grew through its cracked surface

After a while he could stand it no longer. He closed his eyes again and realised that to get to the hatch quickly he was going to have to stand up.

Which was impossible.

No, not impossible.

He pushed himself onto his hands and knees then waited until he stopped panting. He struggled into a crouch. Then he stood. He wavered, dizzy and weak. He reached out for support, an instinctive action, rocked, and almost fell. There was nothing to touch. Nothing.

The vast room spun about him.

IV

The workers streamed down the tunnel towards their duty positions. Dressed now in overalls, Nyk slid along the wall, confused, euphoric, desolate, more than ever in need of touch. There was nothing in his mind except Shen. She was no longer in sight, already at her machine, no doubt. He was unable to work out what to do about these unfamiliar and disturbing feelings. There would be opportunities to meet, in the refectory, in the communal cell, when they watched instructional films, but what did he say? How did you do this?

He tried to press himself into the shadows, tried to disappear. But there was little room, too many others in need of the wall.

Nyk was a Components Quality Inspector. He had no idea what the components were for, or how they worked, but he had an instinct, highly prized in the complex. He could tell, by look and touch if the component was sound or faulty. There was no magic, the item either felt *right*, or *wrong*.

Today, however, it was he, Nyk, who was *wrong*.

Thoughts of Shen were constantly in his head. He dreamed of touching her and feeling her touch. He wanted to kiss her, wanted to crush her to himself. The day wore on with dragging slowness. He grew tired more quickly than usual and, unthinkably, dropped behind the quota. More and more devices and components piled up. The other workers on the conveyor system grumbled.

Panic was on him as well, stirred up by the bleak truth that he didn't know how to make this happen. Here in the iron dark, crushed and surrounded by the other workers, unable to be alone with anyone. Not that he could imagine what *alone* was like. He had never been alone, with himself or anyone else, except in his womb cell. The thought of it was too terrifying to imagine.

It was the first time he had ever thought of the complex that way, as a dark place, a place where he was crushed. Crushed? Surely no one could live without being crushed, without crowded tunnels and closed-in walls. The idea puzzled and unsettled him.

Then came the announcement. "Nyk, please report to the Supervisor's office module."

Nyk clanged up the iron stairway to the Supervisor's office. He kept his right arm against the wall and tried to find comfort in the contact. He wanted his womb-unit. He wanted the routine of the conveyor.

He reached the door. Its metal solidity was broken only by a single glass porthole and a huge lever, which Nyk pressed down. The door swung open and he stepped through.

The office was too big.

Nyk stood by the door, crouched against the curved wall, finding what comfort he could from the cold iron surface. The Supervisor was a long way away, sitting behind her desk.

"Nyk? Come along, come along. Sit down." The chair indicated was opposite her distant desk.

Nyk moved slowly round the edge of the spherical room, pressed against the wall. His mouth was dry now, his breathing shallow.

"Hurry up, please. I am very busy, I need to talk to you urgently."

Urgently? Why would the Supervisor want to talk to *him* so urgently?

He pushed himself away from the wall, lunged at the chair and sat down. The chair was big, and seemed to fold itself about him.

The Supervisor templed her fingers, elbows on the desk, which was made of some heavy, shiny brown material. There was little on its surface, some papers, a computation terminal. Tall, slim and sharply beautiful, she wore a suit which was spotless and razor creased. She seemed kind enough. Her smiles were warm and comforting.

So this was what it felt like to be alone with someone. Strange. Nyk glanced round, continually expecting to see other people here, disturbed by the empty spaces.

The wall behind her consisted of a huge porthole. Nyk could see the endless conveyer belts and the distant machineries beyond them, vast structures that dwarfed their operators to tiny specks. The grey, smoke-misted air was punctuated by the flare of furnaces. The office thrummed to the rhythm of giant hammers and presses.

"It has come to our attention —"

Ours?

"— that you would like to touch Shen."

"I'm sorry. I…" Nyk had no idea what to say, but was sure he was supposed to say something.

"It's all right, Nyk. Touching Shen would be a good thing."

"Good?"

"We noticed your reaction to her in the shower."

Nyk opened his mouth again, horrified that his hardness had been seen by the Supervisor and whoever else *our* might mean.

"So we want you to have the chance to touch her." The Supervisor's smile hardened somehow; a smile, but not a smile. "Would you like that chance?"

Yes, oh yes, he wanted nothing more than that -

"Nyk?"

"Yes, I want to touch her."

"In that case," the Supervisor stood and waved towards a second hatch set into the office wall, off to her right, "she's through there."

Nyk stared at her. "You mean…"

"What else could I mean?" The Supervisor sounded irritated now.

Carefully, slowly, Nyk stood then stumbled across the intervening space to the hatch. It opened as his palm hit its surface. On the other side there was a tunnel. Nyk crawled in and scuttled towards a light that glowed at the end. The tunnel was small, tight. It touched him on all sides. The security and comfort of that contact released a hunger in him. She would be waiting for him, down there, in that light.

V

He didn't fall. Dizzy, sick, but standing, he tried to take a step towards the hatch. He lifted his left foot. Now only the sole of the other foot touched the uneven, dirty floor. He concentrated on that part of his body, on that tiny contact and brought his left foot back down. He panicked, grabbed for something to hold on to, but there was nothing.

Breathing hard, Nyk managed to lift his right foot.

He walked, tottered, but walked, keeping his eyes fixed on his destination, feeling that faraway roof bear down on him. He tried not to look up or to look left or right. Nyk was quickly exhausted and wet with sweat, which was chilled by the air. He wondered where the air was blown in from because there were no fans or vents visible. Nothing was visible, no doors, no walls –

The hatch.

There at his feet.

Nyk dropped to his knees, shaking, panting but so happy he laughed. He had walked without touching a wall, without support and now he could go home. He saw the pad, covered it with his palm and felt the familiar electric tingle.

Nothing happened.

But hatches always opened. He touched it again and again then hammered at it until his hand ached, numbed, then bled. He shouted. His shouts became more and more anguished until he was screaming.

The hatch remained shut.

VI

Shen stood in the centre of a huge softly lit chamber, naked. She looked up as Nyk stepped inside and her gaze locked with his. Then she turned to look over to her left. Nyk followed her stare and saw another hatch through which another male worker entered.

A third hatch opened. A third man.

The distance between the hatch and Shen was impossible to traverse. The floor was a flat metal grid through which red-lit machineries could be glimpsed. Their roar and thrum hammered at Nyk's skull and added to his mounting panic. He stared at Shen then at the space. It was as if his whole body had jammed the way the conveyor sometimes locked up and came to a juddering halt.

The second man to his right took a faltering step. His arms were out, as if trying to touch the distant walls of the chamber. The third man dropped to his hands and knees and began to crawl. Good idea. Nyk did the same. He dropped to the floor slowly, carefully and almost cried with relief to feel the floor beneath his knees and palms. It was better, but there was still too much *nothing* around him, a suffocating wall of it.

He looked up and saw the walker was already moving slowly and clumsily towards Shen, who was watching him, *him* and not Nyk.

Nyk dropped to his belly and began to slither towards Shen, the woman he wanted to touch. But it hurt and it was slow, so he raised himself up onto his hands and knees and crawled. The third man stopped and began to whimper then curled himself into a ball and sobbed and was done. Only the walker to beat. He was already halfway across the space, his steps clumsy and slow, but ahead of Nyk and catching too much of Shen's attention.

Then she looked at Nyk and even at this seemingly enormous distance he felt her plea for him to hurry. It gave him strength. He began to crawl, exposed, alone, with nothing but the grid against his hands, knees and shins. He filled his mind with the touch; the feel of Shen's skin under his fingertips, the taste of her. It was beyond imagining, but something in him, some collection of awakened inner senses seemed to know already how it would be.

The walker was almost there.

Nyk scuttled like the cockroaches and beetles that infested the tunnels. Not quick enough. He was going to lose her. Suddenly he felt a new emotion, anger, not the irritation, the occasional shouted arguments and brief flurries of blows and shoves that were part of a normal day. This anger was as strong as his need for Shen. It shuddered through him and splintered the bright glow of imagined touch with images of blood and fists.

Crawling was too slow.

He needed to walk.

The realisation was too immense to grasp. He needed to walk, here, now, across the remaining vastness of the chamber.

Slowly, Nyk hauled himself first into a crouch, then up onto his feet. He wavered, reached out for walls that were too far away to offer anything more than a taunt of unattainable security. He held his breath, dizzy, paralysed then collapsed back onto his knees.

A moment later the walker lurched the few remaining steps into Shen's arms.

She held him tight, but gazed at Nyk over his shoulder with eyes that held longing and a disappointment so intense it might have been scorn.

The hatches burst open and four bulky-suited Keepers rushed in. Two of them prised the weeper roughly from the floor. The other two bore down on Nyk, who managed to get to his feet but too late. They grabbed his arms and hauled him towards the hatch. He screamed Shen's name until something metallic and sharp was pressed against his neck. There came a hiss, a stab of pain and darkness.

When he woke he was in the great nothing.

VII

When Nyk finally stopped howling at the hatch to open and was curled on the floor, nestling his bruised and bloodied hands to himself, he understood that he must be *outside*.

The thought was too awful to accept. It had slipped into his mind and, no matter how much he tried to push it away, the reality of it had already seeped into every nerve of his body. It rang in his ears, it painted the dark of his tight-shut eyes with barely-understood images of endless space and loneliness, starvation and death.

And they, *they*, the Supervisor and the Directorate, that amorphous, featureless smudge of authority imprinted in his view of the world, they had done this to him. What crime had he committed? The Supervisor told him that wanting to touch Shen was a good thing. He had done as he was told. He had tried to get to her.

But failed.

So he was outside.

His fear once more fractured into anger.

He did not have to die.

He must not die, because *they* wanted him to die.

His mouth was so dry it was difficult to swallow. It had never been difficult to swallow before. He had never even noticed swallowing. But now his throat worked against an almost impenetrable thickness that made him gag. Water, he needed water.

Perhaps there were other hatches. To find them, however, he would need to walk around the room. Well, so be it. He sat up and tried to look away from the floor and at the space around him. Above him, the steam clouds were thickening. Some had turned grey. The ventilation had been turned down as well. The air was now cold enough to make him shiver. Nyk struggled up onto his knees then onto his feet again. He swayed, dizzy. He closed his eyes for a moment then opened them and looked down at the floor, which seemed too far away. He started to walk, slowly, carefully. He concentrated on each step, which was good because it meant that he stopped thinking about the space around him.

Where did this place end? He had always known where things ended. He had always known what was around the corner of every tunnel he traversed through the complex. There was a structure ahead, formed into a tunnel although its sides were ragged and made up of columns. The roof was a web of what looked like green fabric or netting that waved and hissed in the moving air. As he entered the tunnel the light faded and the air cooled further still. A tunnel must lead somewhere. The thought eased his hunger and thirst a little and gave him hope.

The columns were strange, their surfaces roughly textured. Other columns could be seen stretching away into the dark green space behind the tunnel walls. Devices flitted between the columns and in the roof. Fast and agile, they twittered and whistled, but appeared to have no purpose that Nyk could see.

He came to the end of the tunnel and the room opened up again. Its floor sloped away into a distance that drove Nyk back against one of the columns where he wept and whimpered and covered his face with his hands.

He forced himself to open his eyes again. The floor sloped down, rough, brown, grey and green, then rose up again a terrible distance away. The far floor was hidden within another of the sprawling green structures.

Water flowed along the bottom of the slope, silver-grey, wide and fast moving. Objects protruded from its surface and broke the flow into swirls of foam.

Water.

Nyk tore himself away from the shelter and security of the structure and stumbled down the slope. There was water down there and he had to drink.

When he reached it, however, the fear came back and drove him onto his belly.

The water was wide, the floor running along its edges empty and broken. Nyk clutched at the floor, pressed his cheek to the coarse green fabric that protruded between the cracks and stared at the raging, deafening torrent. He relished the feel of the floor against the length of his body. The space around him pressed in, the light, dulled now but all-pervading, seemed to burn into his eyes.

Slowly, he slithered towards the edge of the water. He had to drink. He would stay here. Someone would come looking for him. Wouldn't they? He reached the edge of the water, where the swirl and rush was gentler. The floor here was cold, smooth and dark grey. The floor was wet and unpleasant. Nyk splashed water at his face, then, without thinking, he formed his hands into a cup shape and scooped water up and into his mouth. The cold was shocking on his tongue but it slaked his thirst.

Exhausted, he crawled back towards a group of columns that stood a little way from the edge of the water. The roof had darkened, now completely covered by the grey steam which seemed frozen into bulging, heavy shapes. The air had changed, had become heavy, cold and somehow damp. Then the water came. Great drops of it thudded onto the floor and onto Nyk's head and back. The drops quickly became more frequent, heavier, faster, until the world was turned into an icy, grey blur and Nyk was beaten onto his belly by its relentless hammering.

Desperation drove him to his feet again, hunched double, barely able to see where he was going in the water-drenched mist, he launched himself at the structure, careered over the rough floor and grabbed at the nearest of the columns. Then he collapsed again. The structure leaked badly, but gave some shelter. He clutched at the nearest column, unheeding of its roughness and the grazes it made on his already damaged hands and face. He held it tight, curled up and escaped into darkness.

He woke, suddenly, breathless, confused. The light had changed to night-dark, broken into an uneven patchwork of absolute shadow and silvery grey.

There was a noise, something moving, nearby.

VIII

Wet, shivering and disorientated, Nyk pushed himself away from the column and peered into the dark. Nothing -

No, movement again, the sound of feet rustling through the fabric on the uneven floor. The sound of breathing. Not good breathing, but human breathing nonetheless.

"Hello?" Nyk called out. He was frightened but he needed these people. "I'm Nyk, I'm a Quality Inspector. Who are you?"

He was answered by a brutal fit of coughing, and voices that sounded rough and angry.

Nyk tried again. "I'm over here. I need to get back to the complex."

Something deep inside him, some unease – a voice almost – clamoured for him to keep quiet, to run away. But he was alone, he shouldn't be alone, and these were people.

Then they came.

Three, four, rushing at him from the shadows, their movement shambolic but fast. The closest burst into a pool of silver light and Nyk saw long hair, ragged clothes.

The man grabbed Nyk's throat and they crashed to the floor. The man stank, his body, his breath. The smell was ripe and overwhelming, sweat, rotten food, and something else Nyk could not name. He grabbed at his attacker's wrists. The man's grip loosened and he seemed to simply give up. Nyk shoved him away and he rolled off and onto the floor, into a pool of light.

The man's face was a ruin, his skin distorted by huge swellings, some of which had burst to bleed thick, foul-smelling, fluid. Nyk stood over him, breathing hard, fists clenched, but the man made no move to get up. He began to shake, curled himself into a ball and trembled and whimpered, then coughed.

A moment later, Nyk was shoved aside by another of the figures who knelt beside the man and began to cry. This second person was a woman. Her sobs were chesty, wet, wheezing noises, punctuated by fits of coughing.

"Help us, please." It was the third of the group. A man. He sounded young.

Nyk backed away, sensing more of them, closing in through the shadows. These people were ill. Illness meant infection, contagion, terrible words he understood only by their use in the complex. Anyone who became ill was taken away. Nyk had seen it, weak, coughing, shivering men and women hauled off their conveyor belt stations, out of the showers or the communal hall, by the Keepers. They were never seen again.

If someone became ill, you had to get as far away from them as possible, which was not far in the complex, but was very far out here in this vast and awful room. Suddenly the nothing out here was no longer a bad or frightening thing. Nyk ran, as best he could out of the structure and across the rough, broken floor, following the water, for no reason other than it was a marker, a *way*.

His chest was tight, it was hard to breathe and now he was afraid that *he* might be ill. It had never happened to him, he didn't know what it felt like. He slowed to a walk. He was tired but too frightened to rest. There might be more ill nearby.

He looked up. The roof had changed.

The sight of what it had become stopped him dead.

The action was impulsive. He *had* to stop and feel this... this vast strangeness. He reached out to it and opened his hands and grasped at the emptiness, He was looking up at a roof now lit by a huge silver illuminator, and scattered with countless sparkling white lights. And for the first time the empty vastness of this place filled him with wonder. For the first time, this *nothing* felt good in his hands.

Someone shouted his name.

He turned and saw bulky figures detach themselves from the shadows; shapeless suits, burred, artificial voices. Keepers.

Now his fear was edged with anger. They had torn him away from the complex and thrown him outside. He didn't want to run away from them any more, he wanted to fight, to strike back at them, to hurt them. For a moment, crazed with desires and thoughts of punching, beating and kicking, he almost ran *at* them. But there were too many, and they wore those suits and would be armed with tranquiliser sprays and electrosticks, or worse. So, face burning, rage boiling through him, he broke into a run.

He stumbled over the rough floor, crashed through the structures, dodging and darting, the way he had learned to run in the complex; see a gap in the never-ending flow of people, take it, weave, dodge. On and on until he was too weak to go any further.

Clawing for breath, he staggered to a halt, one palm against a column. Beyond, the room opened out again, and this time to expose ruin.

It stretched away as far as he could see, structures: some squat and ugly, others vast and thrust high towards the light-speckled roof, but all crumbling, broken. He staggered to the nearest wall and found it rough and caked with dirt. He huddled against it, drinking in the comfort of touch. In the silver-black dappling he saw a debris-choked passage, roofless and wide, walled by the ruined structures. There were broken vehicles, many much bigger than the runners that dashed through the tunnels of the complex. Somewhere at the distant heart of the ruin there was a dazzling, stark glow that filled the roof and washed out the other more beautiful lights.

If he stayed here he would be caught. He had to move. He pushed himself away and ran. The darkness helped.

The water was channelled between two crumbling walls, the far wall many metres away. There was a walkway beside it, cracked and pierced by that odd fabric that seemed to grow from every floor. As he picked his way along the path, he saw other vehicles in the channel, dark hulks, rotting where they floated. The fast-running water slapped at their flanks.

Voices, up ahead this time, his name, orders to stop and wait. He looked and saw more Keepers moving towards him. He glanced behind and saw his original pursuers, closing in. There was no other choice. He pushed himself away from the wall and out into the water.

The cold stabbed him with a million knives, seared into his flesh and paralysed his muscles. He couldn't breathe, couldn't move. It was as if his life was swirling away from him, bleeding into the wild writhing of the water. He thrashed and struggled but was thrown and shoved by the torrent. It sucked him down where the roar became muffled and overridden by the pound of his own heart, then up again and away. He stopped fighting, let it take him.

No.

He began to beat and thrash at the water again, weakly, ineffectually, but he could not let it take him.

Solidity smashed into him and knocked the breath from his lungs as he careered into the side of one of the hulks. He saw a rope connecting the vehicle to the water and grabbed at it, found it cold and slimy but held on. He closed his eyes. Why not let go? Why not just let the water take him down into the comforting dark?

He held on.

Until the Keepers came.

IX

"Tough is an understatement. We were supposed to find you curled up and whimpering by the complex's exit hatch like all the others. You led us a merry dance, Nyk." The speaker, a woman, was sitting in the entrance to the womb module in which Nyk had awoken hours (days) ago. "And better still, you're immune."

"Immune?" Nyk was bruised, aching, but warm in clean overalls and safe in the module's padded closeness.

"To the plague. You were in close proximity to victims over twenty-four hours ago but your bloods are clear and you're showing no symptoms."

The victims, those weak, frightened sobbing wretches who had tried to attack him. "Why are they outside? Why aren't they in a womb like this one?"

The woman had long hair, light brown and fine. Hair he wanted to touch. She wore an overall which was white and clean. "There's nothing we can do for them." She sounded sad and wouldn't look at him as she spoke. "The plague was almost the end of everything. Ironic, though, what started as a weapon of war brought humanity together in time to build the complexes, and the arks."

Arks?

The woman smiled. "Come and eat. I want to show you something." She held out her hand. "I'm Sara by the way, from Recruitment and Psychology."

Nyk held her hand and found it to be soft and warm. He was reluctant to release it.

They seemed to be in a complex, one that was much less crowded and more spacious than Nyk's own. Its tunnels were too

211

wide and high, though comfortingly metallic and utilitarian. Nyk found that he was able to walk the tunnels now without his natural terror of space overwhelming him completely.

There was a communal eating hall, large and disturbingly open. A huge window formed one wall, through which the outside could be seen. It was daytime, the sky once more hidden by grey steam. Water ran down the other side of glass.

The view was of the ruin, and something else; an unthinkably huge cylinder held in place by a web of girders and towers and bathed in stark, white light. Its flanks were decorated with an endless mosaic of tubes and pipes which issued clouds of white steam or smoke. The cylinder tapered to a point at its summit, which was so high that at moments it was obscured by the water and grey steam. Even from here, it bore down on Nyk, filled him with both awe and the need to hide from its immensity. The thing seemed alive with some barely restrained violence.

"Impressed? You helped build that, Nyk, you and the other workers in complexes all over what's left of the world."

"What is it?" Nyk asked.

"Hope," Sara said. "An ark. One of five. There's nothing left here, we have to find another home for our children. The ark is a giant womb, mother to a billion embryos, all tended by a handful of crew."

"Why was I sent outside?" Nyk asked.

Sara was obviously taken aback by the sudden question. "It was cruel," she said. "Certain people are watched, people with potential. Shen was offered to you as a test –"

"I failed."

"No, the man who got to her first was bold and reckless, good breeding stock. The weak ones who were too afraid were sent straight back to work. You, though, you were cautious, but brave enough to try. Once outside you became a walker, an explorer, one of the few who have enough fight in them to leave the teat and survive." Sara tapped the glass with her fingertip. "The type we need as crew. The people we'll send to the stars."

"Stars?"

"You saw them, that night you were outside. You saw the stars Nyk."

"Yes," Nyk said quietly. "I saw them, I wanted to touch them."

"It's not all romance," Sara said. "The arks' living quarters are a little cramped; economy of space and mass. It would be premature burial for someone like me, your Heaven, my Hell." She held both his hands, gazed straight into his eyes. "The choice is yours. You're free to go home, back to the complex. We owe you that."

Nyk felt a rush of relief; home, the tunnels and press of his fellow workers.

But then there were the stars.

Nyk pressed his forehead against the cold glass, only millimetres from the grey water that streamed from the distant roof, and experienced an odd panic he had never felt before.

He could not decide because both paths frightened him.

X

The alarm shattered Nyk's sleep with its announcement of a new workday. The lights in his womb-module snapped on; white, bright, stark and cold. Nyk forced his eyes open. They stung, as always, as he blinked against the sudden wash of light. He twisted his head and latched onto the nutritube. There would be wholefood later, but for now it was a sweet, puree that assuaged his wake-up hunger and energised him for his shift.

The womb module door swung open and, naked, Nyk joined the other workers as they travelled the narrow curve-walled metal tunnel. Once in the shower he saw Ynna, who glanced shyly at him. She showered quickly, but as she hurried away, looked back and offered Nyk a smile before disappearing to her workplace.

Pulling on his clean overalls, Nyk scuttled the remaining distance to his own post. He climbed through the hatch into the control module. The module was small and enfolded him on all sides. Its walls were made entirely of glass. Outside was night-black vastness beyond comprehension, and all splintered by the sharp-bright glitter of uncountable stars.

SURVIVORS

The worst thing about interstellar flight, worse than the psychedelic insanities of worm-hole travel, worse than the needle-and-haystack probability of finding life out there, or even a world we could call a second home, worse than the meteor strike and the loss of sixty-eight members of the crew, was time dilation.

Time dilation, the knowledge that when you finally limped home, damaged and grief-stricken, there would be no one left who was there to wave you goodbye twelve years before. Twelve ship-years, that is. Almost two hundred of Earth's.

We took our families. The pain of partings would have been unspeakable, untenable, funereal. The ship was a travelling micro-world on which marriages were made and broken, and children were born.

And now we were back.

God knew how we did it; half the vessel a holed, uninhabitable crematorium, one drive dead, the other three overworked and nearing catastrophic overload.

Seeing Earth, home, for the first time in twelve subjective years was too intense, too overwhelming, for immediate emotion. One hundred and seventy four survivors and ship-born stood on the cavernous community deck, to stare at the wall-sized view port, and barely a tear shed or word spoken between us.

Earth was not as I remembered it. Earth should be noisy with electronic chatter. This Earth was silent. Earth should be blue, broken by handprints of brown and green, smudged with whorls of white. This Earth was concealed by unbroken, grey cloud, a hidden, worrying place.

But it was home.

A landing party was selected, me among them because I was one of the few left who could pilot the remaining shuttle. No one was certain that the damn thing could still fly. Its pod had been on the periphery of the meteor strike. We would return to the original European launch site; a place that was once Heathrow Airport.

There were four of us, me, Lieutenant John Michaels (ship's pilot and mission commander), along with Engineer (and second pilot) Avni Singh, Doctor (Medical) Alistair Nqbe and Security Officer Marta Hammer.

The descent was a cloud-blind, out-of-control, helter-skelter. Touchdown was not gentle either; a tube blew at the last moment, upsetting our precarious balance and deceleration. The landing gear collapsed, pieces of hull, fin and engine were ripped away. But the restraints held and the womb-seats remained inflated. Everyone answered my shaky roll-call. No one, it seemed, was seriously injured.

We emerged from the wounded shuttle. It was arctic cold. The sky a brutal lowering weight of cloud. All structures, buildings and whatever craft had once used the airport, were white-encrusted ruins. A relentless, icy gale whipped snow into gusts of white mist and would have flayed us alive and frozen our lungs if it wasn't for our therma-parkas and masks. We had come prepared.

There were people, headed our way, anonymous figures obscured by the restless snow-fog. We waited. If they were hostile, well, what would we gain by running? The shuttle was in no fit state to get us out of there. As they came closer we saw that the party were muffled in shabby, patched-up parkas and furs.

"We're humans," I shouted above the wind. "We've come home." My words sounded clumsy in my own ears, almost as if I'd asked them to take us to their leader. Hardly surprising, I hadn't seen or spoken to a stranger for twelve ship years.

One of them, tall, dark-skinned, a woman I realised when she was near enough for me to see her properly, called back to us; "Where are you from?"

"We've... We've been away, out in space. We're explorers. The Fiennes Expedition."

"From Before." It was not a question.

"Before what?" Marta asked, diplomacy not her main strength.

"The war, the end, of civilisation. Before the clouds came and the seas froze."

"Have you heard of us?" I said. "Everyone knew about us... Before."

The woman glanced at the others, then shrugged. "We've had other things on our minds." She regarded us carefully. "Are there more of you?"

"Yes," I answered then glanced skywards, the action, a reflex. "Up there, in the ship, the Fiennes."

"Are they coming?" The question was matter of fact, not concerned, but not welcoming either.

It was Avni who answered. "Depends if we can repair the shuttle." And that was when the reality of the situation came crashing in. If we couldn't repair the craft, we would never see our friends, families, our people, again. And those, trapped in the Fiennes could not come home. They wouldn't starve to death or run out of oxygen, the ship's hydroponics and recycling plants would see to that. But the frustration, the emotional devastation at being so close to Earth yet unable to return to her surface, would be unbearable. There were already tensions, cliques. The ship's social structure was fragile.

"We can help you," the woman said. "There's plenty of spare parts. This is a graveyard full of dead machines. And we're engineers, of a sort."

They lived in the remains of a hotel, one of the big expensive ones in the airport environs. The place reared out of the snow, its windows blank empty holes, its paintwork blotched and peeling. It bled wires and pipes, steelwork and panelling. The reception area was a snow crusted slush-floored cave, its concrete ceiling visible between islands of mouldering ceiling tiles. Naked lights were strung out on cables, which were secured to any protuberance available. The light was yellow and uncertain. On our trek here from the shuttle, we had passed a large copse of industrial-scale wind turbines, blades spinning effortlessly in the endless gale. At least this corner of the post-Before world had electricity.

We were led upstairs, the lifts presumably out-of-order. I lost count of how many floors we ascended, a struggling worm of parkas, our panted breath manifest in rhythmic puffs of vapour. Where there was glass in the windows, the view was obscured by frozen snow. Where there was no glass, the relentless wind reached in to claw at my bones and burn my lungs.

We finally ended our climb. A faded, wall-mounted, plastic number informed us that this was the eighth floor.

We were taken into what was once a function room. Now it looked to be a communal dining hall. Men and women were seated at the long rows of age-battered wooden tables, intent on their food and drink. These tables were probably the originals, used for countless meetings and team building sessions. Before. All present wore rough, practical clothes; overalls, combat slacks, frayed sweaters and hooded tops. There was little chatter, and no laughter. They were haggard, intense, undemonstrative. Survivors, that most insular, hard-bitten of species.

It took me a few moments to realise that there were no children.

"Eat," said the woman. She had introduced herself as Lana during one of her rare and brief bursts of conversation, shouted above the gale as we walked.

We sat awkwardly, in a gap on a bench made for us by the shuffling and the redistribution of its occupants. The food was scooped out of a large vat and slopped into metal bowls. Both items of tableware looked homemade, the metal beaten, skilfully, from some scavenged sheet of steel. Apart from the ladle used to serve the portions, there was no cutlery.

The food was a hot, brownish mush. It tasted of meat, interspersed with things that crunched. Its texture and monotonous flavour made it hard work, but these people seemed to live on the stuff, so it wasn't likely to poison us. There was drink as well, a syrupy yellowish liquid that was almost unbearably sweet.

No coffee or tea.

"You mentioned a war." It was the first time Nqbe had spoken. He sounded nervous.

"About a hundred years ago," Lana answered. "The weather turned bad, crops failed. Water ran out in some places, others places

218

were flooded. People fought to survive. It got out of hand; chemicals, germ-warfare, nuclear weapons. The human race punished itself by committing suicide."

"Didn't succeed, did it," Marta said.

"No," Lana smiled, faintly, ruefully I think. "It didn't."

"How does this work?" Marta asked. "I mean, you say you're engineers. Where does the food come from? Are you the only ones left?"

"We live in communes and we trade skills. There are farmers out there, and itinerant construction gangs who keep these ruins from falling down. There are also gangs of scavengers who trade oil and petrol. It's how we heat our living areas at night. And only at night. Fuel is precious, finite. We scavenge a living from the corpses of aeroplanes and space hulks. We make things and repair things."

Space hulks? Did that mean that humankind had continued pushing outwards after we left, desperately clawing its way into the void, until everything collapsed.

They gave us a room, a few more floors up. It was empty, its window sealed with a sheet of mouldy plywood. Apart from sacking spread over the bare concrete floor there were no comforts. We would retrieve our thermal sleeping bags, torches etc. from the shuttle and make it our temporary home.

Nqbe sat down in the corner of the room, face in hands. I crouched beside him. "You okay?"

"We shouldn't have come back, John. This isn't our world."

"We always knew it wouldn't be the same one we left."

"We could have stayed on Rigel IX."

He was right. Though riven by apocalyptic storms and erratic, almost hourly temperature changes, the planet had oceans, supported plant life and was enclosed in a breathable atmosphere.

"I couldn't stay, not there," I said. "A lot of us couldn't bear it, you know that."

"I... I'm sorry John, of course."

My wife and two daughters were among the thirty or so, killed on Rigel IX.

*

219

The Engineers used a giant hanger as their workshop. They wanted to move the shuttle inside. I was reluctant. Avni disagreed with me. She said that the weather was too brutal for us to conduct repair work outside. I wanted the shuttle in a place from which we could make a fast getaway if the need arose.

"Why will we need to run away?" she demanded. We stood by the hanger doors, away from the Engineers who were, nonetheless, watching us, silent and impassive. Nqbe and Marta were slumped against the hanger wall, further inside, waiting resignedly for us to finish our argument. "These people are helping us."

She was right about that, of course. They were under no obligation. But, I didn't trust them. Their quiet acquiescence and acceptance of our sudden presence amongst them unnerved me, as did their lack of protest over the possible influx of an entire community to their starved, ragged world.

I was tired of the dispute. "Okay, Avni, let me put it to you another way. It's an order. The shuttle stays out there. We work on it out there. Now, it's getting dark, we need to fetch our kit."

Later, in our room, in the warm, blackness, I felt Marta unzip my sleeping bag and climb in. She held me tight and I nuzzled her long, fine hair, gently kissed her eyes and for a few moments, the feel of her eased away the memories that haunted my nights. I clawed at her and she hushed me and touched me and I sank into her and forgot until the dark came and I was –

– digging into the mud with my bare hands as the rains of Rigel IX tore the clothes from my back. They were under there, suffocated beneath a river of black-grey slime. They were screaming their silent screams, begging me to release them, so that they could breathe, oh Christ all they wanted to do was breathe –

"John!" Hissed into my ear. I felt Marta shove back the flap of the sleeping bag and sit up. "Can you hear it? Listen!"

I did so, bleary and uncomfortable in the stifling heat of the room. A heat at odds with the gale battering at the shattered window's plywood covering.

"What is it?"

"Outside the room. There's a rustling noise."

"There are people in the building."

"I know, but this isn't people. Can't you hear it?"

Marta was making me nervous. I listened, and, yes, there it was, above the steady rhythms of Nqbe's and Avni's breathing. Rustles and scrapes. Marta was on her feet, wrestling with her overall, then making for the door.

"No," I said. "Stay here –"

Too late. The door was open. I scrambled to my feet, grabbed my own overall, and woke Avni in the process.

She mumbled blearily. "Woz'appening?"

"Marta thought she heard something. Wait here."

I didn't give her time to protest.

The corridor was as warm as the room. There were no lights, but I saw a torch bobbing into the darkness up ahead. It swung round to dazzle me.

"God, Marta."

"Sorry. I can see movement. I think it's... Christ!"

I felt my way to where she stood. Marta grabbed my arm. "Look." She swept the torch beam along the skirting and I saw it too. Insects. Thousands of them, cockroaches, beetles, a mixture of species swarming along the join between floor and wall, racing out of the light. Some were huge, gleaming, things, all were fast. Something clattered past my face, wings brushed my skin. I recoiled. The torch beam shot up, to trap a spiral of flying creatures; moths, flies, wasps, and others too fast to identify.

Survivors, like the engineers and the farmers and fuel scavengers, and possibly the most adaptable of all life forms on earth, the insect.

"The warmth must have brought them out of hiding," I said.

"They should be eating each other, not swarming together like that."

"Things have changed, survival is survival, Marta."

I heard Avni call my name and a moment later felt her hand on my shoulder. Her disgust was palpable. Something batted at my face and I waved it away. More of them whirred past my ear.

Marta moved off again. We had no choice but to follow. The flying insects were so dense now I had to look downwards to protect my eyes and mouth. Avni's hand was tight about mine as we stumbled, in Marta's wake, out onto the lobby.

"Fuck!"

Marta shone the torch round the space. Every inch of wall, ceiling and floor were hidden beneath a heaving carpet of insects. Avni released my hand and staggered back, beating at her face and hair. "Shit, get them off me. Get them off me!" I heard her move away, towards the room, running, bumping into the wall, swearing and sobbing.

It wasn't weakness. We were tough and travel-hardened, us interstellar adventurers, but we were also fragile; minds, hearts and souls fractured by what we had found out there.

"They're coming from below," Marta said.

She shone the torch onto the stairs and I saw them streaming up from the shadows pooled below us. Many were now mating, coupled on the wing or as lumbering double creatures, struggling over the floor.

Wherever I stepped, I could feel them crunch under my boots. Each time I lifted my foot, it was like dragging it from soft sand.

Or mud.

"We're going back, now."

"This is wrong. We need to find –"

"Back," I snapped. "Marta, that's an order."

We stuffed one of our sleeping bags along the crack under the door. I couldn't sleep, Marta was tense in my arms. I could hear Avni, shivering and murmuring in uneasy slumber. The rustling and scraping noises grew louder. Flying things pattered against the door. Some of them must have found their way in here. I began to feel them on my face, in the sleeping bag. Imagination, reality, either way, there was little I could do about it, but wait for morning.

At some point in the deep, hot dark, the noises gradually died away.

Next day we started work on the shuttle. The cloud broke a little and let in touch of sunlight. It felt like a good omen, although it brought no warmth. If anything, the momentary brightness made everything seem even colder.

With the engineers' help, we stripped out the damaged parts and drew up a list of replacements, which the engineers would scavenge for us.

There were decisions to be made if we managed to get this craft back up the Fiennes. We had found only one non-terrestrial planet fit for human life. I and many others did not want to go back there, even though not that many of us would survive the journey. Damaged as it was, the Fiennes would have to take its time. Rigel IX belonged to our children.

But this was no longer home, either.

The sunlight weakened. Clouds closed over the bright-lit wound. Night was coming.

We had not mentioned the insects to Lana. I hadn't requested our silence. It was an unspoken agreement.

That night we ate in the refectory, and the near silence of the engineers began to unnerve me. Apart from Lana and a big, shaven headed guy, they barely seemed aware of us. The food, the mush, made me gag. My head ached from caffeine starvation. When we returned to the room, I felt besieged.

I was woken from an edgy, dream-laden sleep by the rustling. There were other sounds; buzzing and whirring, the pitter-patter of flying creatures. My skin crawled. Marta sat, torch focussed on the door, until she collapsed from exhaustion. When my own dreams returned, they were full of urgent, scuttling movement.

We worked through the daylight hours. We had little rest. I drove the others on, put up with their protests, their discontent. The cold was enervating. The grey sky bore down on us, the wind burrowed into my skull and danced on my nerves.

And at night, the insects came.

I could no longer find comfort in Marta's arms. She was suspicious, restless and argumentative. Nqbe was becoming withdrawn. Avni was working herself to destruction. Squabbles broke out. The fabric was frayed.

Then, on the fifth night, Marta disappeared.

I woke hot, my head pounding, as grey light seeped in through the gaps around the blocked-up window. The wind moaned, rain or sleet lashed at the plyboard covering. I rolled over and was alone, not unusual any more. Marta spent too many nights sitting cross-legged, facing the door, listening to the endless noise of the insects.

This morning she wasn't in the room at all.

Okay, it was light. Her agitation could have driven her out early.

But I knew different. I could feel it, in the vacuum of her absence.

"Stay here," I told the others. Then I was out in the corridor.

I met Lana on the stairs. There was no reason for her to be there. It was as if she had been waiting for me.

"What's wrong?" she asked. Her question was a lie. She knew what was wrong.

"One of our people, Marta, she's missing."

Lana shrugged "We'll look for her."

"Don't lie to me. You know where she is."

"Repair your vessel. Go back to your ship."

"Where is Marta?" I was angry now.

"Your people need to come home." She turned from me and walked away. I reached out, grabbed her arm.

I felt.

Movement.

Under her skin.

A brief wrongness. Gone. Never there.

Lana wrenched her arm free, stared at me for a moment. Then walked away. I slumped against the wall, dizzy from exhaustion.

There was no choice but to continue working on the shuttle. I fetched the others. We finished our dry rations. I kept them away from the engineers, hauled them, cold, tired, and hungry out to the shuttle. The engineers had done a lot of work, the major structural problems had been dealt with, the fin replaced, the torn belly patched. They had crawled over the thing like ants. Moved Heaven and Earth.

By nightfall, we were testing the power plant. She was raw and wounded, but there was a chance the shuttle would make it back to the Fiennes tomorrow, where full repair could be effected.

Before I left the shuttle, I discreetly armed myself with a knife and one of the small flamers concealed under the pilot's seat.

As the light began to fade and we prepared to set-off back to the hotel, I took a last look around at the snow blurred horizon beyond the airport perimeter and wondered what the hell was out there. The desolation, and the mystery of it, was terrifying.

I was always going to search for Marta.

Avni and Nqbe were asleep, exhaustion saw to that. Their sleep was far from easy, however, and was disturbed by mumbled terrors and fraught twisting and turning in their sleeping bags. Grabbing a torch and pocketing the flamer, I opened the door as carefully as I could and stepped out into the corridor. Before I could shut the door again, I felt some of the insects scuttle over my feet and into the room. I headed for the stairs. Tiny bodies crunched under my boots. Moths and other winged creatures danced in the torch beam. The walls seethed with invertebrate life. Things dropped on my head. I scrabbled at my hair, felt the hard, skittish bodies.

As before, the stairs were alive with the things. Surging upwards, frantic in their mating dances. I took a breath then set off downwards. The creatures swirled about my feet, over the insteps, so many of them that walking became difficult. I felt them on my legs and quickly gave up trying to brush them away.

I made it to the lobby, which was a scuttling, squirming lake of living things. I felt my gorge rise. I had to keep going. I had to find her. I had left those I loved on Rigel IX. Never again.

The source of the insect flow seemed to be a doorway to the right of the lobby. I drew the flamer from my pocket.

Through the doorway now, deeper into the hotel. There was a smell, a mixture of mustiness, and a bloody, meaty stink. When I passed through the next doorway I found myself in the kitchen. Food bowls were piled up on the worktop, as were the big serving vats. The sweet liquid we drank, was stored in huge glass flasks. There was a walk-in freezer.

I opened the door, looked in.

A moment later, I was sick.

There were human bodies in there, hanging upside down on meat hooks; arms limp hair trailing, mouths open – death open.

My stomach heaved again and again, because now I knew what we had been eating.

Marta was not among them, thank Christ.

She was in what had probably been the restaurant, and she was not alone.

The tables were locked together to form a set of long platforms that filled the room, end-to-end. The engineers were prone on the tables. I moved among them and there she was, pale as a corpse in the torch light, and not to be woken. She was breathing, though. There was a pulse, her skin was hot, flushed.

I shone the torch in her face.

A cockroach emerged from her left nostril and scuttled over her cheek then dropped to the floor. Another struggled from her left ear. A third scuttled in from the dark edges of the disc of torch light and disappeared back into her ear. Gagging once more, I shone the torch round wildly. Insects were entering into, and emerging from, the others, glimpsed horrors, caught in the wildly dancing torch light.

Then I remembered that odd movement under Lana's skin.

With no plan but to get out of this place, I carried Marta outside, and made for the shuttle. I hugged her close to me, tried to keep her warm as I stumbled and tripped through the snow.

There were no insects out here in this frozen version of Hell.

The freezing gale whipped the snow into a blinding fog that raked my face and drove into my lungs. Marta grew cold in my arms. She stirred and moaned. I told her I loved her. Over and over again. It became a litany. I had never used the word with her before. I thought she was mere comfort in my grief, but now she was going from me, I realised how much I needed her.

I felt the insects stir beneath her skin. I felt them scuttle over my hands as they emerged from her body. Something bit me, a sudden vicious pinch of pain on my hand.

More bites.

Stings.

Exhausted I stumbled on –

— towards the roar of the mudslide, and the screams and shouts of alarm. I was running, back towards the base camp, back towards the great tongue of slime that stretched from the hillside above and covered everything. Everyone. The lightning-riven sky boiled green-grey, and rain slashed down with such force it tore my overall and my skin. I fell to my knees and dug. I howled their names and slithered into the murk like a worm, sobbing and shouting and burying myself until I was dragged back by the others, who were also weeping and shouting and offering their grief to the storm. Almost thirty souls lost, the roll-call of names, soon to be added to the ones we would lose to the meteor strike.

We could have stayed. We would have learned. We had the resources, the expertise. We allowed our grief to drive us back into space, in the vain hope we would find succour back on Earth. We forgot the rules of interstellar travel. We forgot the brutality of time dilation. We forgot why we had brought our families with us —

Marta stirred, coughed wetly and shuddered. Her eyes opened, showed her confusion, and fear.

"John?" Her voice was hoarse, choked, as if she was speaking around something lodged in her throat. "Help me... Please... kill me..."

I couldn't. I stared, helpless, mumbled that I would take her back to the Fiennes.

She struggled weakly in my arms. I felt movement under her skin, a flurry of activity in her arms, her neck. "No..." she said. "I can't go back, not now."

There were engineers ranged around the shuttle, armed, with rifles and flamers, but they made no move towards us. Their patience was terrifying. One of them stepped forward. Lana.

"Survival," she shouted above the storm. "We give them warmth. They give us life. Humanity was a mewling child, poisoned and dying."

Lana and the others took us to the hanger at gunpoint. I sat on a tool chest, Marta beside me. She was quiet, vacant. Someone had given her a sweater and a parka. I helped her to dress. Her flesh rippled. I held her hand and felt them moving inside her. I wondered how long the process took, and how painful it was. She made no sound but I could see the terror in her eyes.

Kill me, she said. *Please...*

I stared out of the door. It was snowing again, huge clumps of white swirled through the grey and across the bright beams of the arc lights.

"There are two species who will always find a way to survive," Lana said. She had stayed with us while the other engineers had gone to fetch Nqbe and Avni. "No matter what; one able to find a hiding place and thrive even in Hell, the other able to shape the world around them, even when the world is broken."

"Symbiosis?" The word seemed too scientific, too clinical, to describe what had happened here.

"Yes, I suppose it is."

"Is she still Marta?"

"Marta?" Lana frowned. "She is... she. A part of us."

For a moment I felt an urge to kill them all, even Marta, to destroy this abomination, but I knew I couldn't, and the urge faded. "So, this airport, this community, is a hive?"

Lana shrugged. "We defend it, we sustain it. We trade, and we fight."

I remembered the carcases, hanging from those hooks. "And steal human flesh."

"We survive."

"You have no feelings? No emotion or... guilt?"

Another frown. "We survive."

"Jesus Christ."

Marta gave a cry and dropped to her knees. She was in pain. Lana made no move to help her. Whatever metamorphosis was taking place, it had to be suffered alone.

"The shuttle is ready to fly," Lana said. "Avni can take it back to your ship and start bringing your people home."

Of course, I would not be allowed to go, or be anywhere near Avni and Nqbe. They were not to know the truth.

And the rest would come, the people trapped on the *Fiennes.* They wouldn't be able to help themselves. They would be driven here by the need to come home, and when they arrived...

*

I waited. A moment, then I saw them. A couple of engineers and two other figures, Nqbe and Avni. They held each other, looked lonely and afraid. Lana went out into the snow to join them.

I don't know what my colleagues had been told, but they must have believed it because they did not appear to be under coercion. Probably that Marta and I had died, exposure perhaps.

There was little time, and even less chance of success. We had been left alone. There was no need to guard us. There was nowhere to escape to.

I grabbed Marta's hand and ran.

I ran and shouted their names.

Marta struggled but was too weak to fight. Lana turned and shouted at me to stop. I yelled back. I saw Avni stop and turn. I shambled to a halt, wrenched Marta to myself and felt the disgusting ripple through her flesh. I saw Avni, take a step towards me. Lana as well. She was armed, a handgun.

"I love you Marta," I whispered then shouted Avni's name. She stopped and turned.

Before Lana could shoot, I slashed upwards with the knife and opened Marta from navel to breast. I heard Avni's wind-snatched scream. I saw Nqbe vomit as the insects poured from Marta onto the red, red snow. Lana fired. Something knocked me backwards, but not off my feet. Nqbe grabbed Avni and hauled her towards the shuttle. I realised I was on my knees now, I felt the warmth of my own blood spread across my stomach. Lana was firing at the fleeing Nqbe and Avni.

I felt a second bullet rip through my right side, a third, shattered my left shoulder blade. I didn't feel the rest, but lay in the snow, clutching Marta to myself. As I watched the shuttle flee spaceward on a pillar of liquid flame, I felt the first of the insects crawl over my face, seeking warmth, and knew that I was not going to die.

ABOUT THE AUTHOR

College lecturer, electrician, actor and musician, Terry Grimwood is also the author of numerous novels, short stories and novellas, including the British Fantasy Award-nominated *Interference*. Three of his plays have been performed on the stage, directed by the author. While most of his work lies in the science fiction, horror and fantasy genres, Terry often strays outside their boundaries, which he considers a must for all genre writers and a cure for writer's block. He has co-written a number of engineering textbooks for Pearson Educational Press, penned a romance for *People's Friend* magazine and his novella *Joe* is inspired by a true story. Terry lives by a lake with his wonderful wife, Debra. In his spare time, Terry is vocalist and harmonica player with The Ripsaw Blues Band.

ALSO FROM NEWCON PRESS

Queen of Clouds – Neil Williamson
Wooden automata, sentient weather, talking cats, compellant inks and a host of vividly realised characters provide the backdrop to this rich dark fantasy. Stranger in the city Billy Braid becomes embroiled in Machiavellian politics and deadly intrigue, as the weather insists on misbehaving, putting the Weathermakers Guild in an untenable position…

Sparks Flying – Kim Lakin
The first ever collection from critically acclaimed author Kim Lakin, spanning fourteen years of writing. Her very best short stories, as selected by the author herself. Fourteen expertly crafted tales that span myth, science fiction, industrial grime and darkest imagining.

Polestars 1: Strange Attractors – Jaine Fenn
First full collection from an award-winning author of innovative science fiction and off-kilter fantasy; features her finest short stories, selected by the author, drawn from more than two decades of publication, including the BSFA Award-winning "Liberty Bird", a Hidden Empire story, and a new tale, "Sin of Omission", written specifically for this collection.

Polestars 2: Umbilical – Teika Marija Smits
Debut collection from one of the finest short story writers to emerge on the genre scene in recent years. Her storytelling relies on keen observation of the world and people around her interpreted through the lens of her imagination, dancing between science fiction, realism, and horror.

Polestars 3: The Glasshouse – Emma Coleman
Contemporary tales of rural horror from one of genre fiction's best kept secrets. An avid haunter of libraries, Emma's fiction is steeped in local colour and rooted deep in her native Northamptonshire, drawing on her love of nature, her passion for literature, and her keen eye for detail. Her fiction is atmospheric, mesmeric, and frequently disturbing.